Rabindranath
Selected Writings fo

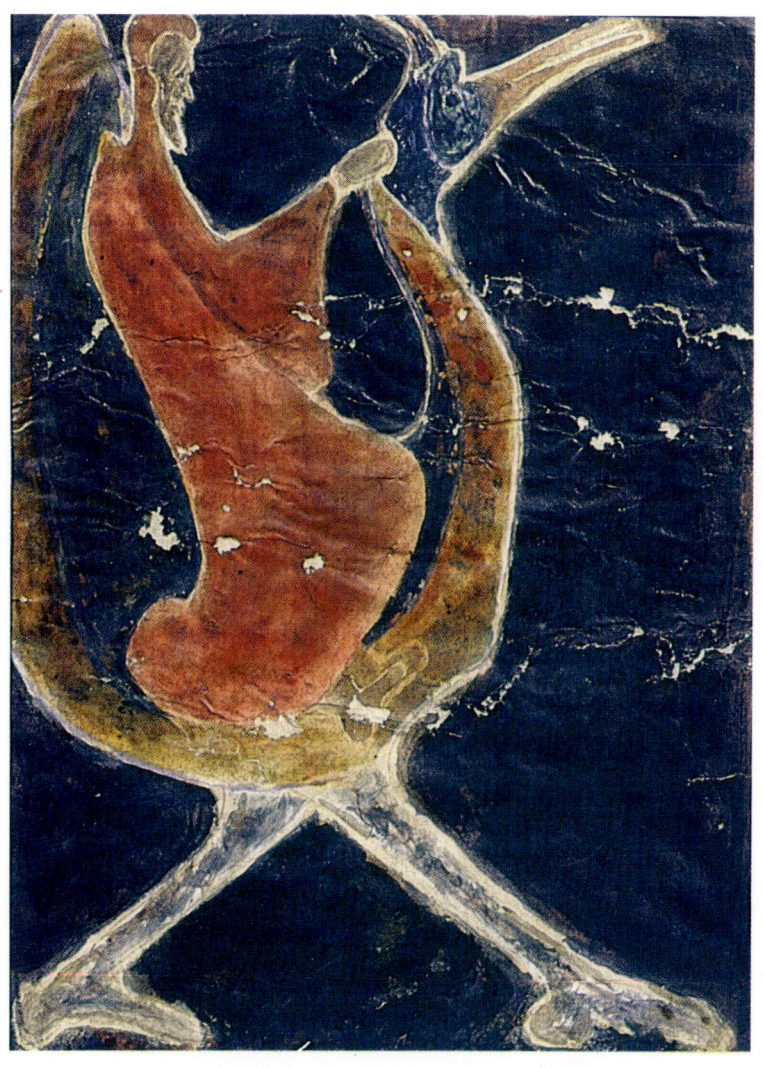

Painting by Rabindranath. Rabindra Bhavan, Visva-Bharati.

THE OXFORD TAGORE TRANSLATIONS

Rabindranath Tagore
Selected Writings for Children

General Editor
SUKANTA CHAUDHURI

Advisory Editor
SANKHA GHOSH

Introduction and Notes by
SUKANTA CHAUDHURI

OXFORD
UNIVERSITY PRESS

YMCA Library Building, Jai Singh Road, New Delhi 110001

Oxford University Press is a department of the University of Oxford. It furthers the
University's objective of excellence in research, scholarship, and education
by publishing worldwide in

Oxford   New York
Auckland Bangkok Buenos Aires Cape Town Chennai
Dar es Salaam Delhi Hong Kong Istanbul Karachi Kolkata
Kuala Lumpur Madrid Melbourne Mexico City Mumbai Nairobi
São Paulo Shanghai Singapore Taipei Tokyo Toronto

with an associated company in Berlin

Oxford is a registered trade mark of Oxford University Press
in the UK and in certain other countries

Published in India
By Oxford University Press, New Delhi

© Oxford University Press 2002

The moral rights of the author have been asserted
Database right Oxford University Press (maker)

First published 2002 by Oxford University Press
jointly with Visva-Bharati

All rights reserved. No part of this publication may be reproduced,
or transmitted in any form or by any means, electronic or mechanical,
including photocopying, recording or by any information storage and
retrieval system, without permission in writing from Oxford University Press.
Enquiries concerning reproduction outside the scope of the above should be
sent to the Rights Department, Oxford University Press, at the address above

You must not circulate this book in any other binding or cover
and you must impose this same condition on any acquirer

ISBN 019 565873 6

Typeset in Adobe Garamond in 11/13
by Excellent Laser Typesetters, Pitampura, Delhi 110 034
Printed in India at Pauls Press, New Delhi 110 020
Published by Manzar Khan, Oxford University Press
YMCA Library Building, Jai Singh Road, New Delhi 110 001

General Editor's Preface

Few people outside Bengal know of the extent and variety of Rabindranath Tagore's writings for children. Hence, this volume is a specially valuable addition to the Oxford Tagore Translations.

We have tried to present the entire range of Rabindranath's writings for children, except for pieces patently written as school texts. However, some of the verses come from an enchanting Bengali textbook, *Sahaj Path*. For the rest, the poems include whimsy, nonsense and fantasy, but also moral pieces, social narratives and historical tales. The prose writings comprise a variety of stories, again ranging from the moral to the fantastic. There is a selection of short humorous plays, and extracts from the poet's own account of his childhood.

In other words, the range of this book is much wider than the standard fare in most children's collections. Rabindranath did not wish to confine children to certain narrow limits of reading and feeling. He credited them with powers of absorption that adults may well lack, and laid before them the entire range of human experience: the comic, the fantastic and the reassuring, but also the tragic, the philosophic, even at times the grim and horrific. All these matters are scaled down in formal complexity but not in intrinsic depth. A child who goes through this book will have extended her mind in many directions. This may be even truer of an adult.

Like any other volume of the series, this book needed notes, explanations and data; yet blatant academic commentary would have been out of place. We have divided up the material so that it does not thrust itself upon the reader. Some essential information has been placed at points where it cannot be missed. All other material is gathered in the 'Explanations' and 'Notes on Texts and Publication' at the end of the volume. Readers of every age and intent can browse through these and pick out what they want. Some data for scholars—dates, texts, provenance etc.—has been placed in a separate sequence.

Whimsy and fantasy are hard to translate. Many other matters important to the young are too local and specific to be rendered precisely in the terms of another language and culture. Hence, translations of such material necessarily end up by taking certain liberties. A few crucial departures and omissions have been pointed out in the notes. For the rest, we have diverged from the literal text only in order to preserve its spirit. We can fairly claim not to have diverged too much or too often.

Every volume of the Oxford Tagore Translations includes some illustrations, but this book is full of them for obvious reasons. Many of the illustrations go with the texts: the two were conceived together. Others have no organic link, but blend remarkably to provide a total aesthetic experience, a single world of the imagination. We wanted to open up this world to readers who do not know Bengali, or even light up some corners of it for readers who do.

We are grateful for assistance from Sm Vijaya Mukherjee, Professor Gautam Bhadra and Professor Tapobrata Ghosh. Special thanks are due to the Director and staff of Rabindra Bhavan, Shantiniketan, for supplying most of the visual material so readily and so efficiently; as also to Dr Amlan Das Gupta for generous technical help with the illustrations.

SUKANTA CHAUDHURI

A Note on the Contributors

SUVRO CHATTERJEE teaches at St Xavier's School, Durgapur.

SUKANTA CHAUDHURI is Professor of English at Jadavpur University.

SANKHA GHOSH is a noted Bengali poet and critic. He retired as Professor of Bengali from Jadavpur University.

SUKHENDU RAY retired as Managing Director of Guest Keen Williams Ltd.

Contents

INTRODUCTION	1
AT THE START	13
GRANDFATHER'S HOLIDAY	15
VERSES	17
FLOWERS	19
OUR LITTLE RIVER	21
THE VOYAGE	23
THE RUNAWAY CITY	25
BHOTAN–MOHAN	27
THE FLYING MACHINE	28
THE BLAZE	30
THE TIGER	31
THE PALM TREE	33
SUNDAY	35
THE UNRESOLVED	36
THE STARGAZER	38
THE HERO	42
THE WISE BROTHER	46
BIG AND SMALL	48
ASTRONOMY	51

CONTENTS

STORIES 53
THE SCIENTIST 55
THE KING'S PALACE 60
THE BIG NEWS 63
THE FAIRY 66
MORE-THAN-TRUE 69
THE RATS' FEAST 72
WISHES COME TRUE 75

PLAYS 81
THE WELCOME 83
THE POET AND THE PAUPER 87
THE ORDEALS OF FAME 90
THE EXTENDED FAMILY 98
THE FREE LUNCH 103

THAT MAN 113

MORE VERSES 141
MOVING PICTURES 143
AT SIXES AND SEVENS 148
THE INVENTION OF SHOES 154
THE KING'S SON AND THE KING'S DAUGHTER 160
FRAGMENTS 163
BHAJAHARI 167
THE BUILDER 170
MADHO 173
TWO BIGHAS OF LAND 176

THE MAGIC STONE	179
THE FAKE FORTRESS	181
THE CAPTIVE HERO	183
THE REPRESENTATIVE	187
THE BEGGAR'S BOUNTY	191
MY CHILDHOOD	195
DESTRUCTION	231
EXPLANATIONS	235
NOTES ON TEXTS, DATES, AND PUBLICATION	254
LIST OF ILLUSTRATIONS	259

Introduction

Rabindranath Tagore (whose name is really 'Thakur' in Bengali) wrote a great deal for children. His collected works already run into thirty-one volumes, with more to come. Out of this, enough matter for at least two volumes consists of writings for young people. This is a much bigger proportion than with any other of the world's great poets, writers or philosophers.

Of course, some of these pieces are not really for children. In November 1902, Rabindranath's wife Mrinalini died, leaving behind five children. The next year Rabindranath brought out a group of poems called *Shishu* (*The Child*) in his Collected Poems appearing at the time. Much of *Shishu*, with some other poems, was translated into English in 1913 as *The Crescent Moon*. Some of the verses were written to comfort and amuse the younger children: they had just lost their mother, and one, the second sister Renuka, was seriously ill. These poems really are very funny, or exciting and amusing at the least. But others in the collection are sad and thoughtful pieces—sometimes about mothers who have lost their children—while yet others talk about children in sentimental and philosophic ways. The young Tagores could not have understood them properly; or if they

Rabindranath and his eldest daughter Madhurilata. Pastel drawing, 1887.

did, they would have felt all the sadder. Obviously their father had written these particular pieces for grown-ups to read.

That still leaves a great deal of writing meant for young people, and read widely by them in Bengal from that day to this. Rabindranath was attracted to children's literature generally. He must have known the English works of Lewis Carroll and Edward Lear, and no doubt much else. His writings show their traces and memories. More importantly, he had a deep life-long interest in children's rhymes and tales from Bengal: in fact, it was largely owing to his efforts that these began to be recorded and studied seriously. He wrote a long essay on Bengali nursery rhymes, to show how deeply these verses had entered Bengali life. He also made a collection of 81 rhymes, and got the learned Academy of Bengali Literature (Bangiya Sahitya Parishad) to publish them in its journal. He also encouraged his nephew Abanindranath and many others to collect and publish such verses. He wrote an enthusiastic introduction for a classic collection of fairy tales called *Thakurmar Jhuli* (*Grandmother's Bag of Tales*), written in wonderfully lively and original style by a great children's writer, Dakshinaranjan Mitra Majumdar.

Rabindranath wrote scores of stories for grown-ups—in fact, he was virtually the first writer of short stories in Bengali. These stories contain many motifs and elements taken from fairy-tales, reworked in the light of real life and adult experiences. This means that the line between grown-up stories and children's, fairy tales and realistic ones, is sometimes hard to draw. The story, 'Wishes Come True', included in this volume, is printed like any other piece among his collected short stories for adults.

Again, Rabindranath wrote a quantity of short humorous plays which were finally collected under the titles *Hasyakoutuk* (*Fun and Laughter*, 1907) and *Byangakoutuk* (*Satire and Laughter*, 1907). (The latter collection had stories as well as plays.) A few of these pieces were acted, chiefly in the Tagore family circle. One, 'The Ordeals of Fame', was even adapted for the public stage and acted five times at the Emerald Theatre in Calcutta in 1895. These days, they are often acted by children.

But these playlets had been written for reading rather than acting. They appeared from 1885 in the children's magazine *Balak*, which was later merged with the grown-ups' magazine *Bharati*. There they had been called *Heanli Natya* (*Riddle-Plays*), because they act out certain Bengali words, syllable by syllable, as in a game of charades. Later on, even their writer felt that this aspect of the plays did not matter very much. More importantly, while some plays afford pure laughter, others make fun of human attitudes or social traits. They can be, and were, enjoyed and even acted by adults no less than children.

This is true of many other works as well. This book contains an uproarious story-poem, 'The Invention of Shoes': it appeared in an adult collection called *Kalpana* (*Imaginings*). Another such volume called *Sonar Tari* (*The Golden Boat*), rich in philosophic pieces, includes 'The King's Son and the King's Daughter'. This poem is phrased like a fairy-tale and sub-titled as such; but what it describes is obviously a real boy and a real girl falling in love, as real people do thinking they are entering a fairy-tale world. Rabindranath's works are full of adult fairy-tales. He knows that adults go on being children, while children are already adults.

Hence, his writing for children reflects various styles, sometimes in a very serious vein, because he thinks children should be taken seriously. The story 'Wishes Come True' has a clear moral. So do many other poems and stories (like 'The Magic Stone' in this volume), and some of the playlets make satirical points. Besides moralizing, Rabindranath tried to teach his young readers all kinds of other matters. Some of these works, in fact, were written as text-books for the school founded by him on his ancestral property at Shantiniketan, about 100 miles from Calcutta.

This school was part of a whole ashram, or spiritual community, that he conceived to make true his ideals about learning, living and working for society. He attracted many famous and talented people to live there—sometimes for a short space, sometimes all their lives. He called his institution Visva-Bharati, which might be explained as 'the seat of the world's wisdom'. Today it is a big university, but it still includes the school he set up, as well as a major centre for farming, village work and social uplift.

Rabindranath was unhappy with the education system of his time. In his own school, he tried to ensure that learning was relaxed and pleasurable; that it brought the children in contact with nature,

Open-air class at Shantiniketan, taught by W. W. Pearson. Woodcut by Ramendranath Chakrabarti from Shantiniketaner Brahmacharyashram, Visva-Bharati.

and blended with a natural and productive way of life. Classes at Shantiniketan were held out of doors under the trees. (Some of them still are.) The children would be taken round the countryside, shown the stars and planets at night, told about plants and animals and, above all, about the country life of Bengal, whose model was worked into the community life at Shantiniketan.

Rabindranath prepared many of the school-books himself, and made sure they were enjoyable to look at and to read. In 1930 at the age of 69, long after winning the Nobel Prize and becoming something of a sage in the world's eyes, he brought out an alphabet-book and primer called *Sahaj Path* (*Easy Learning*) that was like no other alphabet-book. It was full of witty, imaginative rhymes and stories— very much for children, yet conveying some of the pleasures that grown-ups get from reading literature. Some pieces are amusing, some wistful, while others show up vivid and even harsh aspects of real life.

They also promise a feast of sheer delight in language. Rabindranath's first important poem for children, *Nadi* (*The River*) had appeared in 1896 in book form, and later been included in *Shishu*. It was written in a novel metre that Rabindranath had to explain to adults, though he had seen how easily children grasped it. *Sahaj Path* too has a trick poem that can be read in two different metres. (It has been translated in this book as 'Flowers', but of course we could not bring out the trick metre in English.) There are ingenious stories woven out of words containing the complicated joint consonants that make the Bengali alphabet rather hard to learn: but these are worked into the stories as a sort of game, and are absorbing for that reason. The books are full of pictures, specially drawn by Nandalal Bose or Basu, an inmate of Shantiniketan and one of the great artists of modern India.

I shall have more to say about illustrations later on. Let me carry on now with the poems and stories. The *Sahaj Path* pieces were so delightful that they were included in other books, often with illustrations, purely to give pleasure to people young and old. Rabindranath brought out several such books: *Shishu Bholanath* (*The Young Shiva*)[1] in 1922; *Khapchhara* (*At Sixes and Sevens*); *Se* (*That Man*) and *Chharar Chhabi* (*Pictures for Rhymes*) in 1937; *Galpa-Salpa* (*Chats*) just before his death in 1941. *Chhara* (*Rhymes*), being prepared around that time, appeared a month after his death. Many poems from these and other books were put into two new collections later on: *Chitra-Bichitra* (*Varied Pictures*) in 1954, and *Sankalita* (*A Collection*) in three volumes in 1955.

[1] Shiva is the god of destruction, but the name 'Bholanath' alludes specially to his intoxicated, entranced, unworldly state. The poet gives the name humorously, but also philosophically, to a destructive young toddler.

Much of this writing, especially in *At Sixes and Sevens* and *That Man*, consists of pure nonsense, whimsy and fantasy. In *At Sixes and Sevens*, most of the little poems draw their fun from ingenious rhymes for hard Bengali words, sometimes made up by the poet: these cannot be translated into any other language. That is why, rather sadly, this book contains few pieces from this famous collection.

The whimsy and fantasy link up with a crucial activity of Rabindranath's later life. With very little formal training or preparation, he developed into a prolific and markedly original painter. He had once tried painting at an earlier stage of his life, but began practising the art seriously from about 1924, when he was 63. His first exhibition was held in Paris in 1930. He has left behind hundreds of oil paintings as well as great quantities of drawings and sketches, sometimes to illustrate his own writings. This great store of art-works is like nothing drawn or painted previously in India, or indeed hardly anywhere else. It seems to have sprung from a very special, very original way of seeing that Rabindranath had conjured up from the depths of his own mind.

By this time, Rabindranath had a worldwide reputation as poet, thinker, commentator and, in fact, a kind of sage or prophet. One imagines that in these formal public roles, he could not always be himself. His paintings and drawings may have provided a means of escape. Here he could really express his most private, intimate being.

Most grown-ups lay by their childhood memories and fantasies within their innermost selves. This would be particularly true of a poet like Rabindranath, in whose imagination childhood had always been a precious ingredient; and equally of a celebrity like Rabindranath—on public duty most of the time, forced to turn a formal face to the world. That is why his fantasies for children have a special importance—not only for their literary value, but as bringing out a different, informal and intimate side of the poet-sage. That is also how his children's writings link up with his paintings and drawings. He paints figures looking very like himself—as a clown, a dancer or musician or (as in the frontispiece of this book) as riding a strange bird.

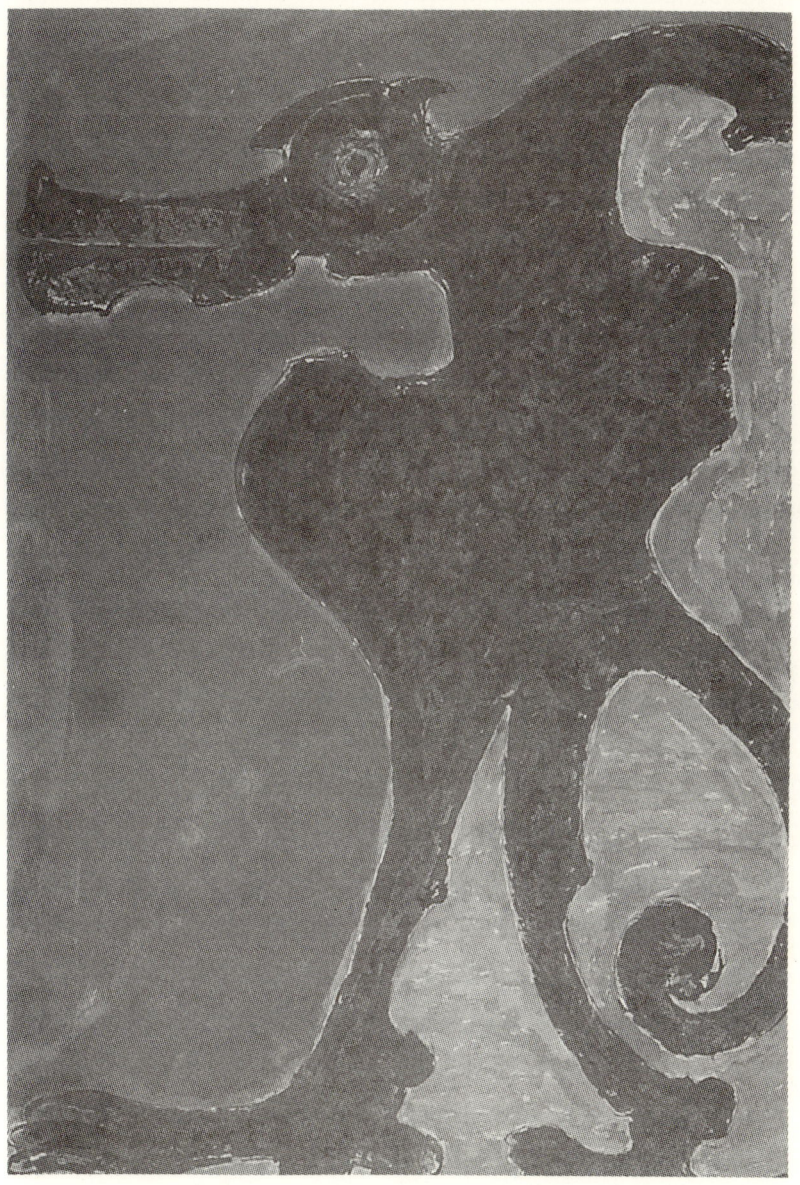

Painting by Rabindranath. Rabindra Bhavan, Visva-Bharati.

Rabindranath's art is uniquely the work of his free and relaxed imagination. Around 1924, he started drawing doodles on his manuscripts, joining together the words he had crossed out. He created all sorts of designs and images in this way, above all of weird animals. He then went on to make full-fledged drawings and paintings of strange birds and animals. The doodles scattered through this book show how he worked this vein of his imagination.

That is why we have filled this book with pictures alongside the stories and verses. Many of the pictures were not drawn to go with these texts. (Many others, needless to say, were.) Yet in a deeper sense, they all belong together. They lead us into a very rich, very colourful treasure-house in a particular chamber of Rabindranath's mind, which we only glimpse from time to time in his serious, formal writings. Again, people both young and old, can enter this chamber side by side: there is no line to divide grown-up territory from the child's.

But we must pass from this rare vein of imagination to other, more normal and formal ones: those too have a prominent place among Rabindranath's writings for children. As we have seen, many of his pieces contain some kind of moral or lesson. We tend to be suspicious of morals and lessons; but Rabindranath is always careful to convey his point through an exciting story, a witty build-up or at least a vigorous turn of language.

For instance, he has an 1899 collection of sharp little anecdotes and allegories which he calls *Kanika* (*Fragments*). These too can be read equally by grown-ups or children. Some are rather abstract and philosophical; others, like the ones in this book, are as philosophical at bottom, but their point is brought out through sparkling little fables.

Then again, he has a great number of story-poems. We could put only a few in this book, as they are rather long. The biggest collection of these, put together in 1908 by combining material from earlier volumes, is called *Katha o Kahini* (*Legends and Tales*). A good many poems draw on religious sources, particularly the life of the Buddha; others on Indian history—especially the deeds of the Marathas, Sikhs and Rajputs, celebrated as models of courage and honour. This book contains an example of each type.

Rabindranath also has a very different class of story-poems, set in his own times. We must not forget how different those times were from ours. Hence some very moving poems, like a famous one called 'The Old Servant' (*Puratan Bhritya*), might seem outdated in the way they present the relation of master and servant, rich and poor. But generally, even in his writings for children, Rabindranath kept up a consistent line of protest and criticism against social evils. Of the poems in this book, 'Two Bighas of Land' is famous as a condemnation of the tyrannous zamindari system. The zamindars or landlords (actually tax-collectors) had been empowered by a 'Permanent Settlement' of land tax made by the British rulers in 1793. Most zamindars squeezed and oppressed their tenants, and the system was rightly blamed for the poverty and degradation of the Indian peasant. 'Madho' also opens against the background of the zamindari system, but moves on to new types of oppression brought in by the coming of industry. Even the whimsical collection *Galpa-Salpa* contains 'Big News', a perceptive allegory about rich men and poor, the rulers and the ruled; and 'Destruction', an open lament about the way peace and love are destroyed by the conflict of nations. We have put this last piece separately at the end of the book, to match the seriousness of its theme.

People think of Rabindranath as a philosophic and romantic-minded poet. That part of his mind is actually balanced by an intense concern for social evils and problems in Bengal, India and the world. This appears chiefly in his prose writings but also in his poems. His writings for young people show the same total concern for reality as well as imagination, the lives of men and women alongside the creations of his mind.

That is why we have rounded off this collection with some of Rabindranath's accounts of his own childhood. He published two books of memoirs, *Jiban-Smriti* (*Memories of My Life*) in 1912 and *Chhelebela* (*Childhood*) in 1940. The two books are of different kinds. The first was written for grown-ups, the second for children; the first in the so-called *sadhu bhasha* or 'chaste language' used in formal Bengali writing till quite recently, the latter in the *chalit bhasha* or 'popular language' that Bengalis always spoke and nowadays write in. (Rabindranath did more than anyone else to bring about this change.) But once again, there is a definite link in spirit, and of course in material, between the two books. The excerpts printed here pass easily from one to the next, regardless of which book they come from.

Something must be said about the illustrations in this volume. Of Rabindranath's own paintings and drawings I have spoken already; but a lot of the pictures here are by other people, belonging to his family or associated with the Shantiniketan community. Some of them were drawn specially for the pieces they accompany. In other cases there is a common subject, and in yet others only a common spirit. But all of them, in one way or another, draw on the material and ambience of Rabindranath's life and work.

The first people to mention must be the poet's two nephews, Gaganendranath (1867–1938) and Abanindranath (1871–1951). Among the most eminent artists of modern India, they were also children's authors in their own right—Abanindranath in a big way. Both of them illustrated their uncle's work. Abanindranath, for instance, contributed paintings to a sumptuous edition of *The Crescent Moon* in 1913. Gaganendranath made a number of plates to illustrate Rabindranath's memoirs (*Jiban-Smriti*). And they both have pictures that fit in wonderfully with one or other of Rabindranath's works, though not actually drawn to illustrate it.

The most important name in Tagore illustration is that of Nandalal Bose (1883–1966). Another of the giants of modern Indian art, Nandalal went to live at Shantiniketan in 1920, and soon became head of the Kala Bhavan or Art School there. Shantiniketan is full of his works—most prominently the murals he drew on the walls of many buildings. The girls of a dormitory called Santoshalay have the happy experience of living among walls painted by him and his pupils, chiefly with pictures of animals. Nandalal has left his 'signature' in a corner of Santoshalay: a picture of himself being hugged by a bear.

Nandalal drew the pictures for many of Rabindranath's books for children. He decorated the Bengali primer *Sahaj Path* with a classic series of woodcuts and line drawings. One striking group of woodcuts accompanies the alphabet-rhymes. Like the rhymes themselves, they sketch a number of enchanting little scenes, both realistic and fanciful. We have worked them into the margins of another group of poems, here entitled 'Moving Pictures'. Many of the other pictures in this book are also by Nandalal.

Shantiniketan attracted other well-known artists, and trained more. The greatest of them was a sculptor of genius, Ramkinkar Baij; but many others filled the Shantiniketan art scene over many decades, like Asitkumar Haldar, Binodebehari Mukhopadhyay, Mukul Dey and

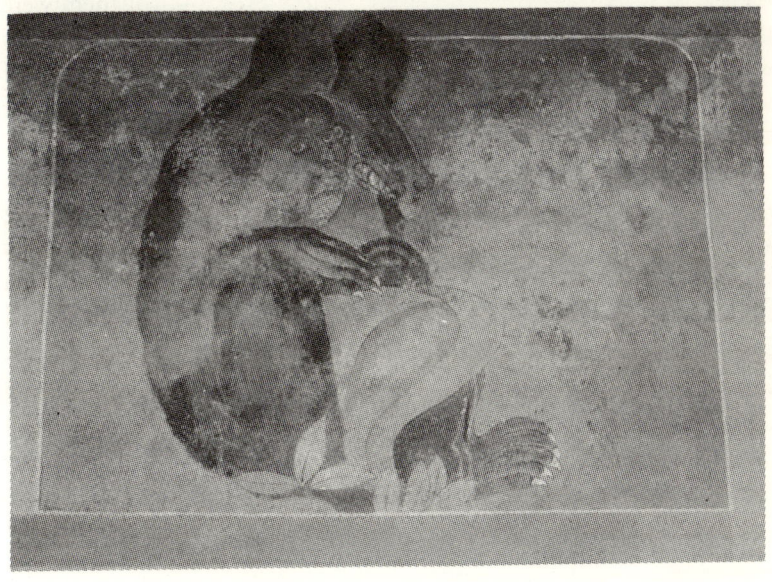

Nandalal Bose hugged by a bear: Mural by Nandalal and pupils. Santoshalay, Visva-Bharati.

Surendranath Kar. In this book, you will find illustrations by some of them, as well as others who trained or worked at Shantiniketan.

Rabindranath conceived of a rich and full way to live one's life, drawing on art and music as well as poetic language. He used all these means to understand the world around us, in its practical and even harsh aspects as well as the pleasant and fanciful ones. He thought a lot about young people and did a lot for them. Above all, he wanted them to know the happiness that comes from looking at the world, engaging with it and expressing oneself by every possible means. This book shows the ways in which he tried to convey this involvement.

At the Start

Before we begin, it may be helpful to explain a few points relating to many of the pieces.

Dada and *Didi* mean 'elder brother' and 'elder sister' respectively. But they are also used of cousins, and in fact of other people in a friendly or respectful way. Finally, they are used between grandparents and grandchildren. *Baba* means 'father', but is also used of older men, small boys, and holy men.

Khoka and *Khuki* are terms of affection for small boys and small girls respectively.

Babu is added after the first names of men as a polite way of addressing or referring to them. It is also used, by itself, by servants towards their masters, and humble people generally towards those of higher social rank.

In Rabindranath's day, Indian money consisted of the rupee, divided into 16 annas with 4 paise (singular *paisa*) to the anna — i.e., 64 paise to the rupee. Today, the decimal currency divides the rupee into 100 paise.

Rabindranath often refers to Indian seasons and the months of the Bengali year. In this book, we have sometimes rendered these in general terms as 'spring', 'summer', 'the rains', 'autumn' or 'winter'. But where the exact reference seemed important, we have kept the Indian names, so that the following table might be useful. (As the terms are used in other Indian languages as well, we have spelt them according to their basic Sanskrit forms.)

Summer (*grishma*) : Vaishakh, mid-April to mid-May
Jyaishtha, mid-May to mid-June

Rains or monsoon (*varsha*) : Asharh, mid-June to mid-July
Shravan, mid-July to mid-August

Early autumn (*sharat*)	: Bhadra, mid-August to mid-September Ashwin, mid-September to mid-October
Late autumn (*hemanta*)	: Kartik, mid-October to mid-November Agrahayan, mid-November to mid-December
Winter (*sheet*)	: Poush, mid-December to mid-January Magh, mid-January to mid-February
Spring (*vasanta*)	: Phalgun, mid-February to mid-March Chaitra, mid-March to mid-April

Rabindranath also refers to many plants, flowers and birds that have no English names. We have explained these only if it is not clear from the text what they might be, or if some special feature about them needs pointing out.

A few poems and stories cannot be understood without a little information, which we have put at the start of the piece or section. All other information has been collected in the endnotes. Many readers, especially Indians, will not need it all; but it is there if you want it. We suggest you glance at the 'Explanations' anyway: they contain some material you may not think of looking for, but which will help you to appreciate the works better. An obelisk (†) in the text indicates that there is a note at the end about that word or phrase. You will also find a lot of information in the Introduction.

As scholars may also need—or even like!—to read these works, we have put in a separate set of material for their use. If you are simply reading for pleasure, you can ignore these notes.

Grandfather's Holiday

Your holiday's among blue skies,
Your holiday's along the steps
Under the tamarind tree it lies,
Among the parul creepers,
Your holiday hope's a-tremble
Your holiday joy is dancing
your holiday's in the meadows,
down to the fathomless lake.
in a corner of the barn,
in every bush and brake.
in the fields where young rice grows,
in waves where the river flows.

I am your old grandfather:
I'm caught up in the spider's web
My holiday goes in the garb
And in your voice, my holiday's
My holiday along the path
At the heart of your holiday,
through spectacles I peer,
of all the world's affairs.
of your own holiday,
sweet-piping music plays.
of your dancing eyes is sped:
my holiday lies hid.

Your holiday's a ferry-boat
The shiuli grove your holiday-basket
Your holiday companion
Voyaging through the chilly night
And when among the opening buds
It comes draped in a mantle
where autumn plies the oars.
fills with its white flowers.
is the dewy wind that breaks
from Himalayan mountain-peaks.
the autumn dawning glides,
with your holiday colours dyed.

You leap, you run around my room:
My piled-up work, my ledger-books
your holiday's in flood.
all tremble at the thud.

O come and leap into my lap, come hug me in your play—
Set up a storm within my heart, my endless holiday.
He who grants you your holiday, who knows what He might mean?
My holiday I gain from you, and that is where I win.

—*Translated by Sukanta Chaudhuri*

Verses

Flowers

I couldn't see
Upon this tree
    A single flower
        Yesterday,
And now it's full:
Can the gardener tell
    How it could happen
        Just this way?

At hide and seek
The flowers peek,
    Within the trees
        They come and go.
Where do they hide,
Where do they bide
    With faces veiled?
        Does someone know?

Hidden from looks
Within their nooks
    They watch and wait
        With open ear,
Until the breeze
Among the trees

>   Whistles a call
>   They somehow hear.
>
> At frantic pace
> They scrub their faces
>   For there's just
>   No time to lose;
> Then on they press
> In coloured dresses
>   From their homes,
>   And out they cruise.
>
> Where is that home
> From which they come?
>   Is it upon
>   The earth close by?
> Dada says no:
> He seems to know
>   It's far away,
>   Up in the sky.
>
> There all the day
> Upon their way
>   Colourful clouds
>   Sail to and fro;
> The sunlight pours
> Through secret doors
>   And in their midst
>   The breezes blow.
>
>   —*Translated by Sukhendu Ray and Sukanta Chaudhuri*

Our Little River

Our little river twists and turns:
It's just knee-deep when summer burns.
How easy is it then to cross:
Cattle and carts just ford across.
The banks slope gently, though they're high,
And in the summer, always dry.

No dirt, no mud: it's all so clean.
The sand glints with a golden gleam.
And to one side, there stands a bed
Of kash,† with white flowers overspread.
Flocks of mynahs† gather there
And with their chatter fill the air,
While deep at night the jackals prowl,
Piercing the silence with their howl.

Groves of palm and mango trees
Upon the other bank one sees.
Nestling beneath their leafy shade
The village houses stand arrayed.
Along the bank the children play,
Splash each other, duck and spray,
Or sometimes, having had their bath,
Catch small fish in bits of cloth.

The village women by that spot
Scrub with sand their pans and pots.
They wash their clothes and have their bath,
Then back they take the homeward path.

And then, after the rains begin,
The river fills up to the brim.
It rushes then upon its course
In muddy whirls and deafening roars.
Upon the banks, among the woods,
A call rings out in joyful mood;
And all the village wakes again
To mark the festival of the rain.

  —*Translated by Sukhendu Ray and Sukanta Chaudhuri*

The Voyage

Beside the landing-stage
A little boat would wait:
It danced among the ripples
When I went down to bathe.

But when I went today
The boat was far away,
Floating upon the ebb-tide
Among the waves at play.

So who can really tell
To what land it might sail—
Among what unknown people,
And how they dress and dwell.

Yet sitting here at home,
I wish that I could roam
Freely afloat just like the boat
And to new countries come,

Where by the distant seas
Among the ocean breeze,
Row upon row, there stand to view
Groves of coconut trees;

Or mountain peaks arise
Against the azure skies
Although no one can ever cross
The tracks of snow and ice;

Or unknown forests where
Among plants new and rare,
All sorts of strange new animals
Roam freely with no care.

Though many nights are gone,
The boat still wanders on:
Why must my father go to work
And not to lands unknown?

—Translated by Sukhendu Ray

The Runaway City

O what a dream of dreams I had one night!
I could hear Binu crying out in fright,
'Come quickly and you'll see a startling sight:
Our city's rushing in a headlong flight!'

    Tottering and lurching
    Calcutta goes marching
    Beams and joists battling
    Doors and windows rattling
    Mansion houses dashing
    Like brick-built rhinos crashing
    Streets and roads jiggling
    Like long pythons wriggling
    While tumbling on their backs
    Tramcars leave their tracks
    Shops and marts go sprawling
    Rising and then falling
    One roof with another
    Bang their heads together
    Rolls on the Howrah Bridge[†]
    Like a giant centipede
    Chased by Harrison Road[†]
    Breaking the traffic code

See the Monument[†] rock
Like a jumbo run amok
Waving its trunk on high
Against the troubled sky
Even our school in merry scoot
Books of maths in hot pursuit
The maps upon the walls aswing
Like a bird that flaps its wing
The school bell tolls on ding dong ding
Without a sense of when to ring

Thousands of people with Calcutta plead,
'Now stop your madness, where will all this lead?'
The city hurtles on and pays no heed,
Its walls and pillars dance with drunken speed.
But let it wander where it will, I say—
What if Calcutta travels to Bombay?
Agra, Lahore, or Delhi if it goes,
I'll sport a turban and wear nagra[†] shoes.
Or even England if right now it reaches,
I'll turn Englishman in hat, coat and breeches.

Then at some sound, my dream came to a pause
To find Calcutta where it always was.

—Translated by Sukhendu Ray

Bhotan-Mohan

Little Bhotan-Mohan dreams
    In a coach-and-four he courses.
His carriage is a banana-gourd,†
    And four bull-frogs his horses.

With a kingfisher to serve as guide,
To Chingrighata's bank he rides,
And there floats the banana-gourd
With a heap of bell-flowers laid aboard
    To sail upon the tides.
Bhotan-Mohan's full of glee:
    He laughs to split his sides.

—Translated by Sukhendu Ray

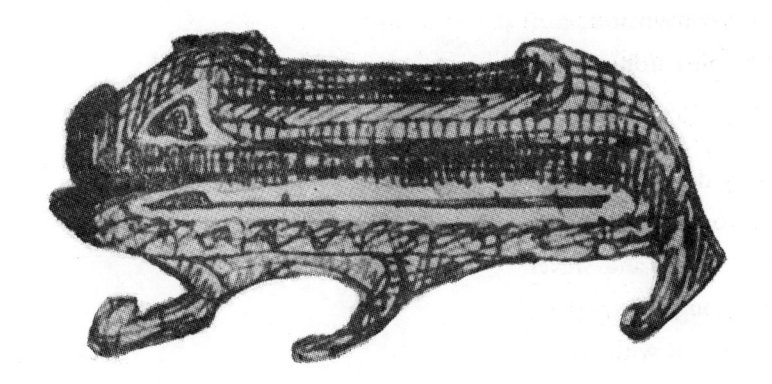

The Flying Machine

A mechanical bird!
How absurd!
A weird creature,
Fire-eater,
Sweeping the sky
Miles high,
Great wings sprawled—
What should you be called?

Did a monster kite
Or adjutant bird[†]
Lay a giant egg
That gave you birth?

Where is your nest?
In a banyan tree,
Or some iron branch
We never can see?

Why don't you sing
As you fly on your trips?
You whine and snivel
As though some devil
Beats you with whips.

Yet man has tamed
Your iron wings:
You're dumb, you're blind:
Caught in a bind
In your iron cage
Like a puppet on strings.

What a sad fate!
No savour, no sweet:
No voice of your own—
Hedged in by men
All day, all night.

You may gnash your teeth
And tower like a giant,
But we're not scared:
We stand defiant.

You carry people
On your back
Through night and day:
We little birds
Salute you—but
From far away.

—Translated by Sukhendu Ray

The Blaze

'Wake up, good sir!' the servant called.
The old man wouldn't heed at all.

He said, 'I can't go venturing:
My alarm clock has yet to ring.'

'Your house is on fire, can't you see?
Forget the alarm, get up and flee.'

'If I wake up too soon, I get
A dreadful pain inside my head.'

'Now your window's in a blaze:
Get going—there's no time to waste.'

'Don't pester me,' the old man groaned.
'Go away now, leave me alone.'

'Just as you wish,' his servant cried,
'But don't blame me if you get fried.'

'Your house is crumbling into dust.
Sleep on the street, if sleep you must.'

—Translated by Sukhendu Ray

The Tiger

A black-striped tiger, big fat beast,
Marked down a man for his evening feast.
He saw his quarry take a broom,
And stalked him as he swept the room.
The man fled; but it came to pass
The tiger found a looking-glass
And saw his face, and raved and ranted:
'How were these stripes upon me planted?'

He left the room, and in a trice
Came where Putu was husking rice.
Puffing his whiskers out, he roared:
'Give me at once some glycerine soap!'

'I simply don't know what you mean,'
Said Putu. 'Where d'you think I've been?
Of lowly parents I have sprung:
I never learnt the English tongue.'

The tiger yelled, 'You're telling lies.
I've got the use of my two eyes.
To lose your stripes you couldn't hope
Unless you had some glycerine soap.'

Putu replied, 'You make me laugh.
I swear I've never touched the stuff.
I'm black and grimy, won't you grant?
Do I look like a memsahib's[†] aunt?'

The tiger said, 'You've got some gall:
I'll crunch you up, flesh, bones and all!'

'O no!' cried Putu in alarm,
'The very thought will do you harm.
For don't you know I'm lowly born,
To Mahatma Gandhi's following sworn?[†]
If on my flesh you come to feed,
You'll lose your caste with utmost speed!'

The tiger quaked in mortal funk.
'Don't come near me, or I'll be sunk!
In Tigerville my name will stink,
With no one could I eat or drink,
Or marry off a single daughter.
Why then, good-bye to soap and water!'

—Translated by Sukhendu Ray

The Palm Tree[†]

The palm tree stands
    On one leg, sees
      Past other trees
        Into the sky.
He wants to pierce
    The clouds so grey
      And soar away:
        But can he fly?

At length his wish
    He starts to spread
    Around his head
        In big round fronds:
He thinks they're wings,
    To let him roam
    Away from home,
        Breaking all bonds.

The livelong day
    The branches quiver,
    Sigh and shiver—
        He thinks he flies,
In his own mind
    Skirting the stars,
    Racing afar
        Across the skies.

But when the wind
    Is still at last
    And the leaves hushed,
        Back homeward then
He turns his thoughts,
    And Mother Earth
    That gave him birth
        He loves again.

        —Translated by Sukhendu Ray and Sukanta Chaudhuri

Sunday

Tell me mother:
The weekdays come so fast and thick—
Have they a car to reach so quick?
But why does Sunday take so long,
Behind the others trudging on?
Has she the farthest skies to cross?
Is her home as poor as yours?

Tell me mother:
The weekdays are an unkind lot:
To go back home they have no thought.
But why is Sunday so pursued
That she stays half the time she should?
Must she go back to do her chores?
Is her home as poor as yours?

Tell me mother:
The weekdays come with such long faces,
No child can stand such airs and graces.
But when at weekends I get up,
There's Sunday with her face lit up.
She starts to cry when back she goes:
Is her home as poor as yours?

—Translated by Sukhendu Ray

The Unresolved

Did you ask me, mother,
    Where I would like to go?
Back to the land from which I came—
    But how am I to know
Where it might be, and what the road
    To take me there again?
I simply can't remember it,
    Although I rack my brain.

When Father saw how sad I was,
    He smiled and said, 'Afar
It lies beyond the banks of clouds,
    The land of the evening star.'
But you, Mother, said, 'Down below
The earth, from where set free
The troops of flowers rise above
    To blossom on the tree.'

While Aunt tells me, 'You'll find that land
    Beneath the ocean's flow,
Where hidden in a chamber dark
    Bright jewels gleam and glow.'
'You silly baby,' Dada says,
    And pulls me by the hair,

'You'll never see that land of yours:
    It's mingled with the air.'

I hear them talk, and think this land
    Is everywhere around:
But Teacher comes along and says,
    'It's nowhere to be found.'

    —*Translated by Sukhendu Ray and Sukanta Chaudhuri*

The Stargazer

The stars of the night
Twinkling bright—
Who are they?
Mother, can you say?
They never sleep,
But all the night
With earthward eyes
Their vigil keep.
However I try,
I cannot fly:
I have no wings
To make me go.
And they, just so,
Having no feet,
Can never greet
The earth below.

The winding river,
Where you go
Every morning
Pitcher on hip—
That's their mirror,
Where they gaze

THE STARGAZER

Through the night
To see their face,
Knowing no sleep.
They look and think,
'If we had been
Village girls,
To the river's brink
Morning and eve
With pitchers we'd run
And play in fun,
Splash and swim
In the full stream.'

And then they watch
Where up above
In the dense woods
Upon our roof,
A princess sleeps
In the stony keep
Of wicked demons
Until I come on
And, with a wave
Of my golden wand,
The princess save.

They look at me
With great envy
And think, if they
Could be your son,
They too could have

Their share of fun,
Happy at play
All through the day
Upon the roof
And then, at night,
Sleep by your side.

One night I woke
From dream, and looked
Through the window bars
Out at the stars:
They were playing shy,
Dimly spread
In a cloudy sky.
Are they just dreams?
It sometimes seems
They are no more.
Their hours they keep
Just when I sleep,
And then, before
The break of day,
They drift away.

The night is blind:
It cannot find
Its way about,
But looks for light
To guide its sight.
Across the sky
It spreads its mat,

And sitting there
Lost in its dreams,
With the star-beams
In fantasy,
It plays a game of look-and-see.

—Translated by Sukhendu Ray and Sukanta Chaudhuri

The Hero

Imagine that I'm travelling through
Far-off foreign lands, Mother, with you.
    You're riding in a palanquin
    With doors ajar to peep between,
And I on a great chestnut horse
    That canters by your side:
    Its hooves stir up a swirling cloud
    Of red dust as I ride.

It's evening, and the sun is low:
Through the Plain of the Twin Lakes we go.
    There's not a single soul in sight:
    You seem to take a little fright
At such a lonely place, and think
    'Where am I being led?'
'Now, Mother, don't be scared,' I say.
    'That's a dry river-bed.'

The fields are full of prickly grass.
Across them, down a winding track we pass.
    No cow or calf, for all the herds
    At evening have gone villagewards.

We wonder where we're going to—
    One can't tell in the dark.
Then you cry out, 'What is that light?
    I think I saw a spark.'

Just then we hear a 'Ho-ho-ho!'
Who are those people shouting as they go?
    Inside the palanquin you cower,
    Calling to all the gods in prayer;
The trembling bearers run away
    And hide behind a tree.
'Don't be afraid,' I call to you,
    'Just leave it all to me.'

They wave their sticks and toss their mops of hair,[†]
Each with a red hibiscus[†] in his ear.
'Stop!' I call out, 'I'm warning you:
You see this sword? I'll run you through
    If one more step you dare!'
Again they shouted 'Ho-ho-ho!'
    And leapt into the air.

'Khoka, don't go!' you cried in fear.
'Calm down,' I said, 'just see what happens here.'
    I spurred my horse into their midst:
    Shields and sabres clanged and hit.
It really was a fearsome fight—
    You'll shudder when I tell
How many men were scared and fled,
    And heads from bodies fell.

Then, just as to yourself you've said
'In such a fight, my Khoka must be dead!'
    I'd ride up, dripping blood and sweat,
    Calling 'The fight's at end!' And when we've met,
Down from the palanquin you'd step
And kiss and draw me to your lap.
'How lucky Khoka was here,' you'd say,
    'Else I'd have been in dread!'

Each day we hear all kinds of news.
Why can't something like this really come true?
    It would be like the books we read:
    Folk would be stunned to hear the deed.
Dada would say, 'How can it be?
    'My puny little brother!'

The neighbours, though, would say, 'What luck
Khoka was with his mother!'

—*Translated by Sukanta Chaudhuri*

The Wise Brother

Mother, your little girl is very silly—
  Your little girl is really just a baby.
The day that we sent up the fire-balloon,
  She seemed to think a star was rising maybe.
When I am playing 'Suppertime', I set
  Pebbles on a toy dish and set them out.
She thinks they're really something to be eaten,
  And stuffs a handful straight into her mouth!
Or if I hold my reading-book before her
  And tell her, 'Learn your lessons, little one!'
She starts to tear the pages with both fists!
  If that's the way she reads, what's to be done?
If I should put a cloth over my face
  And very slowly creep along to catch her,
Your little girl takes fright and starts to scream—
  She thinks a dreadful witch has come to snatch her!
Sometimes when I am angry, and I frown
  And roll my eyes, and scold and shake my head,
She seems to think I'm simply being funny:
  She isn't scared, but laughs right out instead.
Everyone knows Father's away on travel,
  But if I only call out, 'Baba's come!'

THE WISE BROTHER

She jumps up and starts looking all around her:
    Mother, your little girl's so very dumb!
When I lead off the washerman's baby donkey[†]
    To teach it how to read, she makes a bother,
For every time I tell it, 'I'm the Teacher,'
    She keeps on yelling, 'No, you're my Big Brother!'
She tries to catch the moon; she says 'Ganush',
    She simply can't get 'Ganesh'[†] off her tongue.
Mother, your little girl is very silly:
    Your little girl is really much too young.

                      —Translated by Sukanta Chaudhuri

Big and Small

I haven't really got to grow up yet:
    I'm just a child, and so I'm still quite small.
One day I'll be much older than Big Brother—
    As old as Father is, and just as tall.
If Dada then won't learn his lessons,
But with his pet birds keeps on messing,
I'll really scold him well and good—
'Now just you learn your lessons as you should',
I'll tell him, and 'Be quiet, you naughty boy',
    I'll say, when I'm as big as Father is.
I'll take his bird-cage then, without more words,
And keep the very nicest baby birds.

Or in the morning, when it's half-past ten,
    I won't be in a hurry for my bath,
But slip my sandals on, take my umbrella,
    And on a round of all the neighbours start.
When Teacher came, I'd be right there,
And someone would bring out a chair,
But when he said, 'Now where's your slate?
Bring out your books, it's getting rather late',
I'd tell him, 'I'm no longer just a child,
    I've come to be as big as Father is.'

And he'd say, when he saw how I'd been growing,
'Well, Babu, I suppose I'd best be going.'

When Bhulu turned up in the afternoon
    To take me out into the field to play,
I'd frown at him and say, 'Don't make a noise:
    I'm busy with my work, just go away.'
On Chariot Day† I'd even dare
To go alone to the crowded fair.
Uncle would run up in a stew
And say, 'You'll get lost, let me carry you.'
But I'd reply, 'Uncle, why can't you see
    I've come to be as big as Father is?'
Then he would look and say, 'What a surprise!
Our little Khoka's hard to recognize!'

The day I first grow up, Mother will come
    Back from the river, having had her bath.
'Why is the house so very quiet today?'
    She'd wonder, coming up the garden path.
For I'll have learnt to turn the keys
And pay the maid just what I please
Out of the safe: Mother will say,
'Why now, Khoka, what sort of game is this?'
And I'll explain, 'I'm paying out the wages,
    Now that I've grown as big as Father is.
And once we've used up all we have in store,
Just tell me what you need, I'll get some more.'

In Ashwin,† when the Pujas are at hand,
    The big fair to the market-ground will come.

A boat sailing from far away will land
    At Babuganj, bringing my Father home.
Now Father, being a simple soul,
Will think his son is still quite small:
He'll bring some tiny shoes and clothes
In baby-colours, thinking I'll wear those.
'Let Dada wear them,' I would have to say,
    'Now that I've got to be as big as you.
For can't you see,' I'd say, 'Just look at these!
If I should wear them, they'd be quite a squeeze.'

—Translated by Sukanta Chaudhuri

Astronomy

I'd only said, 'When the full moon you see
Caught in the branches of the kadam tree,
    Can't someone quickly go
    And fetch it down below?'
But my big brother only laughed and said,
'Khoka, there's simply nothing in your head!
    The moon's up there, too far away to touch.'
    'Dada,' I said, 'you can't be knowing much.
    When Mother from the window smiles in play,
    Would you say Mother's very far away?'
But even then, Dada just laughed and said,
'Khoka, there's simply nothing in your head.'

He asked, 'Where would you find a net so tall?'
'Dada,' I said, 'just look, the moon's quite small.
    I'd catch it as it lands
    In my two little hands.'
Once again, Dada just laughed and said,
'Khoka, there's simply nothing in your head.
    If the moon were near, you'd see how big it was.'
    'Dada,' I said, 'what stuff you learn in class!
    When Mother bends her head to give a kiss,
    She doesn't suddenly grow big like this!'

But even then, Dada just laughed and said, 'Khoka, there's simply nothing in your head!'

—*Translated by Sukanta Chaudhuri*

Stories

The first five stories in this section come from a book called Galpa-Salpa (Chats). 'The Rats' Feast' was also added to this collection later on.

The stories in Chats *are presented through conversations between a grandfather and his granddaughter. The latter is an imaginary girl, Kusmi; but Rabindranath must have had in mind Nandini, the adopted daughter of his son Rathindranath. He must also have been thinking of another granddaughter, Nandita, to whom he dedicated the book: she was the child of his youngest daughter Mira. Nandita was grown-up and married by this time; but she nursed Rabindranath through his last year of ill-health, and this must have revived her grandfather's memories of her childhood days.*

All the pieces in this section have been translated by Suvro Chatterjee.

The Scientist

'I can't imagine why you like Nilmani Babu so much, Grandpa.'

'That's the most difficult question in the world. Hardly anyone knows the right answer.'

'Leave aside your riddles. Women don't like men who're slovenly and careless and disorganized like him.'

'Well, that's a good notice for him; it only goes to prove he's a full-blooded man!'

'But don't you know what a fuss he makes over trifles? He's always losing things from right under his nose, and hunting for them all over the place!'

'I'm beginning to admire the man.'

'What on earth for?'

'So few of us ever learn that things which seem nearest at hand are farthest from us; yet this doesn't bother us at all.'

'Give me an example.'

'Why, take yourself, for instance.'

'Haven't you found me?'

'If I found you, you'd lose all your charm. The more I look for you the more amazed I am.'

'There you go again: another riddle already!'

'I can't help it, Didi: you're a great riddle to me still—you're always surprising me.'

Kusmi flung her arms around her grandfather's neck. 'You know, Grandpa, that really does sound good,' she said. 'But ask Uncle Bidhu to tell you about the uproar at Nilu Babu's house yesterday.'

'Come on then, Uncle, let's have the story.'

It was quite amazing, said Uncle. The news spread that Nilu Babu had lost his favourite pen. They'd even searched the top of the mosquito-net. At last he summoned Madhu Babu.

'Hey there, Madhu,' he said, 'where on earth is my pen?'

'I'd tell you if I knew,' answered Madhu Babu.

The washerman was called in his turn, and Haru the barber. When the whole household had given up hope, his nephew walked in and said, 'You've stuck your pen behind your ear!'

When this was proved beyond doubt, he slapped his nephew and said, 'You silly boy, it's the pen I can't find that I'm looking for.'

The commotion brought his wife out of the kitchen. 'What are you making such a row about?' she asked.

'I can't find the pen I'm looking for,' said Nilu.

'Well, why don't you make do with the one you've got?' she said. 'You'll never find the other one anyway.'

'I might find one like it in Kundu's shop,' said Nilu.

'No shop would stock that kind of thing,' said his wife.

'Then it must have been stolen somehow,' said Nilu.

'You always say that when you've mislaid something or the other! Now be quiet and start writing with this other pen, and let me get back to work. You've upset the whole neighbourhood already.'

'Why shouldn't I be able to replace a paltry pen?'

'Because nobody's giving away pens for free.'

'Very well then, I'll pay for it. You there, Bhuto—'

'Yes sir?'

'Now I can't find my wallet.'

'It was in your shirt pocket, sir.'

'Really?' The wallet was found there, but it had no money in it. Wherever could the money have gone? So he started looking for the money. The washerman was summoned once more.

'Where's the money I'd left in my wallet?'

'How should I know?' the washerman said. 'I never washed that shirt anyway.'

Osman the tailor was next. 'What have you done with the money in my wallet?'

'It must be in that iron chest of yours,' Osman shot back angrily.

His wife said, on returning from her daughter's house: 'Well, what is it this time?'

'All these servants about the house—they're nothing but a bunch of thieves!' said Nilmani. 'I've had my pocket picked, that's what.'

'O my fate,' she cried, 'you paid off the landlord the other day with those thirty-five rupees.'

'Did I really? But didn't he serve notice on us because we hadn't been paying the rent?'

'You cleared the debt after he'd done so.'

'What do you mean? I've already rented Nimchand Haldar's house in Badurbagan!'

'Badurbagan!' said his wife. 'Where on earth is that?'

'Wait a minute, let me think,' said Nilmani. 'I can't remember the address. All I know is that I've signed a contract—I've rented his house for a year and a half.'

'Oh, well done!' said his wife. 'Now who's going to pay two rents every month?'

'That's not the point,' said Nilmani. 'It's the address I'm worried about. I've written down in my notebook that it's somewhere in Badurbagan, but I simply can't remember whether I wrote down the street and house number.'

'Why don't you just check your notebook then?'

'That's just the problem. My notebook's missing these last three days.'

'Don't you remember, uncle?' said his nephew. 'You gave it to Didi to write her class notes in.'

'Well, where's your Didi?'

'She's gone to stay with her uncle in Allahabad!'

'Here's a pretty mess. Now however will I find that address?'

At that moment, who should turn up but Nimchand Haldar's clerk. 'I've come to collect the rent on the house at Badurbagan,' he said.

'Which house would that be?'

'Why, no. 13 Shibu Samaddar Lane, of course.'

'Thank goodness! Did you hear that, wife? It's no. 13 Shibu Samaddar Lane. What a relief!'

'What good will that do?' she demanded.

'Why, I've got the address I was looking for!'

'So you have. Now tell me how you're going to pay two rents.'

'Oh, we'll talk about that later. But now we know for sure it's no. 13 Shibu Samaddar Lane.'

He shook the clerk by the hand. 'Thank you, brother, you've saved me. Tell me your name, I'll write it down in my notebook.'

He fumbled in his pocket. 'Oh bother, my notebook's in Allahabad. Never mind, I'll learn it by heart: no. 13, Shibu Samaddar Lane!'

'That business of the pen was just a trifle,' said Kusmi. 'You should have heard the uproar in his house the day he lost one of his sandals. His wife swore she'd go off to her parents. And the servants declared they'd all leave if they were accused of stealing half a pair of sandals—and patched in three places at that.'

Actually, I got to hear about it too, I said to her. When they told me things were getting out of hand, I went over to see Nilu.

'What's all this about a lost sandal?' I asked him.

'It's not lost, Dada,' he said. 'It's stolen—I can prove it!'

This talk of proof scared me. The man's a scientist. If he started drawing out those proofs one after the other, he'd hold me up the whole day. I had to play it safe. 'Well, it must have been stolen then. But I wonder where those thieves hang out who go about stealing single sandals.'

'That's something worth discussing,' said Nilu. 'It goes to prove the price of leather has gone up.'

You couldn't argue with him after that. 'You've hit it, brother,' I agreed. 'Everything's a matter of prices and markets these days. That's why I find the cobbler calls every few days at the Malliks' big house, pretending to re-sole the gatekeeper's fancy shoes; but his eyes are actually glued to the feet of the people passing by.'

I did manage to calm him down that day. And the sandal was found under his bed. Nilu's favourite dog had had a great time tearing it to shreds. Nilu was heartbroken at recovering the sandal, because it put paid to his proofs.

Kusmi said, 'Grandpa, how can anyone be so silly?'

'Don't you say such things about him, Didi,' I warned her. 'He's a great mathematician. His brain's grown so refined with working out all those sums that ordinary people can't see it any more.'

Kusmi turned up her nose and said, 'What does he do with his precious maths?'

'He makes discoveries,' I told her. 'He may not be very good at figuring out how sandals are lost; but he's sure to know why the moon is a quarter of a second late in going into eclipse. Of late he's plunged heart and soul into proving that the stars and planets, and everything else in creation, are not simply going round and round but hopping about. Zillions of grasshoppers have been let loose in the universe. He's worked out irrefutable proofs of this in his notebook. I don't dare raise the subject for fear he should start bringing them out.'

Kusmi was very annoyed by this. 'Everything about him is chaotic! What an idea, to forget food and sleep and go measuring how grasshoppers jump! No wonder he's in such a mess!'

'His life won't go round and round,' I remarked. 'It'll hop and gambol.'

'Now I understand everything: why this man's always losing pens, why his sandals keep going astray, and even why you like him so much,' said Kusmi. 'You like all sorts of cranks, and it's only people like that who flock round you.'

'Well, let me tell you one last thing, Didi. You think his wife is fed up with a hopeless husband like Nilu. Let me tell you a little secret: it's really just the opposite. She's utterly taken with his sloppy scatterbrained ways. And so am I.'

The King's Palace[†]

'Aunt Iru was a very clever girl: wasn't she, Grandpa?' asked Kusmi.

'Of course she was—cleverer than you are!'

Kusmi stopped short. She sighed a little and said, 'So that's why she managed to cast a spell on you.'

'You've got it all wrong. What gave you the idea that you must be clever in order to charm people?'

'What then?'

'You need to be silly, that's what. There's a simpleton deep inside everyone: that's where you must appeal to charm them, by being truly silly. That's why love is called the art of charming.'

'Tell me how it's done.'

'I've no idea. I was only going to tell you what happens when someone is put under that kind of spell.'

'All right, carry on.'

'I've always had a great weakness, you see: I'm amazed by every little thing. That's what Iru took advantage of. She kept amazing me all the time.'

'But wasn't Aunt Iru younger than you are?'

'Of course she was, by a full year at least. But she was wise beyond her years—I could never catch up with her. She ruled over me as though I hadn't yet cut my teeth. And I could only stare open-mouthed at everything she did.'

'What fun!'

What fun indeed. She worked me up into a state with a story about a king's seven-mansioned palace. I never found out where it was—she alone knew the secret. I was going through the Third Reader then, I remember. I asked my teacher about it, but he only laughed and tweaked my ears.

I would often plead with Iru: 'Tell me where the palace is.'

She would only open her eyes very wide and say, 'Right here in this house.'

I would gape and say, 'No, really—in this house? Show me where it is!'

But she always said, 'You can't see it unless you know the magic words.'

'Then teach me the magic words, please,' I would beg her. 'I'll give you that seashell I splice mangoes with.'

'It's forbidden to tell them to anyone,' she would reply.

'Why, what'll happen if you tell me?' I would ask.

But she would only gasp, 'Oh, goodness me!'

I never found out what would happen if she told me, but her attitude made me shudder. I decided to shadow her one day when she next went to visit the palace; but she seemed to go only while I was at school. I asked her once why she couldn't go at any other time, but she only said, 'Oh, goodness me!', and I was too scared to press her any more.

She would give herself great airs when she managed to impress me. Sometimes, when I had just returned from school, she would blurt out: 'You won't believe what happened today.'

'What was it?' I would ask, all excited.

And she would reply, 'Shan't tell you.'

I suppose it was best that way. I never got to know what happened, so I could go on dreaming of fantastic things.

She would go off to the Hurry-Scurry Fields while I was asleep. A winged horse grazed in the meadows there, and whisked away anyone who came there up into the clouds.

I would clap my hands with joy when I heard this, and say, 'What fun that must be!'

And she would reply, 'Fun indeed! Oh, goodness me!'

Her expression scared me so much that I never got round to asking what the danger might be.

She had even seen fairies keeping house, and not very far from our home either. She had seen them in the gloom among the thick roots of the old banyan tree on the east bank of our pond. They lived only on nectar, and she had made friends by gathering flowers for them. But she only went to visit their houses when we boys were doing our lessons with Nilkamal-Master[†] on the south balcony.

'What would happen if you went at some other time?' I would ask her.

'The fairies would turn into butterflies and fly away,' she would tell me.

She had many other things in her magic bag, but it was that unseen palace that really fascinated me. Just think—a mysterious palace tucked away in our very own house, perhaps right next to my own bedroom, only I could never catch a glimpse of it as I didn't know the magic words! I often went with Iru to the mango grove, plucked green mangoes for her, even bribed her with my precious seashell. She would peel the mangoes and eat them with dill leaves; but every time I asked her about the magic words, pat came the reply: 'Oh, goodness me!'

Then Iru got married and went off to her in-laws, and the secret went with her. And I grew too old to go looking for palaces, so I never found the place after all. Since then I have seen lots of real palaces from afar, but a palace tucked away near my own house—oh, goodness me!

The Big News

'You promised to tell me all the big news of the world, Grandpa,' Kusmi reminded me. 'How else can I be educated?'

'The bag of big news is too heavy to carry around,' said Grandfather. 'It's stuffed so full of rubbish.'

'Well, leave out the rubbish and tell me the rest, can't you?'

'That would leave very little substance: you'd think it wasn't big news at all. But it would be the real news.'

'That's all right, give me the real news then.'

'So I will. You're a lucky girl. If you were reading for your BA degree, your table would be piled high with rubbish; you'd have to trundle round a load of notebooks crammed with lies and nonsense.'

'All right, Grandpa. Tell me some really big news, and try to keep it very short,' said Kusmi. 'Let's see how good you are at it.'

'All right, listen on.'

It was peaceful on board the merchant boat. Then a violent quarrel broke out between the oars and the sail. The oars rattled up in a body and laid their case before the boatman. 'We shan't put up with this any more,' they said. 'That sail of yours, all puffed up with pride, calls us a vulgar mob—and all because we're lashed to the planks down in the hold and forced to wade through the water night and day, while he merrily goes his own way, with no hand to push him along. He thinks that makes him a superior person. You must decide once and for all who's worth more to you. If we're really of no consequence, we'll resign all together. Let's see how you manage your boat without us!'

The boatman sensed trouble. He took the oars aside and whispered to them, 'Don't pay him the slightest attention, my brothers! He's just a windbag. Why, if you strong men didn't do your utmost, this boat wouldn't move at all! That sail's a toff, an empty upper-deck showoff. One strong gust of wind and he crumples up in a heap, without so much as a flutter—whereas I know you'll stay by my side through thick and thin. It's you who carry that monstrous load of vanity through all weathers. How dare he call you such vile names!'

But now the boatman was afraid the sail might have heard his words. So he went up to him and whispered in his ears, 'Dear Mr Sail, there's no one to compare with you. Who says you only run a boat? That's just crude labour, quite unworthy of you. You simply follow your noble fancy, while your lackeys bring up the rear. Maybe you sag a little now and then when you're out of breath, but what of that? Brother, don't listen to the vulgar prattle of those oars. I've fixed them so tightly that labour they must, no matter how much they grumble and splash about!'

At this the sail puffed up his chest and yawned as he looked up at the clouds.

But the signs don't augur well for him. Those oars are tough-boned. They've been lying on their sides a long time, but they'll stand up straight and hit back hard one of these days. The sail's pride will be shattered. The world will learn that it's the oars that move the boats through tide and storm and rain.

'Is that all?' asked Kusmi. 'Was that your big news? You must be joking.'

'It sounds like a joke now,' said Grandfather, 'but one day it'll be seen for the big news that it is.'

'What's going to happen then?'

'Why, your Grandpa will fall in with those oars and learn to keep time with them!'

'And what about me?'

'You'll go about oiling the oars where they creak too much.'

'You understand now, don't you?' asked Grandfather. 'The really important news is always tiny, like a seed. It takes time for a big tree to grow out of it, branches and all.'

'Oh yes, I understand,' said Kusmi.

It was evident from her face that she hadn't understood at all. But Kusmi has the virtue of never admitting that to her Grandpa. It's best not to tell her she's not as clever as her Aunt Iru used to be.

The Fairy

🌷

'You keep spinning such tall tales, Grandpa,' said Kusmi. 'Why don't you tell me a true story for a change?'

I said, 'There are two classes of things in this world. One is the true, the other is the more-than-true. I deal with the more-than-true.'

'Grandpa, people say they can't understand you at all.'

'They're quite right,' I agreed. 'But the fault is theirs, not mine.'

'Why don't you explain what you mean by the more-than-true?'

'Why, just look at yourself,' I told her. 'Everybody knows of you as Kusmi. And that's perfectly true—there are proofs enough. But I have come to know that you're a fairy from fairyland. That's more-than-true.'

Kusmi was pleased. 'But how did you find out?' she asked.

I said: 'Once you had an exam the next day, and you were sitting up in bed, learning your geography, until at last you began to nod. Your head sank upon the pillow, and you fell fast asleep. It was a full-moon night, and the moonlight came pouring in through the window and fell on your face and your sky-blue sari. I saw quite plainly that the Fairy King had sent a scout to look for his runaway fairy. He came sailing past my window, and his white shawl swept into the room. He looked you down from head to toe, but couldn't decide whether you were that runaway fairy. He thought you might be a fairy of this very earth: you might be too heavy for them to carry away. Meanwhile the moon climbed higher; the room was cast in shadow. Standing under the shishu tree, the scout shook his head and went back. Then I knew you were a fairy from fairyland, trapped down here by the weight of the earth.'

'How did I reach here from fairyland, Grandpa?' Kusmi asked.

I said, 'You were skyriding on a butterfly's back in a forest of asphodel, when you caught sight of a ferry-boat moored at the horizon.

Painting by Rabindranath. Rabindra Bhavan, Visva-Bharati.

It was made of white clouds, and it rocked in the wind. You got into the boat on a fancy, and it drifted off till it reached the earth, where your mother picked you up in her arms.'

Kusmi clapped her hands in delight. 'Is all this really true, Grandpa?'

'There you go again!' said I. 'Who ever said it was true? What do I care for the truth? This is more-than-true.'

Then she asked, 'Can't I ever go back to fairyland?'

'Perhaps you can,' I answered, 'if a strong breeze from those parts should touch the sails of your dream boat.'

'Suppose that does happen, how shall I find my way back? Is fairyland very far away?'

'It's very close by,' I replied.

'How close?'

'As close as you are now to me. You won't even have to get out of this bed to go there. Just wait for another night when the moonlight comes through the window, and if you look out, you shan't have any doubts left at all. You'll see the cloud-ferry floating down the moonbeams towards you. But that boat won't do for you any more: you're an earth-bound fairy now. You'll leave your body behind in bed, and only your spirit will go with you. Your truth will remain here on earth, while your more-than-true soars up, up and away, where none of us can reach.'

'Very well then,' said Kusmi, 'on the next full-moon night I'll watch the sky from the window. Grandpa, will you hold on to my hand and come with me?'

'No, but I can tell you the way even as I sit right here. I have the power—I'm a dealer in things more-than-true.'

More-than-True

'Grandpa, that more-than-truth you were talking about the other day—is it to be found only in fairyland?'

'Not at all, my dear,' said I. 'There's a lot of it in this world of ours. You only need to look. But of course you must have the eye to spot it.'

'Can you see it?'

'That's one power I do have. I suddenly catch sight of things that aren't meant to be seen. When you sit by my side learning your geography, I remember my own studies. That Yang-tse-kiang river of yours—every time I read the name, it conjured up a kind of geography that was absolutely no use in passing exams. Even now I can see that long caravan with its enormous loads of silk. I once found a place on the back of one of those camels.'

'Come off it, Grandpa! I know you never rode a camel in your life!'

'Really, Didi, you ask too many questions.'

'Never mind, go on. What happened then? Where did you get a camel from?'

'There, another question already!—I never worry about finding camels: I simply climb on to one. Whether or not I visit other lands, nothing stops me from travelling. That's the way I am.'

'Well, what happened after that?'

'After that I passed through so many grand cities one by one—Fuchung, Hangchow, Chungkung; I crossed so many deserts, finding my way at night by the stars. And then I came upon the jungle at the foot of the Ush-khush Mountains†—past olive groves, through vineyards, along pine forests. I fell among thieves, and a great white bear rose on its hind legs in front of me.'

'When did you find the time to wander like that?'

'Oh, I travelled while the class was busy with their exams.'
'But how did you pass the exams then?'
'That's easy—I never did pass.'
'All right, get on with the story.'

'Now shortly before I set out on that journey I had read in the *Arabian Nights* about the beautiful princess of China. And wonder of wonders! I chanced upon her in my travels. It was on the bank of the Fuchao river. The landing-place was paved in marble, leading up to a pavilion of blue stone. There was a champak tree on each side, with a stone lion at its foot. Incense burned in gold censers, and the smoke rose in coils. One maid was doing up the princess' hair, while two others fanned her, one with a yak's tail. I somehow appeared before her all of a sudden. She was feeding her milk-white peacock with pomegranate seeds. She gave a start and asked: 'Who are you?'
'I remembered in a flash: I was the crown prince of Bengal!'
'How could that be? You were only—'
'Questions again! I'm telling you I was the crown prince of Bengal for that day, and that's what saved me: otherwise she would have had me thrown out there and then. Instead she gave me tea in a golden cup—tea laced with chrysanthemums, bearing the most marvellous scent.'
'Did she marry you after all that?'
'Now that's something very secret. Nobody knows to this day.'
Kusmi clapped her hands: 'It happened, I know it happened! You married the princess in the very grandest way.'
Plainly she would be very upset if it didn't work out like that. 'Yes, in the end she married me all right. I got my Princess Angchani, and half the kingdom of Hangchow as well. And then—'
'Then what? Did you set off on your camel again?'
'Else how did I come back to be your Grandpa? Yes, I climbed back on to my camel, the camel that went nowhere. The fusung bird flew carolling over my head.'
'The fusung bird! Where does it live?'
'Oh, it lives nowhere, but its tail feathers are blue, its wings yellow, and there's a brown patch on its shoulders. They flew off in great numbers, and perched on the hachang tree.'

'I've never heard of the hachang tree.'

'Nor have I—I only just thought of it as I was telling you the story. That's the sort of person I am: I'm never ready beforehand—I tell you whatever I see, even as I'm seeing it. Today my fusung bird has flown across the sea. I haven't had news of it for ages.'

'But what about your marriage? And the princess?'

'I won't answer you there, my dear, so you'd better stop asking. And anyway, you mustn't let it upset you. You weren't even born then, remember.'

The Rats' Feast

'It's an outrage,' said the boys. 'We shan't study under a new teacher!'

They were going to have a new Sanskrit teacher, Kalikumar Tarkalankar[†] by name.

The vacation was over, and the boys were on the train going back to school. A wag had already changed the new teacher's name into *Kalo Kumro Tatka Lanka*, 'Black pumpkin and red-hot chilli', and made up a rhyme called 'The Sacrifice of the Black Pumpkin.'[†] They were belting it out in chorus.

At Arkhola an elderly gentleman boarded the train. He had a bedroll with him, a few bundles, a big trunk and two or three large earthen pots, their tops bound with cloth. A tough boy, whom everyone called Bichkun, yelled at him at once: 'Get down, you old fool, there's no room here. Go to another carriage.'

The old man said, 'The whole train's packed, there isn't a seat to be found anywhere. Don't worry, I'll sit in a corner here; I won't trouble you at all.'

He left the whole seat to them, rolled out his bedding on the floor, and settled down on it. Then he turned to them and asked, 'Where are you going, my sons, and for what?'

'To settle somebody's hash for him,' said Bichkun.

'And who might he be?' asked the old man.

'*Kalo Kumro Tatka Lanka*,' came the reply, and the boys merrily took up the chant:

> Black pumpkin and red hot chilli,
> We'll soon make him look pretty silly!

At Asansol the train stopped for a while, and the old man got down to have a wash. The moment he came back Bichkun shouted, 'Get off this coach if you know what's good for you, mister.'

'Why, what's the matter?'

'There are rats all over the place.'

'Rats! You don't say so!'

'Look for yourself. See what they've done to your pots over there!'

The old gentleman saw that all the sugar balls in one pot were gone, and not a morsel was left of the sweets[†] in another.

'They've run off with whatever you had in that bundle of yours too,' said Bichkun.

The bundle had held five ripe mangoes from his garden.

'Poor creatures,' he said with a smile, 'they must have been very hungry!'

'Oh no, they're always like that,' Bichkun told him. 'Even if they're not hungry, they'll tuck in all the same!'

The boys roared with laughter: 'That's right, mister. If there had been anything more they'd have eaten that too!'

'It's my fault,' said the man. 'If I'd known there would be all these rats on the train, I'd have come better stocked.'

The boys felt rather disappointed when they saw the old man wasn't angry. They would have enjoyed seeing him lose his temper.

At Bardhaman there was an hour's wait. They had to change trains. The gentleman said, 'I won't trouble you young men any more. I can find a seat in another coach this time.'

'Oh no, you must come with us,' they clamoured. 'If there's anything left in your bundles, we'll guard it all the way. We promise you won't lose anything else!'

'Very well,' said the gentleman. 'You go ahead and board the train; I'll be along in a minute.'

They climbed into the new train. A little later a sweet-seller came trundling his cart to their window, the gentleman beside him.

He handed each of them a paper bag full of sweets, saying, 'This time the rats won't go hungry.' The boys gave a hurrah. Next a mango-seller came along with his basket, and mangoes were added to the feast.

The boys asked the gentleman, 'Tell us where you're going and why.'

'I'm looking for a job,' he told them. 'I'll go wherever I can find one.'

'What sort of work can you do?' they asked.

'I'm a schoolteacher,' he said. 'I teach Sanskrit.'

They clapped their hands. 'Then you must come to teach in our school!'

'But why should they have me?'

'We'll make them,' they assured him. 'We shan't let Kalo Kumro Tatka Lanka set foot in the neighbourhood, you'll see.'

'You're making things difficult for me. Suppose your secretary doesn't like me?'

'He'd better—else we'll all quit the school together!'

'Very well then, my sons—take me to your school.'

The train puffed into the station. The secretary of the school committee was waiting in person on the platform. Seeing the old gentleman get off, he came up to meet him.

'Welcome, Master Tarkalankar, sir. Your rooms are ready for you.' And he bent down to touch the old man's feet.

Wishes Come True

Subalchandra's son was called Sushilchandra. But a name does not always reflect the person. 'Subal' means 'strong', but he was rather frail; and 'Sushil' was not particularly well-behaved, though his name meant just that.

The boy was always vexing the neighbours with his pranks, so his father would often run after him to punish him. But the father was rheumatic, while the boy ran like a deer, so the blows did not always find their mark. When Sushilchandra did get caught, however, he met with no mercy.

It was a Saturday, when school closed early at two o'clock; but Sushil did not feel like going to school at all. There were several reasons for this. First, there was going to be a geography test; and second, there would be a firework show in the evening at the Boses', for which they were going to prepare from the morning. Sushil had planned to spend the whole day there.

After some hard thinking, he went back to bed when it was time for school. His father came and asked, 'What's wrong? Why are you in bed? Aren't you going to school?'

'I've got a tummy-ache. I can't go to school today,' said Sushil.

Subal could easily see that the boy was making it up. So he said to himself, 'Wait—he needs to be taught a lesson.' Aloud, he said, 'A tummy-ache, is it? Then you'd better stay at home all day. Hari can go by himself to see the fireworks at the Boses'. And I suppose you shouldn't have any of those toffees I got for you. Just lie down quietly while I mix you some of that bitter medicine!' He locked the boy in and went off to prepare it.

Sushil was in a fix. He loved toffees just as much as he hated the bitter fever-medicine. And on top of it, he had been longing since last night to go to the Boses': even that might not be possible.

When Subal Babu returned with a huge bowl of medicine, Sushil sprang up from bed and announced, 'My tummy's stopped aching! I think I'll be off to school.'

'No, no,' said his father, 'just drink this up and rest.' He forced the boy to swallow the stuff, locked the door again, and left.

Forced to lie in bed, Sushil cried to himself all day and kept thinking, 'If only I were as old as my father! I could do just as I pleased—no one could lock me up!'

His father Subal Babu sat brooding outside, thinking, 'My parents pampered me too much; that's why I didn't care to get a proper education. If I could get back my childhood! This time I'd study properly and not waste my time.'

Now the Lady of Wishes happened to be passing by at that very moment. She overheard the wishes of both father and son, and said, 'Well, let me make their wishes come true for some time and see what happens!'

So she appeared before the father and told him, 'You will have what you desire. Tomorrow you will be your son's age.' To the son she said, 'You will be as old as your father tomorrow.' Both of them were delighted to hear this.

Old Subalchandra did not sleep well at night; he fell asleep only towards the morning. But today a curious thing happened: he leapt out of bed at the crack of dawn. He discovered that he had grown very small. He had got back all his teeth, and lost his beard and moustache. His clothes were now much too big for him—the sleeves dangled nearly to the ground, the neck of his shirt fell halfway down his chest, and the loose end of his dhoti trailed in such a way that he was in danger of tripping.

Meanwhile our Sushilchandra, who would be up to his pranks from daybreak, just could not get up today. When at last he was woken up by his father's shouts, he found that he had grown so much overnight that his clothes had burst their seams. His face was covered with grey stubble, and his hair had vanished completely. Feeling his head, he encountered a shining bald pate. He did not feel like getting up at all. He yawned over and over, and tossed in bed for a long time. The noise made by his father finally made him get up, in a perfectly foul mood.

Their wishes had come true, but it only made trouble for them. Sushil had always imagined that if he grew up and could be free like his father, he would climb trees, dive into pools, eat green mangoes, plunder birds' nests and roam around all day long; he would come home and eat whatever he liked whenever he liked, with no one to scold him. But strange to say, that morning he felt no urge to climb a tree. He shuddered at the sight of the scummy pond, feeling quite sure that he would shiver and catch fever if he plunged into it. He rolled out a reed mat on the porch and sat there, thinking quietly to himself.

Once he thought he should not give up all games so suddenly— he should at least try. So he got up and tried to climb an amra tree nearby. Only yesterday he had climbed it like a squirrel; today his old body protested. As soon as he tried to pull himself up by a thin, newly-sprouted branch, it broke under his weight and he fell to the ground. Passers-by laughed themselves hoarse to see the old man playing childish pranks. With lowered head, Sushil returned mortified to his mat on the porch, called the servant and said, 'Boy, bring me a rupee's worth of toffees from the market!'

Sushil had always been fond of toffees. Every day, at the shop near his school, he saw sweets of many colours, and bought some whenever he was given a few paise. He had always dreamt of stuffing his pockets with them when he had lots of money like his father. Today his servant brought him a big pile, a whole rupee's worth. He took a piece and started to suck it with toothless gums; but the old man did not care for children's sweets. 'Let me give them to my child-father,' he thought; but at once decided, 'No, it'll make the boy sick.'

All the little boys who had played kabaddi with Sushil till yesterday came as usual, saw the old man and ran away. Sushil had always thought he would play kabaddi with his friends all day long if he were as free as his father; but now the sight of Rakhal, Gopal, Akshay, Nibaran, Harish and Nanda only irritated him. 'Here am I sitting in peace,' he thought, 'and along come these boys to bother me!'

Earlier it had been old Subalchandra's habit each day to sit on the porch on his mat and think, 'When I was young, I wasted my time in mischief. If I could get my childhood back, I'd shut myself in my room and study quietly all day. I'd even forgo hearing stories from my grandmother in the evenings, and instead go over my lessons by lamplight till ten or eleven o'clock.' But having got back his childhood, he revolted at the idea of school. Sushil would prod him in the morning: 'Baba, won't you go to school?' Subal would scratch his head, lower his eyes and mumble, 'I've got a tummy-ache, I can't go to school.' Sushil would grow angry at this: 'Oh, can't you? I've had lots of tummy-aches in my day when it was time for school. I know all the tricks!'

Indeed, Sushil had avoided school in so many ways, and so recently, that his father couldn't hope to hoodwink him. Sushil began sending his little father to school by force. On returning home, Subal wanted to run about and play for a while; but old Sushil wished to stick his glasses on his nose and read aloud from Krittibas's *Ramayana*[†] in a sing-song voice at the time. Subal's noisy games disturbed him, so he would make Subal sit down with his slate and do sums. They were such long sums that his father took a whole hour to work out a single one. In the evenings, a group of old men gathered in Sushil's room to play chess. To keep Subal quiet during that time, Sushil hired a tutor, who kept Subal busy till ten at night.

Sushil was equally strict in the matter of Subal's diet. He remembered that when his father had been old, he suffered from indigestion if he overate in the slightest degree; so now he forbade him from having hearty meals. But poor Subal, being young now, had acquired a huge appetite—he could have scrunched up stones and digested them. The less Sushil gave him to eat, the more desperate he became for food. He grew so thin that his bones began to stick out. At this Sushil, thinking that he was suffering from some serious illness, began to stuff him with medicines.

Old Sushil too got into all kinds of trouble. Nothing he had liked doing as a child agreed with him any longer. Earlier, whenever he heard that a jatra[†] had arrived in the neighbourhood, he would escape from home, be it rain or shine, to see the show. When the old Sushil tried doing so now, he came down with a bad cold and body-ache, and took to bed for three whole weeks. He had always taken a dip in the pond: on doing so now, his joints grew stiff and swollen, and he was so crippled by rheumatism that it took him six months to recover. After that he only bathed once every two days in warm water, and refused to let Subal bathe in the pond either. If he ever jumped out of bed as he had done as a child, all his bones would shiver in protest. No sooner did he put a paan[†] in his mouth than he found he had no teeth to chew it with. Absentmindedly taking up a brush and comb, he would be reminded that he had no hair left. If he ever forgot himself so far as to hurl a stone at old Aunt Andi's earthen pitcher, people came rushing to scold the old man for such childish tricks: he did not know where to hide his shame.

Subalchandra, too, sometimes forgot how young he was. Imagining himself as old as before, he would turn up at old men's gatherings where they were playing at cards or dice, and begin to talk like a grown-up. They would box his ears and send him away, saying, 'Less of your impertinence—run away and play.' There were days when he said to his teacher, 'Give me the hookah—I'd like a smoke.' The teacher would order him to stand on the bench on one leg. He would ask the barber, 'Why haven't you come to shave me all these days?' The man would think the boy was quite a wag, and retort, 'I'll come in ten years' time!' At times Subal even tried to beat Sushil out of old habit. Then Sushil would lose his temper and shout, 'Is this what you're learning at school? You dare to hit an old man, you little rascal!' And people came running to scold and thrash him for his impudence.

At last Subal began to pray earnestly: 'If only I were as old as my son Sushil, and free to do what I liked!' And Sushil would pray, 'O Lord, make me as young as my father, so that I might play again to my heart's content. I can't control my father any more—he's become much too naughty, and I'm worried about him all the time.'

The Lady of Wishes now came again to ask, 'Well, have you had enough of your wishes?'

Both father and son bowed their heads as low as her feet. 'Yes, mother, we've had enough. Please turn us back into what we were before!'

'All right,' she said, 'you will both be yourselves again tomorrow morning.'

Next morning Subal was the same old man as before, and Sushil woke up as the little boy he used to be. Both imagined they had been dreaming. Subal called his son gruffly and said, 'Sushil, aren't you going to start learning your grammar?'

Sushil scratched his head and said, 'Father, I've lost my book.'

Plays

All the pieces in this section have been translated by Suvro Chatterjee.

The Welcome

❦

SCENE I

[A village road.
Chaturbhuj Babu has come back to the village after passing his MA examinations, hoping that everyone will make a great fuss over him. There is a plump Afghan cat with him.
Enter Nilratan.]

Nilratan: Hello there, Chatu Babu. When did you arrive?
Chaturbhuj: Directly the MA exams were over. I—
Nilratan: Ah, you've got a fine cat there!
Chaturbhuj: This year the exams were very—
Nilratan: Tell me, where did you find that cat?
Chaturbhuj: Bought it. The subjects I'd offered—
Nilratan: How much did you pay for it?
Chaturbhuj: I don't remember. Nilratan Babu, has anybody passed any exams in our village?
Nilratan: Oh, lots of them. But you won't see a cat like that in these parts.
Chaturbhuj: (to himself) Confound him, he can't talk about anything but cats—it doesn't seem to matter that I've just passed my MA!

[Enter the Zamindar.†]

Zamindar: Ah, Chaturbhuj—what have you been doing in Calcutta all this time?
Chaturbhuj: I've just finished my MA, sir.

Zamindar: Finished off your daughter?† Your own *meye*! How could you do it?

Chaturbhuj: You've got me wrong—after passing the BA I—

Zamindar: Married her off! And we didn't get to hear of it?

Chaturbhuj: Not a marriage†—a BA—

Zamindar: Oh, it's all the same—what you city people call a BA, we call a *biye*† in these backwaters. Anyway, let it pass—this cat of yours is a stunner, I must say.

Chaturbhuj: You're mistaken, sir, my—

Zamindar: No mistake about it. You won't find another such cat in the whole district!

Chaturbhuj: But we're not discussing cats!

Zamindar: Of course we are—I'm telling you you won't find another cat like this!

Chaturbhuj: (to himself) Confound him!

Zamindar: Why don't you drop by my place with your cat sometime this evening? The boys would be delighted.

Chaturbhuj: Of course—I quite understand. They haven't seen me for a long time.

Zamindar: Yes, I suppose so... but what I mean is, even if you can't come yourself, send Beni round with the cat—I want the boys to see it. *(Exit)*

[Enter Uncle Satu.]

Satu: How are you, my boy? Been away a long time, haven't you?

Chaturbhuj: That's right. There were so many examinations—

Satu: This cat of yours—

Chaturbhuj: (furiously) I'm going home. *(About to leave)*

Satu: Hey, wait a minute—this cat—

Chaturbhuj: No, sir, I've got work to do.

Satu: Oh come on, now, answer a civil question. This cat— *(Chaturbhuj strides away without another word)* Just look at that. It's education that's ruining these young people. We know what they're worth, but they're stuffed full of conceit!

SCENE II

[Inside Chaturbhuj's house.]

Maid: Mother, Dada Babu has come home in a blazing temper.
Mother: Why, what's the matter?
Maid: I don't know.

[Enter Chaturbhuj.]

Little Boy: Dada, can I have this cat?
Chaturbhuj: (slaps him hard) Cat, cat, cat the whole day long, is it?
Mother: No wonder the poor boy's angry! He comes home after such a long time and these brats start annoying him at once.—*(To Chaturbhuj)* Let me have the cat, son. I'll give it some rice and milk that I've put by.
Chaturbhuj: (furiously) Here, mother, you can have the cat and feed it all you want. I shan't stop to eat—I'm leaving at once.
Mother: (plaintively) What makes you say such a thing?—Your meal's ready and waiting, dear. You can sit down to it as soon as you've had your bath!
Chaturbhuj: No, I'm leaving. You're all crazy about cats in these parts. No one cares for men of worth. *(Kicks out at the cat)*
Aunt: Don't hurt the cat—she hasn't done any harm.
Chaturbhuj: When it comes to a cat you're all heart, but you have no pity for human beings! *(Exit)*
Little Girl: (looking out) Come and see, Uncle Hari—what a big fat tail!
Hari: Whose tail—Chaturbhuj's?
Girl: No, the cat's.

SCENE III

*[On the road.
Enter Chaturbhuj, bag in hand, without the cat.]*

Sadhucharan: Sir, where's that cat of yours?
Chaturbhuj: It's dead.

Sadhucharan: How sad! How did it happen?
Chaturbhuj: (irritably) I don't know!

[*Enter Paran Babu.*]

Paran: Hello! What's happened to your cat?
Chaturbhuj: It's dead.
Paran: No, really! How?
Chaturbhuj: The same way all of you'll die—by swinging at the end of a rope!
Paran: Good God, he's positively furious!

[*A swarm of urchins run after Chaturbhuj, clapping and teasing him with cries of 'Pussy cat, pussy cat!'*]

Curtain

The Poet and the Pauper

❦

[Enter Kunjabihari Babu, the celebrated poet, and Bashambad Babu.†]

Kunja: What brings you here, my good man?

Bashambad: Sir, I'm starving. You'd talked about a job...

Kunja: (interrupting hurriedly) A job? Work? Who thinks of work in this sweet autumn weather?

Bashambad: No one does so of choice, sir; it's this hunger that—

Kunja: Hunger? Fie, fie, what a mean, paltry word! Pray do not repeat it before me!

Bashambad: Very good sir, I won't. But I can't help thinking about it all the time.

Kunja: Really, Bashambad Babu! All the time? Even on a serene, tranquil, beautiful evening such as this?

Bashambad: Yes indeed. I'm thinking even more about it now than I usually do. I had a little rice at half-past ten before I set out job-hunting, and I haven't had a bite since then.

Kunja: Does it matter? Must you eat? *(Bashambad scratches his head in silence.)* Doesn't one wish, sitting in this autumn moonlight, that a man might live without gorging himself like a beast? That these moonbeams, the nectar of flowers and the spring breeze might suffice for all his needs?

Bashambad: (terrified, softly) Sir, that would hardly suffice to hold body and soul together—one needs something more substantial to eat.

Kunja: (heatedly) Then go away and eat! Go stuff yourself with gobbets of rice and dal† and curry! This is no place for you—you're trespassing.

Bashambad: I'll go at once, sir. Just tell me where I might find that rice and dal and curry! *(Seeing that Kunja Babu looks very angry)* No,

Kunja Babu, you're quite right: the breeze from your garden is enough to fill one's belly, one doesn't really need anything else.

Kunja: I'm glad to hear you say so—spoken like a man! Well, let's go outside, then. Why stay indoors when there's such a lovely garden to walk in?

Bashambad: Yes, let's. *(Softly, to himself)* There's a chill in the air, and I don't even have a wrap...

Kunja: Wonderful! How charming autumn is!

Bashambad: That's right—but a little cold, don't you think?

Kunja: (wrapping his shawl closely around himself) Cold? Not at all.

Bashambad: No, no, not at all! *(His teeth chatter.)*

Kunja: (looking up at the sky) What a sight to gladden the eye! Fleecy puffs of cloud sailing like proud swans in the azure lake, and amidst them the moon, like—

Bashambad: (has a violent fit of coughing) Ahem, ahem, ahem!

Kunja: ...the moon, like—

Bashambad: Cough, cough—ahem!

Kunja: (nudging him roughly) Do you hear me, Bashambad Babu? The moon, like—

Bashambad: Wait a minute—ah, ah, ahem, cough, cough!

Kunja: (losing his temper) What sort of philistine are you, sir? If you must go on wheezing like this, you should wrap yourself in a blanket and huddle in a corner of your room. In such a garden...

Bashambad: (frightened, desperately suppressing another cough) But I have nothing—*(aside)* neither a blanket nor a wrap!

Kunja: This delightful ambience reminds me of a song. Let me sing it.

> This bea-oo-tiful gro-o-ve, these bloo-oo-ming trees,
> The winsome bakul—

Bashambad: (sneezes thunderously) Ah - h - choo!

Kunja: The winsome bakul—

Bashambad: Ahchoo! Ahchoo!

Kunja: D'you hear? *The winsome bakul—*

Bashambad: Ahchoo! Ahchoo!

Kunja: Get out. Get out of my garden!

Bashambad: Just a minute—ahchoo!

Kunja: Get out at once, you...

Bashambad: I'm going, I'm going, I don't want to stay here a moment longer. If I don't leave at once my life will take leave of me—ahchoo! The liquid sweetness of autumn is overflowing through my nose and eyes—I'll sneeze my life out in a moment—ahchoo! ahchoo! Cough, cough, cough... But Kunja Babu, about that job—ahchoo! *(Exit)*

[Kunja Babu draws his shawl closer and gazes silently at the moon. Enter Servant.]

Servant: Dinner is served.
Kunja: Why so late? Does it take two hours to get the food ready? *(Hurries out)*

Curtain

The Ordeals of Fame

SCENE I

[Dukari Datta, lawyer, seated on a chair. Enter Kangalicharan—timidly, subscription book in hand.]

Dukari: What do you want?
Kangali: Sir, you're a patriot—
Dukari: Everybody knows that, but what brings you here?
Kangali: For the public good, you have been trying with might and main—
Dukari: —to make a living out of lawsuits; that's common knowledge too. What have you got to say?
Kangali: Sir, it's nothing much, really.
Dukari: Well then, why don't you get it over?
Kangali: If you think a little you will have to agree that *Ganat parataram nahi*†—
Dukari: Look here, I can't think or agree about anything until I know what it means! Translate that into Bengali.
Kangali: I'm not sure what it would be in Bengali, but what it means is that music is delightful to hear.
Dukari: Not to everybody.
Kangali: He who doesn't like music is—
Dukari: —the lawyer Dukari Datta.
Kangali: Don't say such a thing, sir.
Dukari: Why not? Would you rather I lied?
Kangali: In ancient India the sage Bharata was the first great singer to—
Dukari: Is there a lawsuit involving him? Otherwise cut your lecture short.

Kangali: I had a lot of things to say—
Dukari: But I have no time to hear them.
Kangali: Then I shall be brief. In this great metropolis we have founded an organization called the Society for the Advancement of Music, and we'd like you, sir, to—
Dukari: Give a speech?
Kangali: Oh no!
Dukari: Preside over a function?
Kangali: Not at all.
Dukari: Then what is it you want me to do? I'm warning you, I can neither sing nor listen to people singing.
Kangali: Oh, rest assured, sir, you shan't have to do either. *(Advancing the subscription book)* Only a small donation—
Dukari: (with a violent start) Donation? O calamity! You're a very devious man—creeping in timidly in that harmless kind of way...I thought you might have got into a lawsuit. Get out this minute, and take that subscription book with you, else I'll file a police case for trespass!
Kangali. I came for a donation, and you're throwing me out![†] *(Under his breath)* But just you wait—I'll fix you.

SCENE II

[*Enter Dukari Babu, newspapers in hand.*]

Dukari: Here's fun! Someone called Kangalicharan has told all the papers that I've donated five thousand rupees to the Society for the Advancement for Music. Donation be damned, I nearly thrust the man out by the neck! This is good publicity, though—it'll give my practice a boost. They'll gain something too—people will think it must be a really big organization if it can draw five-thousand-rupee gifts. They'll get fat subscriptions from all kinds of other places. Anyway, I'm a lucky man.

[*Enter Clerk.*]

Clerk: So you've donated five thousand rupees to the Society for the Advancement of Music, sir?

Dukari: (scratching his head and smiling) I—Oh, that's just something people are saying. Don't take it seriously. But suppose I have given it, why make a fuss?

Clerk: What modesty! First he gives away five thousand rupees, then hushes it up as a trifle—truly no ordinary man!

[*Enter Servant.*]

Servant: There's a crowd of people downstairs.

Dukari: (to himself) There you are! My custom's swelling already. (*Aloud, happily*) Call them up here one by one, and fetch some paan[†] and tobacco for them.

[*Enter First Visitor.*]

Dukari: (pulling up a chair) Come in, please. Have a smoke. Boy, get the gentleman some paan.

First Visitor: (to himself) What a charming personality! If he doesn't fulfil my heart's desire, who will?

Dukari: Well, sir, what brings you here?

First Visitor: Sir, your magnanimity is well-known through the land.

Dukari: Why do you listen to these rumours?

First Visitor: Such modesty! Sir, I'd only heard about your greatness, now my doubts have been laid at rest.

Dukari: (to himself) I wish he'd get to the point...there are a lot of people waiting. (*Aloud*) Ah, yes—so what can I do for you?

First Visitor: For the uplift of the nation the heart must—

Dukari: —That, of course, goes without saying—

First Visitor: True, true. Large-hearted gentlemen like yourself who, for the sake of India's—

Dukari: I admit everything, my dear sir; forget all that and proceed.

First Visitor: It's the sign of a modest man that when he hears himself praised—

Dukari: For God's sake, man, come to the point!

First Visitor: The fact is, our country's fortunes are declining day by day—

Dukari: —Only because we can't keep our speeches short.

First Visitor: India, our sacred motherland, engenderer of golden harvests, is floundering in the dark pit of penury....

Dukari: (clutching his head in despair) Go on.

First Visitor: —in the dark pit of penury, day by day—

Dukari: (in a stricken voice) I don't know what you're talking about!

First Visitor: Then let me come to the crux of the matter.

Dukari: (eagerly) That's much better.

First Visitor: The British are looting us.

Dukari: Fine—just get me the evidence. I'll file a suit in the magistrate's court.

First Visitor: The magistrate is looting too.

Dukari: Then in the district judge's court—

First Visitor: The district judge is a very brigand!

Dukari: (startled) I don't understand you at all.

First Visitor: The country's wealth is being shipped abroad.

Dukari: How sad.

First Visitor. Therefore, a public meeting—

Dukari: (alarmed) A meeting!

First Visitor: Here's the subscription book.

Dukari: (gaping) A subscription book!

First Visitor: A small donation—

Dukari: (leaping off his seat) Donation! Get out—get out—get out.... *(Upsets the chair, overturns a bottle of ink. First Visitor runs off, falls, rises again. Confusion.)*

[*Enter Second Visitor.*]

Dukari: What do you want?

Second Visitor: Sir, your well-known magnanimity—

Dukari: Enough, enough—I've heard that already...have you got anything new to say?

Second Visitor: Your profound concern for the country's welfare—

Dukari: Confound it, this fellow's saying just the same things!

Second Visitor: Your interest in all kinds of patriotic initiatives—

Dukari: Here's a nuisance! Just what is it you want?

Second Visitor: A meeting—

Dukari: Another meeting!

Second Visitor: Here's the book.

Dukari: Book! What book?

Second Visitor: The subscription book—

Dukari. Subscriptions? *(Dragging him up by the hand)* Get up, get up, get out—get out if you value your life—

[*The subscription-hunter flees without another word. Enter Third Visitor.*]

Dukari: Look here, I've heard everything about my patriotic spirit, my generosity, my modesty—all that's over. Start from after that.

Third Visitor: Your breadth of vision—cosmopolitanism—liberality—

Dukari: That's better, it sounds a bit different. But sir, let's dispense with all that too—start talking in plain prose, will you?

Third Visitor: We're thinking of a library—

Dukari: A library? You're sure it's not a meeting you mean?

Third Visitor: No sir, not a meeting.

Dukari: Thank heavens. A library—excellent! Carry on, carry on.

Third Visitor: Here's our prospectus.

Dukari: You don't have any other kind of book as well, do you?

Third Visitor: No sir, not a book, only some printed papers.

Dukari: I see. Go on.

Third Visitor: A small subscription, if you please.

Dukari: (leaping to his feet) Subscription? Help! My house has been attacked by robbers today. Police! Police!

[*Third Visitor flees in breathless haste. Enter Harashankar Babu.*]

Dukari: Is that Harashankar? Come in, come in! We haven't met since we left college—I can't tell you how glad I am to see you.

Harashankar: Yes, we must have a long chat some time, old friend—but later on. Let me dispose of a serious matter first.

Dukari: (delighted) I haven't heard of a serious matter for quite some time—go right ahead, it'll be music to my ears. *(Harashankar draws out a receipt-book from under his wrap.)* Good lord, another receipt-book!

Harashankar: The boys in our neighbourhood are planning a meeting—
Dukari: (startled) A meeting!
Harashankar: That's right, a meeting. So I've come for a small subscription—
Dukari: A subscription?—Look here, it's true we've been friends for a long time, but if you utter that word before me again we'll have to part company for ever. I'm warning you.
Harashankar: Is that so? You can squander five thousand rupees on some obscure Music Society in Khargachhia, but you can't sign up for five rupees to oblige an old friend! Only a shameless scoundrel would set foot in this house again.

[Storms out of the room. Enter another Stranger, book in hand.]

Dukari: Another of those infernal receipt-books! Get lost!
Stranger: (scared) But Nandalal Babu said—
Dukari: I don't want to hear about any Nandalal. Get out, I say!
Stranger: Sir, about the money—
Dukari: I won't give you a paisa. Get out!

[The stranger flees.]

Clerk: Sir, sir, what have you done? He came to pay the money Nandalal Babu owes you! We must have that money today at all costs.
Dukari: Good heavens! Call him back, call him back.

[Exit Clerk. Re-enter presently.]

Clerk: He's gone, I couldn't find him.
Dukari: Now here's a pretty mess.

[Enter a man carrying a tanpura.†]

Dukari: What brings you here?
Musician: Oh, sir, where shall I find such a connoisseur of the arts? What have you not done to encourage music! I've come to sing for

you. *(Promptly starts strumming on his tanpura and singing in the yamankalyan raga.)*

   Of Dukari Datta is my ditty—
   The world has never seen the like of his charity... *(etc.)*

Dukari: Heavens, what a noise! Shut up, will you?

[Enter another musician with tanpura.]

  Second Musician: What does *he* know about music? Listen to this—
   Dukari Datta, glory be—
   Who knows your greatness, if not me?
  First Musician: Cha-a-a-ri-i-i-te-e-e-...
  Second Musician: Du-u-k-a-a-ri-i-i...
  First Musician: Du-u-ka-a-a...
  Dukari: (stopping his ears) Help! For God's sake help!

[A drummer walks in with a tabla set.[†]]

  Drummer: How can you sing without a beat?

[Gets going at once. Enter Second Drummer.]

  Second Drummer: What does this fool know about accompaniment? He hasn't even learnt how to hold the drums properly.
  First Drummer: Shut up, you rogue!
  Second Drummer: Shut up yourself.
  First Drummer: What do you know of music?
  Second Drummer: What do you know about it?

[The musicians argue furiously, and finally start beating each other. The drummers also argue, and start pitching their tablas at each other. Hordes of singers, players and subscription-hunters invade the room.]

  First: Sir, a song—
  Second: Sir, a donation—
  Third: Sir, a meeting—

Fourth: Your munificence—
Fifth: A khayal† in the yamankalyan raga—
Sixth: The country's welfare—
Seventh: Shori Miyan's† tappa†—
Eighth: Hey you, clam up for a second—
Ninth: Let me get a word in, will you?

[They all start tugging at Dukari's clothes, everyone yelling 'Listen to me, sir—', 'No, to me, sir—'.]

Dukari: *(to the clerk, desperately)* I'm leaving for my uncle's place. I'll be away for some time. For God's sake don't give anyone the address!

[Exit. The excited musicians fight among themselves. The clerk struggles to break them up until he drops down, battered, in the evening.]

Curtain

The Extended Family

❦

[Enter Daulatchandra and Kanai.]

Daulat: When the soul is on fire, all the Company's[†] fire-engines can't put out the flames. I spoke at great length at the meeting on the extended family system. The chairman had fallen asleep, so there was no one to stop me. In the end two young ruffians came up and dragged me away. Oh, I was so inspired that day!

Kanai: Why not? It's an inspiring subject. What did you say?

Daulat: I told them that living in an extended family was the only way to practise selflessness. When your whole life's bound up with others' support,[†] you don't have to think of yourself at all! The newspapers have given good reports of my speech—they're all saying it's a great pity that Daulat Babu has to live all alone, with no one to call his own. *(Sighs deeply)*

[Enter Jaynarayan.]

Jaynarayan: God bless you, my boy! I'm your uncle—your father's sister's husband.

Daulat: What do you mean, sir? My father didn't have a sister!

Jaynarayan: Alas, no longer, she has passed away.

Daulat: No, I mean he *never* had one!

Jaynarayan: (with a slight smile) How can that be, dear boy? How else could I be your uncle? *(To Kanai)* What do you say, sir?

Kanai: Of course, quite right.

Daulat: So be it. And what brings you here?

Jaynarayan. Nothing in particular, really. I heard the papers were saying it's a shame that we live apart, so I've come to stay with you.

Daulat: Do you have any property?

Jaynarayan: Nothing at all, no troubles of that sort. I only have a cousin—he'll turn up soon, no fear.

Daulat: I see. Well, what about him—does *he* have anything?

Jaynarayan: Nothing—no burdens at all. Only two wives[†] and four little children: they're coming too. They'd have been here by now, but the two ladies started quarrelling just before setting out. They were pulling each other by the hair when I left. That's why they're late.

Daulat: Kanai, what am I going to do?

Jaynarayan: Oh, you needn't do anything, they'll come on their own. Don't worry about such trifles. They'll be here by evening.

[Ramcharan enters and prostrates himself at Daulat's feet.]

Ramcharan: Uncle, your speech has put me to shame.

Daulat: Who are you, my man?

Ramcharan: Why, I'm Ramcharan, your sister's son. Send someone round to the station, will you? I've left my baggage and my old mother there.

Daulat: And why are you here?

Ramcharan: To stay with you.

Daulat: Don't you have any other place to stay?

Ramcharan: Oh, I have a place of sorts, but you can't learn selflessness there.

Daulat: (frightened) Kanai!

Kanai: He's taken your advice to heart—it won't be easy to oust him.

[Enter Nitai.]

Nitai: Dada, I've quit my job and come over to save you from infamy. Who's there? Run and get me a green coconut[†] from the garden! I'm terribly thirsty.

[Enter Naderchand.]

Naderchand: Here I am, uncle, come to sacrifice my self-interest at your feet. Here's my broken cooking-pot, my hookah and my pet kitten. The first two I inherited from my father, the last I acquired all by myself. You can't blame me any longer, I'll never part from you again.

[Enter Tailor.]

Daulat: And what relation may you be to me?
Tailor: I'm the tailor, sir, I've come to measure you for some clothes.
Daulat: Go away. I'm rather hard up just now—I can't afford new clothes.
Naderchand: Don't run off, Mr Tailor, you can take my measurements instead. My uncle here is wearing a very nice flowered design. Six pairs of shirts like that should keep me going. If you do your job well Uncle will pay you handsomely, understand?
Tailor: Very good, sir. *(Takes measurements)*

[Enter Pareshnath with child.]

Paresh: *(touches Daulat's feet and speaks to the boy)* Go on, bow before your uncle. Dada, this is your nephew.[†]
Daulat: My nephew!
Paresh: That's right. Why do you look so surprised? Surely having a nephew is no great wonder?
Kanai: What does your son do?
Paresh: Well, I was teaching him myself, but he didn't get very far with the alphabet. So I thought, why bother? With Dada here to look after him, why should he need me? Uncle or father, what's the difference?
Kanai: No difference at all.
Paresh: Dada has said that the joy that comes from forgetting one's own hunger to feed others can only be found in a joint family. I realised at once that he couldn't have tasted this joy for a long time; or if he ever did, he must have forgotten about it long ago. So I brought the boy over out of sheer pity. The fires of hell[†] burn in his belly night and day, I tell you.

[Enter Natabar.]

Natabar: (*tweaking Daulat's ear*) What have you been up to, you rascal? I heard you wept floods at a public meeting over my absence!

Daulat: Who are you, you ruffian? How dare you box a gentleman's ears!

Natabar: Whose ear do you want me to box, if not my own brother-in-law's? What do you say to that, sir?

Kanai: Well, it stands to reason.

Daulat: What's that you're saying, Kanai? I don't even have a wife, so where could a brother-in-law† come from?

Natabar: You mightn't have a wife, but other people do. Just think about it, will you?

Daulat: Yes, lots of people have wives. So what?

Natabar: (*smiling*) Well then!

Daulat: (*angrily*) What do you mean, well then? Just how did you become my brother-in-law?

Natabar: Why, through your own brother. If you can have a brother, *he* can surely have a brother-in-law! You might shrug off a brother-in-law, but you can hardly deny you have a brother.

Daulat: I never knew I did, but the way things are going today—

Natabar: Good, that's settled then. Let's put an end to this wrangling—it isn't seemly to carry on like this before all these honourable gentlemen. (*Pulling out a bolster from behind Daulat*) I think I'll rest awhile. Call for a smoke, will you?

[*Enter Servant with fruit and sweets.*]

Servant: (*to Daulat*) Your food, sir.

Daulat: (*incensed*) Who asked you to bring it here, you fool? Take it inside.

Paresh: Oh, let him be, no harm done. (*To servant*) Here, my man, just bring it round this way. (*Takes the plate and starts eating*)

[*Enter two women, dragging Bidhubhushan by the hair.*]

First Wife: You wretch, when shall we be rid of you?

Daulat: (*hurriedly*) Who are these people?

Jaynarayan: Don't be upset, my son, it's only my cousin. He's arrived at last.

First Wife: You filthy rascal!

Second Wife: Beat him with a broom, beat him with a broom.

Daulat: My dear Kanai!

Kanai: There can't be a better training in tolerance.

First Wife: The old fool has taken leave of his senses.

Second Wife: So many husbands die every day, yet you're left behind!

Daulat: Calm down, calm down, my dears.

First Wife: Why should I calm down, you idiot? Calm down yourself, let all your forefathers die and turn cold.

Daulat: Kanai!

Kanai: Your house is full—

Daulat: My evil planet's at its height.

Kanai: Be that as it may, you don't need me any more. I think I'll beat a retreat. *(Exit)*

Daulat: (shouting) Kanai, don't leave me alone!

Everyone all together: (holding him down) Alone? God forbid! Why should you be alone? We're all here—we shan't budge!

Daulat: You don't mean that seriously, do you?

Everybody: We most solemnly swear we do.

Curtain

The Free Lunch

❦

[Enter Akshay Babu, straight from the office.]

(Laughing to himself) Today I've got him by the short hairs. The rascal keeps talking big while sponging off us all the time, without spending a penny of his own. Imagine—he's been promising me a feast every day for almost a year now, but I've yet to taste it. A quarter of those promises would have been enough for three royal banquets. No matter, I've got an invitation out of him at last. But I've been waiting two hours—where on earth can he be? I hope the fellow's not going back on his word. *(Looking out)* Hey you, what's your name? Bhuto? or Modho?† Or is it Harey?†

Chandrakanta? All right, so be it. Well, my dear Chandrakanta, when is your master going to return?

What was that? He's gone to get lunch for us from a hotel? How wonderful! it's going to be a real feast all right. And I'm rather hungry too. I'll lick the bones on the mutton chops till they glisten like ivory toothpicks. There'll be a chicken curry, of course—but it won't be there for long. And if he throws in two kinds of pudding I'll lick the china clean till they shine like glass mirrors. I hope he brings two or three dozen oyster patties as well—that'll add the final touch to the feast. My right eye's been twitching† since morning—I think we'll have oyster patties today. Here, Chandrakanta, when did your babu go out?

A long time ago? Fine, then he can't be much longer. Why don't you fetch me a hookah meanwhile? I've been asking you for a long time, but you don't seem eager to oblige.

There's no tobacco in the house? Your babu's locked it up? I never heard such a thing in my life!—It's only tobacco, not Company shares!† What's to be done now? I take a little opium now and then, and I can't do without tobacco. Hey, Modho—I mean Chandrakanta—can't you fetch me one small plug of tobacco from the gardener or someone?

You'll have to go to the market? You want some money? All right, if it can't be helped—get me a paisa's worth of tobacco, on the double.

You can't get any tobacco for a paisa? Why ever not? Do you take me for the Nawab of Muchikhola? I can do without amburi tobacco[†] at sixteen rupees a tola:[†] a paisa will be quite enough for the sort I want.

You'll have to buy a hookah too? Your babu has stashed away even his hookah in his iron safe? Why didn't he deposit it with the Bengal Bank instead? Goodness! What kind of a place have I landed in? Here, take these six paise: I'd kept it for the tram fare home. I'll have to recover it with interest from Uday when he returns. This tumble-down house is supposed to be his garden villa. I wonder what his usual residence is like! I hope the rafters don't fall on my head. There isn't even anything to sit on except this broken chair, and it won't take my weight. But I've been on my feet for ages—they're aching. I can't carry on like this much longer—let's sit on the floor.

[Dusts the floor with the loose end of his dhoti, spreads out a newspaper, sits down, and begins to hum.]

> *A free feast daily*
> *Ah, wouldn't that be jolly!*
> *Dish after dish*
> *Of mutton curry, fish,*
> *Washed down with whisky-sodas*
> *In double royal dose!*
> *And someone else's till*
> *Will go to foot the bill,*
> *So I may live in paradise*
> *And never be morose!*

Ah, there you are! Have you got the tobacco? What's this—only the tobacco bowl![†] Where's the hookah? You can't get a hookah for six paise in these parts? The bowl alone cost two annas? Now look here, Chandrakanta, I'm not such a duffer as I may look. Fat I may be, but I'm not a fathead. Now I see why your master needs to lock up even his hookah and tobacco in an iron safe. His only mistake was not to lock up a jewel like you as well. No fear—you won't be at large very long. As soon as the Government gets to hear of you they'll put you away under guard. But I'm simply dying for a puff—here goes. *(Takes a pull at the hookah and begins to cough violently)* Oh my god! where on earth did you find tobacco like this? One should make one's will before risking a whiff of this stuff. Two puffs and Lord Shiva[†] himself would burst his skull, and Nandi and Bhringi[†] fall down in a daze! I'd better not try another pull. Let your babu come back first. But he doesn't seem to be in any hurry. Perhaps he's polishing off the patties one by one. And there's such a fire in my belly that it might set my dhoti ablaze in a minute. I'm thirsty too, but I daren't ask Chandrakanta for water: he's sure to say he'll have to buy a glass, his babu has locked up all the glasses. Let it be—I'll ask for a green coconut[†] from the garden instead.

Here, Chandra, do something for me, will you? Get me a green coconut from the garden, quick—I'm devilish thirsty.

Why can't you get me one? I saw lots of them in the garden.

All the trees have been leased out? So what—surely you can get me one coconut?

You need money? But I don't have any more. All right, let your master come back, then we'll see. I have my salary with me, but I'd rather not give him a large note to change. Who could have thought such a robber was at large in the Company's domain?[†] I wish Uday would come back.

There, he must be coming—I heard footsteps. Thank heavens! Hey, Uday, here, this way! Oh no, it's not him. Who are you?

Babu sent you, eh? It would have been much better if he'd come himself instead. I'm dying of hunger.

The babu at the hotel? The clerk? Never saw him in my life. Has he sent something to eat? Oyster patties perhaps?

He hasn't? He's sent a bill instead? Much obliged, I'm sure. The babu for whom the bill is meant is not here now.

Oh no, it isn't me. Here's a fine mess. I swear it isn't me. Why on earth should I cheat you? I was invited to lunch and I've been waiting here for three hours now. You've come from a hotel, so I'm pleased to make your acquaintance at last. Perhaps if I boiled that wrap of yours

I might at least... No fear, I don't want your wrap, but I don't want your bill either.

I've landed myself in a mess all right. I tell you I'm not Uday Babu, I'm Akshay Babu. You can't be serious! You know my name and I don't? Let's stop this nonsense. Just go and wait downstairs for a while—Uday Babu'll be along by and by.

O God, is this why you made my right eye twitch this morning? No dinner from the hotel but a bill instead?

> Love, look where I've been led!
> I begged the cloud for water,
> And lightning struck instead.

This is fate: one got the nectar of life when the ocean was churned[†] and another got the poison. Will someone get all the fun out of this hotel-churning and another foot the bill? It seems to have been piling up for some time too.

Who are *you* now? Babu sent you? How generous of him! Does he imagine that the sight of your face will quench my hunger and thirst? He seems to be a fine gentleman!

What was that? The tailor's bill? Whose clothes are you talking about?

Uday Babu'll buy clothes and Akshay Babu'll pay for them? What a very reasonable proposition!

Really? How did you make out that I was Uday Babu? Have I put up a sign on my forehead? Why, don't you like my name as it is—Akshay?

Changed my name, have I? All right, suppose I have; but it's not so easy to change my appearance. Tell me, do I look like Uday Babu in any way?

You've never seen him face to face? Just wait a while and you'll have your heart's desire. It shouldn't take long—he's sure to turn up any minute now.

O death, here's another of them. And where might you be coming from, sir? Have you been invited too?

The house rent? Which house would that be? This one? What are your rates?

Seventeen rupees a month? Then will you kindly tell me how much I ought to pay you for three hours and a half?

No, I'm not joking, sir—I'm not in the mood for it. I was invited to this house for lunch and I've been waiting for three hours and a half. If you want me to pay the rent for that stretch of time, work out what it comes to. I've even paid for the tobacco I smoked.

No, my dear sir, you haven't guessed correctly. There's been a slight mistake. My name is Akshay, not Uday. Such a trivial mistake makes no difference usually, but when rents are being collected it's wise to stick to the name your parents gave you.

You're telling me to get out of this house? Sorry, that's one thing I can't do. Here I am, gnawed by the pangs of hunger for three hours and a half, and just when a meal is about to arrive, you expect to turn me out by your insults! I'm not such an ass. You can sit there and rail at me all you want: I'll leave as soon as I've had my lunch.

My throat's dry with talking—I can't stand it any more. I'm hungry enough to swallow my own guts. There—I think I can hear footsteps again. Uday, my dear friend Uday, apple of my eye, treasure of my soul, why don't you turn up? I'm dying for you—come!

Who are you, sir? If you have come to abuse me you can sit there and start right away. These gentlemen will gladly give you company.

Hari Babu wants to see me? How gratifying! He loves me truly, no doubt about it. My best friend who invited me to lunch here is conspicuous by his absence, and people I've never heard of have been paying me attentions since morning—why should that be so? Well, sir, do enlighten me as to why a certain gentleman by the name of Hari Babu should have so impatiently summoned me at such an inconvenient hour.

What did you say? I borrowed a few samples of jewellery from him to show my wife who wanted a bracelet made, and I'm refusing to return them?—I could have said a great many things about this, but only one must suffice for the present: I've never borrowed any jewellery from anyone, and I don't even have a wife! Everything else I wanted to say must wait for another day. You must excuse me—my throat is too parched for conversation. Please wait another half an hour and you'll get to know all. *(Loudly)* Uday—Udo![†] you godforsaken scoundrel, you great oaf, you swine, you lout—my belly's on fire, my throat's dry, my head's ready to burst—you wretch, you rascal, you…!

Oh no, no, gentlemen, I'm not addressing you. Please don't be agitated. I'm famished and miserable, and I'm only calling to my dearest friend. Pray be seated again.

You can't wait any longer? It's late already? You needn't tell me that, I know it's late all right. In that case, why don't you depart? It's been nice meeting you; I enjoyed the charming conversation.

But really, now you're going a bit too far. I assure you I bear none of you the slightest ill-will, but I can't fulfil your present expectations.

Look here, you really are crossing all limits. I dare say you gentlemen dine heartily at regular hours twice a day, so you can have no idea how much a man can be vexed by pangs of hunger. That's why you dare to provoke me in this condition.

Again! Don't you dare! My good man, don't pick a fight with me, I'm more than a match for you. Just look at my bulk, will you? I'm struggling to keep my temper under control so that I don't go berserk. All right, let's see if you can provoke me. Go on, do your worst—you can't make me angry. See—I'm going to sit down, serene as you please.

Oh my God! they seem to be rolling up their sleeves! A beating on an empty stomach would be the last straw. All right, sit down, all of you: tell me all your claims one by one. I'm lucky I have my salary in my pocket, otherwise I'd have had to run for my life, hungry as I am. Let me save my skin for the time being—I can get the money back from Uday later.

You came for only five rupees, sir, but you've hurled fifty rupees' worth of abuse at me: here's your money.

And you, my man, I'm paying your hotel bill today, but remember me if I turn up hungry at your doorstep some day.

You want three months' rent, do you? Well, here's payment for a month: take the rest later. You shouldn't mind; you didn't pull your punches while calling me names—that must have unburdened your heart. Give me your blessings and go home now, there's a good man.

As for you, sir, it won't be easy to return your jewellery. Even if I had a wife and I had indeed given your ornaments to her, it would have been difficult to get them back; but seeing that she doesn't exist and I haven't given her any jewellery, even you ought to realize how utterly impossible it is to return them. If you still insist I suppose I'll have to go and see your Hari Babu by and by, but I must stay a while longer to see whether my lunch arrives.

Oh this is becoming unbearable! Chandra—hey, Chandra! Uday is nowhere in sight; are you going to do a disappearing act[†] now? Ah, there you are. Chandra, surely you know your babu well enough: tell me, do you honestly think he's going to return from that hotel today, tomorrow or the day after?

Not likely, you say? Ah—at last you've said something I'm inclined to believe. Never mind, I'm ravenous now—I don't even have the energy to yell at you. Take this half-rupee and save a life. Get me something to eat—quickly now!

That man lives like a king and never does an honest day's work; we used to wonder where the money came from. Now I'm beginning to see how he manages it. But swallowing so many insults every day, warding off bills and holding off creditors is no joke! It's more than I could have handled: give me a prison sentence any time.

What have you got there? Just plain puffed rice and nothing to go with it? Do I get some loose change back?

Nothing at all? No matter—that puffed rice will have to do. Chandra, I don't mind telling you—I'm so hungry that this stale stuff tastes like nectar from heaven. I've eaten at many banquets, but I never enjoyed a meal more in my life. I see you've got me a coconut too; should I pay extra for that? No? You do have a human streak after all. Now if you'd only whistle up a cab I could get going.

There's no cab to be found hereabouts? Then I'm in deep trouble. I'm too weak with hunger to walk three miles. I did it when there was the prospect of a feast before me. What shall I do now? Oh well, let's start off anyway.

Here's a nuisance! You want me to go and see Hari Babu now? Chandra, you've done me a lot of favours today, do just one more — for pity's sake tell this gentleman here that I'm not Uday Babu but Akshay Babu from Ahiritola.

He won't take your word for it? Can't say I blame him; he's probably known you for a long time. Well, I'm too exhausted to quarrel, so let's go to see Hari Babu then. But my dear sir, I'm in such a state that

I might drop dead on the way, and then you'll have to pay for the funeral. Don't say I didn't warn you.

Chandra, what are you thrusting out your palm at me for? Thanks to you I've had such a feast on the cheap today that I won't be hungry again for a long time. What more do you want?

Oh! baksheesh!† Yes, I suppose I should settle that account too. Since I've done so much already, I shouldn't leave this little thing undone. But I have just one rupee left, and I need twelve annas for the cab fare. If you have some change on you... You haven't? *(Turns out his pockets and hands over his last coin)* Here, keep the whole rupee. I'll step out of this house quite emptied out, like a fruit gnawed hollow by an insect.

But how on earth am I going to recover all the money I've paid out? If I could lay my hands on something of value, I could carry it off by way of security. The only precious thing I've seen around here is that Chandrakanta. But it's beyond me to carry him off against his will—he could stuff me into his pocket if he wished!

(Jerking open a safe in one corner) Ah, a gold watch! Just the thing I wanted. It's got a fine chain too. I think I'll take this with me.

Why, Chandra, what are you so excited about?

The police? Policemen are coming this way?

I've got to run? Why, what crime have I committed? I came here only to honour a gentleman's invitation, and I've been punished enough for that already.

Heavens, they really are coming this way! Where did Chandra disappear? And that man Hari Babu sent? They've all run away.

Here, what do you think you're doing? Don't push me around like that—I'm a gentleman, not a common thief!

Ouch! That hurt! Stop, for heaven's sake stop. My good man, I've eaten nothing but some puffed rice the whole day; this is no time for rough humour of that sort!

Here, constable, you can have something for tea. *(Fumbling in his pockets)* Oh dear, I don't have a paisa left. Officer sahib, if you want to nab a first-class crook, I'll take you to him. There never was such a rogue since they invented prisons.

At least tell me what I'm supposed to have done! Signed for Jiban Babu to take away a watch from Hamilton's?† Constable, aren't you ashamed of making such a monstrous charge against a gentleman?

Hey, be careful, don't pull at that—it's not my watch. If the chain snaps I'll get into trouble.

  What? This is the watch from Hamilton's? Well, take it away then, take it away at once. But why drag me along with it? I'm not a gold chain. I may be the golden Akshay, but only to my parents!

  Well, if you won't let me go, then I must go with you. Everyone loves me—I've had proof aplenty of that today. I'll be forever grateful if I can survive the magistrate's loving attentions now.

> *A free feast daily—*
> *Ah, wouldn't that be jolly!*

Curtain

That Man

These stories were written for Nandini, the adopted daughter of Rabindranath's son, Rathindranath. Her pet-name was Pupu or Pupe, and she herself appears all through the book—listening to, commenting on, or even adding to her grandfather's stories. In fact, That Man *is a continuous story-within-a-story: an outer story or shell about Pupu and her grandfather, enclosing tales about various characters, with 'that Man' stepping in and out of both worlds.*

All the pieces in this section have been translated by Sukhendu Ray.

That Man

❦

Down the ages, God has gone on creating human beings in their millions and billions. But no, that wasn't good enough for those humans. They said, 'We want to produce our own human beings.' So alongside God's games with his living dolls, humans began their own games with dolls they had made themselves. And then children began to say, 'Tell us a story'—in other words, make human beings out of words. Thus were devised the countless king's sons and minister's sons, favourite queens and neglected queens, fables of mermaids, tales of the Arabian Nights, the adventures of Robinson Crusoe. These creations kept multiplying in pace with the world's population. Even grown-ups began to say, when they had a day off from work, 'Make us some human beings.' And so the epic *Mahabharata*[†] was prepared in eighteen books. Now a host of story-makers are kept busy in every land.

At my granddaughter's command, I've been involved for some time in this game of people-making. They are play-people, so it doesn't matter whether they are true or false. My listener is nine years old, and the story-teller has crossed seventy. I started my work all on my own, but Pupu joined in when she found the stuff I worked with was very light. I did call in another man to help me, but more of him later.

Many tales start with 'Once there was a King.' But I'm beginning my tale with 'There is a Man.' My stories are nothing like what people mean by stories. This Man never rode on horseback across the vast fairy-tale fields of Tepantar.[†] Instead, he came to my room one evening after ten o'clock at night, when I was reading a book. He said, 'Dada, I'm very hungry.'

Now in all these tales about princes, we never hear of a hungry prince. Nonetheless, I was rather pleased that my character should be hungry at the start of my story—because, you see, it's easy to make friends with a hungry person. To please him, you don't have to travel farther than the end of the lane to buy him some food.

I discovered that my Man was fond of good food. He'd ask for curried fish heads, shrimps with gourd, or a savoury dish of fish-bones and vegetables. If you gave him malai[†] from Barabazar,[†] he'd lick the bowl clean. As for ice-cream, it was a treat to see him relish one: he would remind me of the Majumdars' son-in-law.

It was raining rather hard one day. I was painting in my room: a landscape of the wide open fields you see in these parts,[†] with a red-clay road going due north; an uneven piece of fallow land to the south with curly-headed wild date-palms; a few toddy-palm trees in the distance, staring avidly at the sky like beggars; behind them a dense black cloud, like a huge blue tiger ready to pounce on the sun in mid-sky. All this was I painting, mixing colours in a bowl, swishing my paintbrush.

There was a shove at the door. When I opened it, in came—not a bandit, not a giant, not even a general's son—but that Man. He was dripping water, his dirty shirt stuck to his body, the end of his dhoti was splashed with mud, and his shoes were just like two lumps of clay.

'How now!' I said.

'It was dry and sunny when I left home,' he said. 'I got caught in the rain midway. Can I have that bedspread of yours? I could then get out of these wet clothes and wrap myself in it.'

Before I could say anything, he snatched my Lucknow bedspread, dried his head with it and wrapped it round himself. It was lucky I didn't have my precious Kashmir jamewar[†] on the bed.

Then he said, 'Dada, let me give you a song.'

What could I do? I abandoned my painting. He began to sing the old-fashioned song:

> *Just think, Shrikanta, you handsome young lover,*
> *Grim death will approach and your life will be over.*[†]

From my expression, he suspected that it wasn't going well. 'How do you like it?' he asked

'Look,' I told him. 'As long as you live, you'd better remove yourself far, far away from human habitation if you want to practise the scales.

After that it's up to Chitragupta,† who writes down all your deeds in a fat register to charge you with after you're dead. That's if he's able to stand your song.'

He piped up, 'Pupe Didi takes music lessons from a Hindustani ustad.† How about my joining her?'

'If you can persuade Pupe Didi to agree, there shouldn't be any problem,' I replied.

'I'm scared stiff of Pupe Didi,' he said.

At this point Pupe Didi, who was listening, broke into peals of laughter. She was delighted by the idea that anyone could be scared stiff of her. She found it very pleasing, as do all the strong men of the world.

But being tender-hearted, she said, 'Tell him he needn't be afraid. I won't say anything to him.'

'Is there anyone who's not afraid of you?' I asked her. 'Don't you drink a bowlful of milk twice a day? Look how strong it's made you. Don't you remember how that tiger met you brandishing a stick, and ran away with its tail tucked under him to hide under Aunt Nutu's bed?'

Our heroine was ecstatic. She reminded me of that other time when a bear, trying to escape from her, fell into the bathtub.

The history of my Man, that I was so far putting together all by myself, now took on additions from Pupe's hands. If I were to tell her that the Man came to see me at three in the afternoon to ask for a razor and an empty biscuit tin, she would add that he had also borrowed her crochet hook.

All stories have a beginning and an end, but my story of 'There is a Man' has no end: it just runs on. His sister falls ill and he goes to fetch a doctor. A cat scratches the nose of his dog Tommy. He jumps onto the back of a bullock-cart and gets into a row with the carter. He takes a tumble in the backyard near the pump and breaks an old brahman lady's earthen pitcher. During a football match when Mohan Bagan† is playing, his pocket gets picked clean of three and a half annas, so he can't buy sweets from Bhim Nag's† shop on the way home. Instead he goes to see his friend Kinu Choudhuri, and asks for fried shrimps and curried potatoes.

And so it goes on, day after day. Pupe adds how one afternoon, he walks into her room and asks to borrow a cookbook from her mother's cupboard because his friend Sudhakanta Babu wants to cook banana flowers. Another day he begs for Pupe's perfumed coconut hair-oil as he's afraid he's going bald. Yet another day he goes over to Din-Da's[†] hoping to hear him sing, but finds him asleep, snuggling his bolster.

Of course this Man of ours has a name; but it's known to just the two of us and can't be disclosed to anybody else. That's where the real fun of our story lies. The king who lived once upon a time had no name; neither did the prince. And that lovely princess, whose hair reached down to the floor, whose smile showered gems and her tears pearls—no one knows her name either. They were quite nameless, yet they are well-known in every home.

This person of ours we just call *Se*—'He', or 'That Man'. When a stranger asks his name, we two just smile and look knowingly at each other. Sometimes Pupe says teasingly, 'Have a guess. It starts with a P.' And people guess it to be Priyanath, or Panchanan, or Panchkari, or Pitambar, or Paresh, or Peters, or Prescott, or Pir Bux, or Pyar Khan.

As I put down my pen at this point, someone piped up at once, 'I hope that's not the end of the story.'

Story! What story? Our hero isn't a prince; he's just an ordinary Man. He eats and sleeps, has a job in an office, likes to see movies. His story is simply his daily routine, which is like everybody else's. If you can build him up clearly in your minds, you'll see him wolfing down rasgullas[†] in the front porch of a sweetshop, with syrup dripping from the bottom of the packet onto his grubby dhoti. That's his story. If you ask, 'What happened then?', I'd say he jumped onto a tramcar, found he had no money, and so jumped off again. And then? Much, much more of the same sort happens then. He goes from Barabazar to Bowbazar, from Bowbazar on to Nimtala.[†]

Someone among the listeners said, 'This Man seems to be an unstable character: he can't find shelter in Barabazar, or Bowbazar, or Nimtala. Can't you make up a story about his waywardness?'

'Well,' I said, 'if one can, one can; if one can't, one can't.'

'Let's have your story then,' the listener said. 'Just whatever comes to your mind—with neither head nor tail, sum nor substance.'

Now that really would be bold. God's creation is strictly ruled by order and system: everything there must be as it should be. It becomes quite intolerable. Let's make fun of Grandfather God, who created this dull system, and do it in such a way that he can't punish us. My story lies quite outside his domain.

Our Man was sitting quietly in a corner. He whispered in my ear, 'Dada, have a go, write whatever you want about me: I shan't take you to court.'

I now need to say something about this Man.

The main prop of the serial story that I keep telling Pupu Didi is a Man built wholly out of words, a Man named after a pronoun—'He'. That's why I can make up any stories I like around him and no questions asked. But as evidence to back up my chaotic creations, I've had to find a man of flesh and blood. If I'm threatened with a literary lawsuit, this man is ready to stand up and testify in my favour. He doesn't mind what he says. Given a hint, even by a petty lawyer like me, he'll swear without batting an eyelid that a crocodile once caught his topknot between its jaws when he was taking a dip in the holy Ganga during the Kumbha Mela[†]—the one held in Kanchrapara.[†] The topknot went down with the crocodile, but the rest of the man, like a flower cut off its stalk, managed to reach dry land. If you wink at him a little more, he can shamelessly declare that some English divers from a man-o'-war rummaged in the mud for seven months and finally brought up his topknot, all but a few hairs. He tipped them three and a quarter rupees. If Pupu Didi still asks 'What happened next?', he'll immediately continue that he went to see the great Doctor

Nilratan Sarkar[†] and implored him, 'Please, Doctor Babu, give me some medicine to fix my topknot, otherwise I can't tie a flower to it.' The doctor applied a powerful ointment that a Holy Man had given him. Now his topknot keeps growing recklessly, like an endless earthworm. When he wears a turban, it swells like a blown-up balloon; when he rests his head on a pillow, his topknot forms a canopy like a giant mushroom. He has to pay a barber full time to shave his head every three hours.

If the hearer is still curious for more, he'll continue his story with a sad face. He'll say he found the Surgeon-General of the Medical College waiting with his shirtsleeves rolled up, bent on drilling a hole at the root of his topknot, plugging it with a rubber stopper and then sealing it with wax to prevent the topknot from ever growing again in this world or the next. He was afraid that this drastic treatment might carry him straight to the next world, so he refused to oblige.

This Man of ours is a rare bird, one in a million: an unparalleled genius in making up lies. I'm very lucky to have found such an artful disciple for my outlandish yarn-spinning. Sometimes I present to Pupe Didi this strange creature from my tale. At the sight of him, Pupe Didi's large eyes grow even larger. She's so pleased that she orders hot jalebis[†] for him from the market. The Man is inordinately fond of jalebis, as well as chamchams[†] from an alley in Shikdarpara. Pupe Didi asks him where he lives; he replies, down Question Mark Lane in Whichtown.

Why don't I disclose his name? Because if I do, he'll be reduced to that name and that name only. There's only one 'I' and only one 'you' in this world; everybody else is 'he' or 'she'. The 'He' of my stories stands surety for all of them.

Let me tell you something else about him, otherwise I'll be to blame. Those who judge him only from my stories form a wrong impression about him. Those who have met him know that he's a handsome man with a serious expression. Like the night sky lit up by stars, his solemnity is lit up by hidden laughter. He's a first-rate person, really. No silly jokes and pranks can hurt him. It amuses me to show him up as a fool in my tales, for the simple reason that he's more intelligent than I am. He doesn't lose face even if he pretends to be stupid.

This is helpful, because it makes for a link between Pupu's nature and his.

(*Se*, chapter 1)

THE HOLY MAN OF THE TREES

Udho: Did you find him?

Gobra: Now look here, Udho. Just because of something you said, I've been scouring all sorts of wild places for a month. I'm worn down to skin and bones, but I haven't yet spotted a hair of his head.

Panchu: Who is it you're looking for?

Gobra: The Holy Man of the Trees.

Panchu: The Holy Man of the Trees! Whoever is he?

Udho: Haven't you heard of him? The whole world knows who he is.

Panchu: Tell me about him.

Udho: Any tree that this Holy Man inhabits turns into a Wishing-Tree. You just stand under it and hold out your hand, and you get whatever you wish for.

Panchu: Who told you all this?

Udho: Bheku Sardar from Dhokar village. The other day this Holy Man was sitting on a fig tree and swinging his legs. Bheku, who didn't know this, happened to be passing under the tree. He was carrying a pot of thick treacle on his head to blend with tobacco. The Holy Man's legs hit the pot, and a stream of treacle ran down Bheku's face: he couldn't even open his eyes or his mouth. The Holy Man is all made of pity. 'Bheku,' he said, 'tell me your wish, and I'll let you have it.' Bheku's a fool. He only said, 'Baba, give me a rag to clean my face.' No sooner said but a towel came floating down from the tree. When Bheku had wiped his face clean and looked up, there was no one to be seen. You see, you can have only one wish and no more, even if you bring the heavens down with your bawling.

Panchu: Oh dear, oh dear! No shawls, no fine clothes, just a towel! What can you expect from a blockhead like Bheku?

Udho: But Bheku hasn't come badly out of this. Haven't you seen the big shed he's built near Rathtala? It may have been just a towel, but it was the Holy Man's blessed towel after all.

Panchu: Really? How did all this happen? By magic, was it?

Udho: Bheku went to the fair at Hondalpara and sat down with the towel spread in front of him. Thousands of people flocked round him and showered offerings on this towel to His Holiness: coins, vegetables, all kinds of things. Women came to ask favours for their children: 'Bheku Dada, please touch my son's head with the Baba's towel, he's been ailing for three months now.' Bheku's fee for his divine services is five quarter-rupees, five suparis,† five measures of rice and five dollops of ghee.†

Panchu: That's fine for Bheku, but do the devotees get anything in return?

Udho: Of course they do. Do you remember Gajan Pal? He filled Bheku's towel with paddy for fifteen days in a row. He also tethered a goat to one corner of the towel. The goat's bleating attracted more people to Bheku. You won't believe me, but in eleven months flat Gajan landed a job in the royal palace guard. His duties are to mix drinks for the Chief of Police and comb and dress his whiskers.

Panchu: Is it really true?

Udho: Of course it's true. You know, I'm sort of related to Gajan: his wife's sister to the wife of a cousin of mine.

Panchu: Tell me, Udho, have you seen this towel yourself?

Udho: Of course I have. It's exactly like the stuff the Hatuganj weavers make: a yard and a half across, pale yellow like champak flowers, with a red border—just the same.

Panchu: Really? But how did this towel fall from the tree?

Udho: That's the miracle. All by the grace of the Holy Man.

Panchu: Let's go and find him. But how do we recognise him?

Udho: That's the problem. No one seems to have really seen him. And as ill luck would have it, that idiot Bheku's eyes were blinded by the treacle.

Panchu: What shall we do then?

Udho: Why, whenever I see anyone anywhere I join my hands and ask him, 'Please, sir, are you the Holy Man of the Trees?' This makes them turn very violent and abusive. One of them was so angry that he splashed the dirty water from his hookah† all over me.

Gobra: Never you mind, we shan't give up. We must find the Holy Man, and we may if we're lucky.

Panchu: Bheku says you can only see him when he's up on a tree, but not if he's down below.

Udho: You can't really put every man to test by asking him to climb a tree. But I'm trying out an idea. My amra tree is loaded with fruit, and I ask anyone I meet to climb up and help himself. All that's happened so far is that there's hardly any fruit left, and even the branches are broken.

Panchu: Now come along, we've no time to waste. If we're lucky we'll surely be able to find the Baba. Now let's call out together, 'O Holy Man of the Trees, dear Merciful Lord, where are you? If you're hiding somewhere among the parul creepers, do come out and show yourself to us poor creatures!'

Gobra: I say, something's stirring! It seems the Holy Man has listened to our prayers!

Panchu: Where? Where?

Gobra: On that chalta tree.

Panchu: What's there on the chalta tree? I can't see anything.

Gobra: Something's swinging there.

Panchu: That dangling thing? But it looks like a tail!

Udho: You're a dolt, Gobra. That's not our Holy Man: it's a monkey's tail. Can't you see it making faces at us?

Gobra: It's the sinful age[†] of the world. That's why the Holy Man has assumed the form of a monkey to elude us.

Panchu: You can't trick us, Holy Man: your black face[†] won't fool us. You can go on making faces as much as you wish, but we're not budging from here. Your holy tail will be our succour and protection.

Gobra: The Lord save us! The Holy Man's running away with enormous leaps!

Panchu: But where can he escape from us? We'll outrun him by the strength of our devotion.

Gobra: There now, he's climbed up the wood-apple tree.

Udho: Panchu, go up that tree.

Panchu: Why don't you go up?

Udho: I'm telling you to go up.

Panchu: No, no: I can't climb so high. Dear Holy Man, have mercy and come down to us!

Udho: Please, Holy Man, bless me that when it's time for me to leave this world, I may close my eyes with your holy tail round my neck.

(*Se*, chapter 3)

That Man dropped in while I was having my morning tea.

'Is there something you want to tell me?' I asked.

'Yes, there is,' he said.

'Then please be sharp about it. I've got to go out right now.'

'Where to?'

'To the Governor's house.'

'Does the Governor often send for you?'

'No, he doesn't. It would have been better for him if he had.'

'Better? How?'

'He'd have known then that I'm far and away better at making up stories than his agents who're supposed to keep him informed. No one, not even a Rai Bahadur,† can match me in this. You know that, don't you?'

'Yes, I do, but what's all this rubbish you're making up about me these days?'

'I've been asked for fantastic stories.'

'Maybe so, but even fantastic stories must follow some pattern. Not crazy drivel that anybody can cook up.'

'Really? Let's have a sample of what you mean by a fantastic story.'

'All right. Just listen to me.'

While keeping goal for Mohan Bagan Club in a football fixture against Calcutta Club, Smritiratna† Mashai let in five goals, one after another. Swallowing so many goals didn't spoil his appetite: on the contrary, he grew ravenously hungry. The Ochterloney Monument† was near at hand; our goalkeeper started to lick it from the bottom up, all the way to the top. Badaruddin Mian, who was mending shoes in the Senate Hall,† rushed up at full speed and cried, 'You're such a learned man, so well versed in the scriptures! How could you defile this huge thing with your licks? Shameful, shameful,' he muttered, spat three times on the Monument, and headed for the office of *The Statesman*† newspaper to report the matter.

It suddenly struck Smritiratna Mashai that he had polluted his tongue. He walked across to the watchman at the Museum.

'Pandey Ji,' he said to the watchman, 'you're a brahman, so am I. You must help me.'

Pandey Ji saluted him and said, fingering his beard, *'Comment vous portez-vous, s'il vous plaît?'*†

Our scholar pondered for a while and said, 'A very baffling conundrum. I need to look into the books of Sankhya philosophy.† I'll give you my answer tomorrow. Not today, as I've polluted my tongue by licking the Monument.'

Pandey Ji lit a Burmese cigar, and after a couple of puffs said, 'In that case, check out Webster's Dictionary at once to find what remedy† it prescribes.'

Smritiratna said, 'Then I'll have to visit Bhatpara;[†] but that can wait. For the moment, lend me your brass-knobbed stick.'

'Why, what'll you do with it?' asked Pandey Ji. 'Have you got coal dust in your eyes?'

'How did you know that?' asked Smritiratna. 'It happened the day before yesterday. I had to run all the way to Ultadanga to see Dr McCartney, the wellknown specialist of liver disorders. He arranged for a crowbar from Narkeldanga, and cleaned my eyes with it.'

'Then what do you want with my stick?' asked Pandey Ji.

'To use as a twig toothbrush.'[†]

'I see,' said Pandey Ji. 'I thought you might be wanting to tickle your nose to force out a sneeze. Had you done so, my stick would have had to be purified by washing it in Ganga water.'

That Man stopped here, pulled my hubble-bubble nearer him, and after a couple of draws on it, said, 'You see, Dada, this is a sample of your style of spinning yarns. Instead of using your own fingers to write, you seem to wield the trunk of the elephant-god Ganesh[†] to scribble your tall tales. You just twist facts, which is easy to do. Supposing you went about telling people that our Governor, after a stint as an oil merchant, has now set up a shop in Bagbazar to sell dried fish, who do you think would laugh at such a cheap joke? Is it worth your while to tickle the fancies of silly people?'

'You seemed peeved.'

'And with good reason. Only the other day you were telling Pupu Didi all kinds of rubbish about me, and she, being just a child, was hearing you open-mouthed. Don't forget, even weird stories need to be made up with some art.'

'Wasn't there any art in my story?'

'Absolutely none. I wouldn't have said a word if you hadn't dragged me into the matter. Suppose you'd said that you'd been entertaining your friends with curried giraffe brain, whalemeat fried with ground mustard, and pilau of hippos freshly caught from the river slime, with a dish of drumsticks made from the trunks of palm trees, I'd have said it was too crude. It's not at all difficult to write such things.'

'Is that so? Then let's have a specimen of your style instead.'

'Fair enough, but I hope you won't be cross. Dada, it's not that I'm more gifted than you: rather the opposite, but that's actually an advantage. Here's what I'd have said:

I was invited to Cardiff for a game of cards.† The head of the family there was a gentleman named Kojumachuku. His wife was Mrs Hachiendani Korunkuna. Their elder daughter, Pamkuni Devi by name, cooked with her own hands their celebrated dish, meriunathu of kintinabu, whose aroma wafts across seven districts. Its fragrance is so strong that it tempts even wild jackals to come out during the day and howl, whether out of greed or frustration I don't know; and the crows desperately flap their wings for three hours with their beaks stuck in the ground. And this was just a vegetable side-dish. Along with that came barrels of sangchani made of kangchuto, with the pulp of their delectable fruit anksuto dunked in it. The pudding was victimai of iktikuti—baskets of it. Before this was served, tame elephants were brought in to crush it under their feet. Then the largest of their beasts, a cross between a man, a cow and a lion which they call gandisangdung, made it somewhat more tender by licking it with their sharp spiky tongues. And finally, before the three hundred places set for the diners, there arose the noise of huge mortars and pestles. The people there say this very din makes their mouths water, and attracts beggars from far and wide. Many lose their teeth while eating this food, and then they make a gift of their broken teeth to their host. The hosts deposit these teeth in the bank and bequeath them to their children. The more teeth a person collects, the higher is his standing. Many people secretly buy other's collections and pass them off as their own. This has been a cause of many celebrated lawsuits. Lords of a thousand teeth are so high and mighty that they won't marry their daughters to families with only fifty teeth. A man with no more than fifteen teeth choked to death while eating a ketku sweet, and not a soul could be found in that quarter of the thousand-tooth tycoons who'd agree to take the body to be cremated. In the end the poor dead man was secretly floated down the Chowchangi River. This created a great uproar among people on both banks of the river. They sued for compensation, and the case went all the way up to the Privy Council.†

By this time I was gasping for breath. I said, 'Will you please stop and tell me what's so special about your story?'

'Just this: it's not a cheap chutney. It's no great crime if we amuse ourselves by embroidering matters about which we know nothing. Not that I claim my story has any superior humour about it. A bizarre story[†] becomes exciting only if you can make incredible things credible. Let me warn you, you'll land in disgrace if you keep on making up cheap popular pufferies that only take in children.'

'Fine,' I said. 'From now on I'll write stories so utterly credible that Pupu Didi will need a witch-doctor to exorcise her faith in them.'

'By the way, what did you mean when you said you were in a hurry to go to the Governor's house?'

'I meant that I can be free if you leave. Once you arrive, you simply stay put. I was just telling you in a roundabout way—go away!'

'Oh, I see. In that case, I'll go.'

(*Se*, chapter 5)

I was sitting one evening on the south terrace of my house, facing a bank of ancient rain-trees that shut out the stars; but they were lit up by fireflies, as though they were winking at me out of a hundred eyes.

Pupe Didi was with me. I said to her, 'You've grown too clever these days. I think I need to remind you that you were once a little child.'

Pupe Didi laughed and retorted, 'That's where you score over me. You must once have been a little child yourself, but there's no way I can remind you of that.'

I sighed deeply and said, 'I don't think there's anyone left who can do so. Yes, I too was a child once, but the only witness to that are those stars in the sky. But let's not talk about me. I was going to tell you about something that happened when you were a child. You may or may not like it, but it'll give me some pleasure to tell it.'

'Then go ahead.'

I think it was in early spring. For the past few days, you had been listening avidly to the story of the *Ramayana* from shiny-pated Kishori Chatto.[†] One morning, as I was reading the newspaper and sipping my tea, you rushed in with startled eyes.

'What's the matter?' I asked.

You said breathlessly, 'I've been stolen away.'

'What a disaster! Who did this foul deed?'

You hadn't yet worked that out. You could easily have said 'Ravana',[†] but you knew that wouldn't be true. Hadn't Ravana died only last evening in battle, when not a single one of his ten heads was spared? So you fumbled and faltered, and then said, 'He's asked me not to tell anyone.'

'That makes it more difficult. How can I rescue you then? Do you know what direction he took?'

'He took me to a new country.'

'Was it Khandesh?'

'No.'

'Bundelkhand then?'

'No.'

'What sort of country was it?'

'It had rivers and hills, and great big trees. It was sometimes light and sometimes dark there.'

'But most countries are like that. Did you see some kind of demon, with his sharp spiky tongue hanging out?'

'Yes, yes, I did. He put out his tongue just once and vanished immediately.'

'Lucky for him, otherwise I'd have caught him by the scruff of his neck. Anyway, the person who stole you away must have taken you away in something. Was it in a chariot?'

'No.'

'On horseback?'

'No.'

'On top of an elephant?'

Suddenly you blurted out, 'On the back of a rabbit.'

That animal was much on your mind at the time because your father had just given you a pair on your birthday.

I said, 'Now I know who stole you away.'

'Tell me,' you said with a little smile.

'None other than Uncle Moon, I'm sure.'

'How do you know?'

'Because Uncle Moon has been a rabbit fancier[†] for a long, long time.'

'Where did he find his rabbits?'

'Not from your father.'

'Then from whom?'

'He stole them from Brahma's zoo.'[†]

'How disgraceful.'

'Disgraceful it was. That's why Brahma branded the Moon with black spots.'

'Serve him right.'

'But did he learn his lesson? Didn't he steal you as well? Perhaps he needed you to feed his rabbits with cauliflower leaves.'

This pleased you very much, and to test me you asked, 'Tell me: how could a rabbit carry me on its back?'

'Because you must have fallen asleep.'

'Does a person weigh less when she's asleep?'

'Yes, of course. Haven't you ever flown in your sleep?'

'Yes, of course I have.'

'Then where's the difficulty? Why a rabbit—even a toad could have carried you on its back and leapfrogged all over the field.'

'No, no, not a toad. How disgusting!'

'Don't worry, there aren't any toads on the moon. By the way, did you meet the Bangama bird[†] on your way?'

'Indeed I did.'

'And how did your meeting go?'

'He flew down from the top of a tamarisk tree and stood very tall. He thundered, 'Who's that running away with Pupe Didi?' As soon as the rabbit heard him, he ran away so fast that Bangama Dada couldn't catch up with him. What happened after that?'

'After what?'

'After the rabbit ran away with me.'
'How should I know? It's for you to tell me.'
'Really, how should I know? Didn't I fall asleep?'
'That's just the problem. That's why I can't trace where the rabbit took you—so I don't know which way I should go to rescue you. Tell me, did you hear any bells ringing when you were being carried away?'
'Yes, yes, I did—ding-dong, ding-dong.'
'Then he must have taken you through the land of the Bell-Ears.'
'The Bell-Ears! Who are they?'
'They have two bells for ears, and two tails that end in two hammers. They beat on their ears with their tails—now one ear, then the other. There are two Bell-Eared tribes. One tribe is rather violent and has a shrill ring to their bells, the other is dignified and gives out deep sonorous rings.'
'Have you ever heard those bells, Grandpa?'
'Of course I have. In fact, only last night, as I was reading a book, I suddenly heard a Bell-Ear walking through the dark night. I couldn't stand it any longer when he struck the hour of twelve midnight. I rushed to my bedroom and threw myself on my bed with my eyes closed and my face buried in the pillows.'
'Are the rabbits and the Bell-Ears friendly?'
'Very much so. When the rabbits walk through the Milky Way, past the constellation of the Seven Sages,[†] they keep their ears alert to hear the Bell-Ears.'
'And then?'
'Then when they strike the hours—one o'clock, two o'clock, three o'clock, four o'clock, and then five o'clock—they reach the end of the Milky Way.'

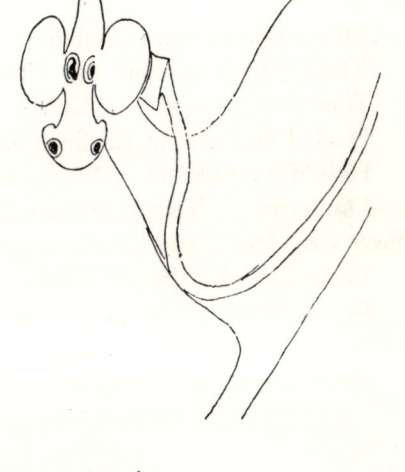

'What happens then?'

'Then the rabbits cross the vast fields of sleep[†] and reach the land of light. Then they disappear from sight.'

'Have I also reached that land?'

'Yes, certainly.'

'Then I'm no longer on the rabbit's back?'

'If you'd been, you'd have broken its back.'

'Yes, indeed. I forgot that I'm heavier now. So now what?'

'Now we must make plans to rescue you.'

'Of course you must. But how?'

'That's what's worrying me. I must take the help of a prince.'

'Where will you find a prince?'

'Well, I was thinking of Sukumar.'

Your face turned very grave as soon as I mentioned Sukumar. You said rather stiffly, 'I know you're fond of him because he takes lessons from you. That's why he's ahead of me in maths.'

There are other simple reasons for Sukumar being ahead, but I thought it better not to bring up the subject. I said, 'It's not a question of whether I like him or not; he's the only prince on call.'

'How do you know he's a prince?'

'He's reached an understanding with me to become Prince Permanent.'

You frowned and said, 'All his understanding seems to be only with you.'

'How can I help it? He doesn't listen to me because I'm so much older than him.'

'You call him a prince? I can't even think of him as the Jatayu Bird.[†] Humph!'

'Calm down now. We're in serious trouble. We don't even know where you are. Just this once, let him help us find you. Afterwards I'll turn him into a squirrel to help build Rama's bridge to Lanka.'[†]

'Why should he agree to help you? He's busy studying for his exam.'

Well, I'm three-quarters sure he'll agree. I saw him two days ago—last Saturday, around three o'clock in the afternoon. I had gone to visit his folk. I tracked him to the roof of their house: he was walking about there, having managed to slip away from his mother's watchful eyes.

'What's going on?' I asked him.

He tossed his head and announced, 'I'm a prince.'

'Where's your sword?'

He showed me a half-burnt stick, left over from a rocket lit on Diwali[†] night, which he'd fastened to his waist with a string.

'Yes, I see you have a sword; but you need a horse.'

'There's one in the stable.'

He ran to a corner of the roof and fetched an old broken umbrella, thrown away by his uncle. He tucked the umbrella between his legs, and with a shout of 'Gee-ho gee-up', he ran round the roof.

'Truly a marvellous horse,' I agreed.

'Do you want to see him with his wings?'

'I certainly do.'

He unfurled the umbrella. Some grains of horsefeed fell out from it.

'A marvel, a marvel!' I cried. 'I never thought I'd live to see a winged horse.'

'Now, Grandpa, I'm flying off. Close your eyes, and you'll see that I've reached the clouds. It's very dark there.'

'I don't have to close my eyes. I can see you quite clearly—flying very fast, and the wings of your horse have disappeared behind the clouds.'

'Grandpa, can you suggest a name for my horse?'

'Chhatrapati,'[†] I said.

He liked the name. He patted the umbrella on the back and shouted, 'Chhatrapati!'

Then, acting the part of the horse, he replied, 'Yes, sir!'

He looked at me and asked, 'Did you think I said "Yes, sir"? Not at all, it was the horse.'

'You don't have to tell me. I'm not so deaf.'

The prince said to the horse, 'Chhatrapati, I don't like sitting here quietly.'

The horse replied, 'Tell me your command.'

'Let's cross the fields of Tepantar.'

'Yes, let's.'

I couldn't stay any longer. I had other things to do. I had to break up the party and say, 'Prince, I believe I saw your teacher waiting for you. He didn't seem to be in a very good mood.'

The prince grew very restless at this. He prodded the umbrella and said, 'Can't you fly me somewhere at once?'

I had to speak for the poor horse. 'He can't fly until it's night. During the day he pretends to be an umbrella, but as soon as you fall asleep at night he'll spread his wings. It's better for you to go down to your teacher now, otherwise you'll be in trouble.'

As he went down, Sukumar said, 'But I haven't finished all I had to say.'

'You can never finish all you have to say,' I answered. 'If it were to finish, there would be no fun left.'

'My lessons will be over by five o'clock, Grandpa. You must come back after that.'

'You mean that you'll have done with your Grade Three Reader. You'll need a change to a grade-one story. All right, I promise I'll come.'

(Se, chapter 10)

Next morning, Pupe Didi brought the breakfast I'd ordered: sprouted chickpeas and molasses in a stoneware bowl. I've set about reviving ancient Bengali food culture in this modern age.

'Would you like some tea?' Pupe Didi asked me.

'No, some date palm juice,' I replied.

She said, 'You look rather strange. Did you have any bad dreams?'

'Shadows of dreams flicker through my mind all the time,' I said. 'Then the dreams dissolve and the shadows pass as well, leaving no trace. But today I want to tell you something about your childhood that keeps coming back to me.'

'Why don't you?'

'One day I'd put down my pen and was sitting on my balcony. You were there, and so was Sukumar. It grew dark: they lit the street lamps. I was telling you, making up most of it, about Satya Yuga,[†] the Age of Truth—ages and ages ago.'

'Making it up, were you? You mean you were turning the Age of Truth into the Age of Lies!'

'Don't call it lies. Just because the ultra-violet ray can't be seen, it doesn't mean that it's unreal—it's a genuine kind of light. The Age of Truth existed in the Ultra-Violet Age of human history. I wouldn't call it prehistoric but ultra-historic.'

'Spare me your explanations and tell me what you were going to say.'

'I was trying to impress upon you that in the Age of Truth people didn't learn from books or from the news they heard. Their knowledge came from Being.'

'I can't follow you at all.'

'Then listen to me carefully. You believe you know me well, don't you?'

'Yes, very well.'

'And so you do; but that knowledge leaves ninety-nine per cent of me out of account. If in your heart of hearts you could have turned yourself into me whenever you wished, then you'd really have known me.'

'Are you telling me we know nothing?'

'Indeed we don't. But we've all agreed to think we know, and all our relations are on that basis.'

'But we seem to be getting along quite well.'

'Maybe, but it wasn't like that in the Age of Truth. That's what I was telling you. In those days there was no Knowing by Seeing or Knowing by Touching, only Knowing by Being.'

Women's minds take hold of concrete things, so I thought Pupu would find my words quite unreal—she wouldn't like it at all. But she seemed interested and said, 'What fun!'

She then went on excitedly, 'Now, Grandpa, they say science these days is playing all kinds of tricks. You can listen to songs sung by someone who's dead, you can see a person who's far away; they say they're even turning lead into gold. Perhaps some day one person will just be able to pass into another by some sort of electrical trick.'

'Quite possibly, but then what would you do? Because then you wouldn't be able to hide anything.'

'Goodness! Everyone has a lot of things to hide.'

'They've got something to hide because they keep it hidden. If nobody hid anything, if it were all like an open card game where you could see what cards everybody held, people would deal with each other on that basis.'

'But people have a lot of shameful things to keep to themselves.'

'If the shameful things about everybody were known, we wouldn't feel so ashamed.'

'Never mind all that. What were you going to say about me?'

'I asked you that day how you'd have liked to see yourself if you'd been born during the Age of Truth, and you promptly said, "As an Afghan cat".'

Pupe was furious. She said, 'I never said anything of the sort. You're making it up.'

'I might make up stories about the Age of Truth, but what you said was all your own. Even a wordsmith like me couldn't have made that up instantly.'

'And I suppose it made you think I'm very silly.'

'No, not at all. I only deduced that you badly wanted an Afghan cat but had no means of getting one, as your father loathes cats. In my view, in the Age of Truth no one would need to buy a cat or get one as a gift; but if you so wished, you could change yourself into a cat.'

'What use would it be to change from a human being into a cat? It's better to buy one: if you can't buy one, it's best not to have one at all.'

'There you are. You can't imagine the glory of the Age of Truth. In that age, Pupe could easily extend her frontiers to include a cat; but she wouldn't wipe out her own frontiers. You'd be both yourself and the cat.'

'What you're saying makes no sense at all.'

'It makes perfect sense in terms of the Age of Truth. Don't you remember how the other day you heard your teacher Pramatha Babu say that light descends in particles like raindrops, but also flows in waves like a stream? Our ordinary sense tells us it must be either one or the other, but science says it's both at the same time. So you too could be at once Pupu and a cat. That's what the Age of Truth is all about.'

'The older you grow, Grandpa, the harder it gets to understand what you say—just like your poetry.'

'Obviously it's a sign that I'll grow quite silent one day.'

'Didn't our conversation get beyond the Afghan cat that day?'

Indeed it did. Sukumar, who had been sitting quietly in a corner, suddenly burst into speech as if he were dreaming: 'I want to see what it's like to be a sal tree.'

You, Pupe, have always looked for a chance to make Sukumar look foolish. You were in stitches when he said he wanted to be a sal tree. The poor boy was very embarrassed. So I took his side and said, 'The wind starts blowing from the south, the branches break out in flowers, an invisible current of magic runs through the heart of the tree and bursts out in a splendid show of beauty and scent. Of course you want to sense this wonderful feeling rising up from inside you. If you don't become a tree, how can you feel the endless thrill of a tree in springtime?'

Perhaps inspired by what I said, Sukumar cried excitedly, 'I can see a sal tree from my bedroom window. When I lie down on my bed I can see its top. It seems to be dreaming.'

When you heard Sukumar talking about a dreaming sal tree, you were perhaps about to say, 'How silly!' But I stepped in and said, 'The whole existence of a sal tree is a dream. It's in a dream that it passes from a seed to a shoot, from a shoot to a tree. The leaves are its dream-talk.'

I asked Sukumar, 'That morning when it was raining heavily from a cloudy sky I saw you standing quietly on the north balcony, clutching the railings. What were you thinking about?'

Sukumar said, 'I don't know what I was thinking about.'

I said, 'These unknown thoughts of yours filled your mind, just as the sky had filled with clouds. When trees stand still, they too are full of unknown feelings. Those unknown thoughts deepen in the shadow of monsoon clouds and sparkle in the winter morning sun. The same unknown thoughts make them murmur through the young leaves and sing through the flower-buds.'

I still remember how Sukumar's eyes grew wide at this. He said, 'If I were a tree, that murmur would climb up my body towards the clouds in the sky.'

You realized that Sukumar was getting too much attention, so you brushed him aside and took the stage. You asked me, 'Grandpa, if the Age of Truth returns, what would you like to be?'

I knew you were expecting me to say that I wanted to be a mastodon or a megatherium, because we'd been talking a few days earlier about creatures in the first chapter of the book of life. The world was young then, its bones still delicate; its landmasses hadn't firmed up, its trees looked like the first uncertain brush-strokes of the Creator. I had told you that human beings today have no clear idea how those huge behemoths lived in that primeval forest in the unstable climate of those times. From what I'd said, you'd sensed an urge to find out about those early days of life's adventure, like the age of the old epic heroes. I'm sure you'd have been pleased if I'd said I wanted to be a primitive hairy four-tusked elephant. It would have been within striking distance of your wish to be an Afghan cat, so you'd have had me on your side. I could have said something like that, but talking to Sukumar had made me think of other things.

I wanted to become a scene, spread over a wide stretch of ground—in the first hour of morning, towards the end of the winter month of Magh. The wind would have risen, making the old banyan tree turn restless as a child, the river break out in sound, and the band of trees along the uneven river-bank grow blurred. Beyond all this there would be the open sky, and in it a sense of distant space—as though the sound of a bell were being wafted on the wind in the faintest possible way across a great expanse, infusing the sunshine with its message: the day's at end.

From your expression, you clearly thought it was much more wayward to imagine oneself as a whole landscape—river, forest and sky—than as a single tree.

But Sukumar said, 'It's rather fun to think of you as spread across everything—the river, the trees. Tell me: will the Age of Truth ever come back?'

'Until it does, we have pictures and poems. They're the best way to forget about oneself and turn into something else.'

'Have you drawn a picture of the scene you're talking about?' asked Sukumar.

'Yes, I have.'

'I'll draw one too.'

On hearing Sukumar speak so boldly, you burst out: 'What makes you think you'll be able to?'

'Of course he will,' I said. 'And when you've finished, I'll have your picture, and you can have mine.'

That's as far as our conversation went that day.

(*Se*, chapter 14)

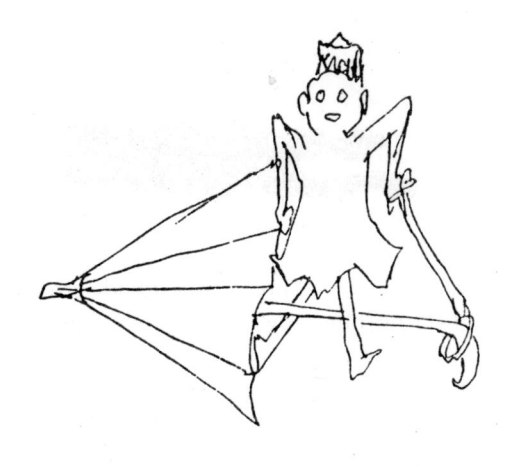

More Verses

Of the poems in this section, 'The Invention of Shoes' and 'The Builder' have been translated by Sukhendu Ray and Sukanta Chaudhuri. All the other poems have been translated by Sukanta Chaudhuri.

More Verses

Moving Pictures

The light green veil is blown away,
　　The face appears to sight.
The air fills with the spreading scent
　　Of the queen-of-the-night.
The Nawab† has three brave Pathans†
　　To keep watch on his garden,
And all the night his greyhounds bark
　　Beside the gate they're guarding.
The shehnais† play a raga
　　Over Kunja Babu's gatehouse:
They're going to act a drama there—
　　Just look at all the great crowds.
Her sari tucked around her waist,
　　The barber's charming spouse is
Conveying a large betel-bowl
　　Past all the Ghoshes' houses.
The cowherd's picking betel-nuts
　　Sitting among the branches—
The betel-leaves he gets as pay,
　　As well as more advantage.

> The oil-wife with a load of sweets
>> Went for a ferry-ride:
> The basket tumbled from her grasp
>> And fell into the tide.
> The greedy fish came swarming in
>> From every finny quarter,
> And lobsters plump rose from the mud
>> To crowd upon the water.
> The feasted carp turned somersaults,
>> Their tails they flapped and flourished.
> The slender chanda[†] grew quite stout,
>> With sugar-syrup nourished.
> The hilsa's[†] stomach turned at last
>> From eating too much sweet.
> I didn't have the heart to ask
>> The chital[†] of his treat.
> And one wife to another said,
>> 'Don't cut these fish in slices:
> Once in the pot, you'll find they're kin
>> To sugar-puffs and spices.'

The air shimmers in noonday heat,
> The sand is simply burning.
To drink their fill, the thirsty cows
> To the pond's brink are turning.
The river's just a trickle now,
> The boats are almost grounded:
In the noon sky, the screaming kite
> His whinnying call has sounded.
Young Lakha sports a parasol:
> He's Gouri's promised groom.

The wedding-drums are beating
  At her Charakdanga home.

The river-bed is nearly dead:
  The water's only calf-high.
Stuck in the mud beside the bank,
  The fishing-boats stand half-dry.
There goes a load of pots and pans,
  All plated with enamel.
They're making cartwheels at the forge—
  They hammer and they pummel.
Beyond the fields, a railway train
  Spouts out its smoke on high
Like a black panther's furry coat
  Laid out against the sky.
The metal-man goes down the street
  Clanging his metalware:
The village dogs can't bear the din—
  They bark and howl and blare.
The maiden sits with her wet hair
  Rolled tightly in a coif:
She's going to cook banana-flowers
  To put before her love.
The tethered cow licks doubtfully
  At her great trough of fodder,

Near where a heap of coal and ash
    Is lying in a corner.
A dancing bear goes down the street:
    I hear a rattle playing.
It shuffles to a bobbing stick
    That a gypsy girl keeps swaying.
The brown cow sits with lazy eye
    Under the peepal branches.
The baby goat in search of grass
    Along the meadow prances.
A great big pile of inky clouds
    Gathers upon the sudden:
The rain comes down in a sharp burst,
    And all the fields are sodden.
The Santhal[†] girls go down the road
    Laughing out loud and clear O,
Their heads protected from the rain
    Under broad leaves of taro.
The marketmen with covered heads
    Are coming back from trading,
The woodcutter goes running home
    With rain-drenched faggots laden.

Up in the sky, the snaky lightning
Groves of leafy bamboos brightening.

Boom! Boom! goes the wedding-drum.
Bullfrogs croak from field and farm.

At Sixes and Sevens

1

Old mother Khanto's grandma-in-law
Has the strangest sisters you ever saw.
Their saris on the stove they keep,
And saucepans on the clothes-horse heap.
From carping tongues to be at rest,
They hide inside an iron chest,
But at the window air their cash
    Without a jot of worry:
They put salt in their betel-leaves
    And quicklime† in their curry.

2

Four ruffians, all warts and blemishes,
Were raiding a shopkeeper's premises.
    They'd started to smash
    The till full of cash,
When who should arrive but the sergeant?
    They saw the police
    And whimpered, 'Oh please,
We're poor homeless waifs without guardian.

To better our prospects through knowledge,
> We made this intrusion
> Led by the delusion
That this was a free evening college.'

3

Don't worry, I'll do all the cooking today
> While you take a rest from your toil.
Nidhu, just measure the water and rice,
> And put the big pot on to boil.
>> I'll count out the platters:
>> But just to help matters,
The wife's very welcome to pick up a ladle
>> And stir at a dish while she's looking—
>>> Or indeed, if she wants, have a go
>>> At kneading and rolling the dough,
>>> While Mahesh's part is
>>> To bake the chapatis:[†]
But yes, I insist—as I've said from the start,
You must let me do all the cooking.

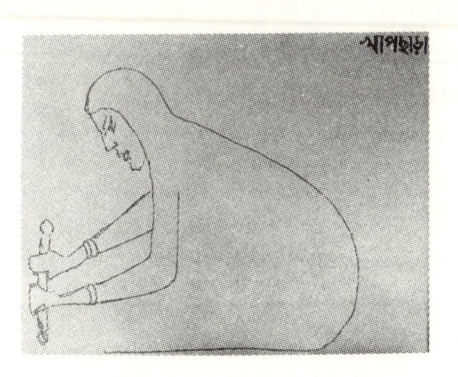

4

The King sits lost in silent meditation:
    While twenty sentries rend the air
    With cries of 'Quiet!' and 'Keep out there!'
The General bellows, as befits his station.

The Grand Vizier in his agitation
    Swishes his beard, and all the time
    Drums and bassoons and cymbals chime
Their warning notes in fearsome orchestration.

The solid earth shudders in consternation.
    The frightened beasts quiver and leap,
    And all the queens in order creep
Behind the curtains in their trepidation.

5

The famed research of Doctor Moyson
Filled the air with deadly poison.
    Until—O pity!—
    In all the city
He left just nine young men alive.
'What grand success!' he said. 'Just hear me
Tell you how it's done: but dear me,
    Who will attend
    Or comprehend
If no-one's able to survive?'

6

 Asleep on the floor
 With sonorous snore
The Sultan enraptured all gazes;
 While wagging his beard
 The Minister steered
His voice through a raga's mazes.
Inspired by the bent of these musical courses,
The General commanding His Majesty's forces

Girded his waist in a colourful skirt
    And charmed the spectators with dances:
        The guards on parade
        Untunefully played
On flutes, having thrown down their lances.

7

Father Giraffe said, 'Really now, my boy,
To look at you gives little cause for joy.
My love grows less each time I view your body:
So tall up front, behind so squat and shoddy.'
'Look at yourself,' his son replied. 'It's true:
Nobody knows what Mother sees in you.'

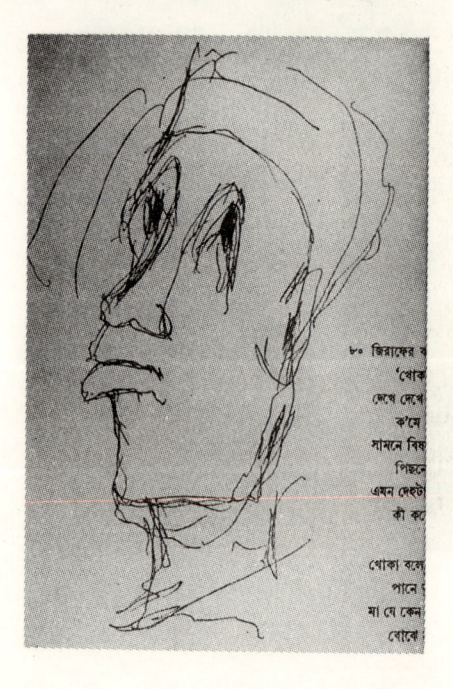

8

If you set out for Khardah
And land up at Khulna instead,
    You may rage and strike terror,
    But that you're in error
Must clearly be taken as read.

If you want to weave garlands
But bring home a deal of sour berries,
    I'll hold with my powers
    That these are not flowers,
Although you drub me till I perish.

If you squat on a sofa
And tell me to give you a swing,
    You might land in a fury,
    But how can you query
I simply can't do such a thing?

If you feel a bit fey
As you sit in your dressing-room chair,
    And brush with great glee
    The crook of your knee,
    It's clearly my duty
    (Though it might sound snooty)
To point out it isn't your hair.

The Invention of Shoes

Said good king Hobu
To Minister Gobu,
    'I've pondered all night: is it just
That whenever my feet
Should land on the street
    They come to be sullied by dust?
Your wages you draw,
But you don't care a straw
    To serve the demands of the King:
It's a rank plot to foil me,
My own soil to soil me:
    I simply won't stand such a thing!
Unless you can find a solution,
You're all doomed to swift dissolution!'

The terrified Minister
At these words sinister
    Broke into cold sweat with fright:
The pandits[†] grew pale,
And the courtiers once hale
    Lay sleeplessly tossing all night.
In the Minister's home

THE INVENTION OF SHOES

There was weeping and gloom,
    The fires in the kitchen grew cold:
Till crazed with fears,
His beard drenched in tears,
    He fell at the King's feet, and told,
'But how can we live, if denied
The dust from your feet sanctified?'

'That's a question indeed,'
King Hobu agreed,
    'But "maybe" should come after "must".
We need to discourse
On this problem of yours,
    But meanwhile—get rid of the dust!
You're getting good money:
I don't think it funny
    You can't tackle problems like these.
There seems little point
Why I should appoint
    These scientists with long degrees.
So deal with the first things first,
Or else be prepared for the worst!'

Thus royally chided,
Poor Gobu decided
    To call the wise men of the land.
Each subtle mechanic
Was summoned in panic:
    They studied and brooded and scanned.
With spectacles perched

On the nose, they researched
    As they took nineteen barrels of snuff,
Then warned: if the crust
Of the earth lost its dust,
    You couldn't grow foodgrains enough.
'Why, what are you wise men worth?'
Said the King. 'Can't you tackle the dearth?'

After some more discussion,
They found a solution—
    Which was, to buy millions of brooms.
The King couldn't breathe,
For the dust from the street
    Was driven right into his rooms.
The people that passed
Were blinded with dust,
    They coughed and they sneezed in a daze.
The dust floated down
And veiled all the town,
    The sun disappeared in the haze.
The King remarked, now really sore,
'To clear the dust, they've added more!'

So to dowse down the earth
And settle the dirt,
    Some two million watermen came:
They drained all the lakes
To fill water-bags,
    And boats couldn't sail on the stream.
The water-beasts died

THE INVENTION OF SHOES

As their element dried,
    While land-beasts struggled to swim:
All business was stuck
In the slime and the muck,
    And fever attacked every limb.
The King said, 'This army of asses
Has turned all the dust to morasses!'

So they held more talk,
And from every walk
    The wise men came to attend.
With reeling eyes
And dazed surmise
    They found of the dust no end.
One man had a thought
To lay out cloth,
    Or cover the land with mats:
Or day and night
To shut up tight
    The chamber where the King sat.
If they kept him enclosed all the time,
His feet couldn't land in the grime.

Said the King, 'That's neat!
It would guard my feet,
    But how could I govern my realm?
If I'm shut in a room,
The land meets its doom:
    I must have my hand on the helm.'
So they spoke again:

'Call the leathermen
    To sew up the earth in a sack.
'Twill make a great story
To his majesty's glory,
    And hold all the dust right back.
A simple device, if we can
Just find out a smart leatherman.'

For such leatherware
They looked everywhere,
    Abandoning all other chores:
But no craftsmen found,
Nor hides to go round,
    Even after they'd knocked on all doors.

THE INVENTION OF SHOES

But just at this while
There rose with a smile
    The leathermen's grizzled old chief.
'My lord, please permit
That I may submit
    A measure to bring you relief.
The whole earth you needn't ensheathe:
Just cover your own two feet.'

'Pooh! Were it so easy,
We wouldn't be busy,'
    The King said, 'pursuing our mission.'
'Let him be impaled,'
The Minister railed,
    'Or bind him and throw him in prison.'
But the old man sat down
At the foot of the throne,
    And in leather the royal feet dressed.
'Why,' Gobu now said,
'This was in my head:
    But how could the blighter have guessed?'
And that is how shoes were invented,
The earth saved, and Gobu contented.

The King's Son and the King's Daughter
A Fairy Tale

MORNING

A king's daughter would go to school,
    A king's son too would go,
And they would meet upon the road.
    (All this was long ago.)
The king's daughter would turn aside,
Down from her hair the flowers would glide:
The king's son he would pick them up,
    Flowers and creepers too.
The king's daughter would go to school,
    The king's son too would go.
The birds upon the branches sang,
    With flowers the road was lined.
The king's daughter went on ahead,
    The king's son walked behind.

MID-DAY

The king's daughter she sits above,
    Below the king's son sits.

They read from books in many tongues,
>   And do arithmetic.
The king's daughter forgets her task,
She lets the book slip from her grasp,
The king's son comes to pick it up—
>   Again she lets it drop.
The king's son sits at work below,
>   The king's daughter atop.
The day is hot, the koel bird
>   From the bakul tree makes moan.
The king's son gazes up aloft,
>   The king's daughter looks down.

EVENING

The king's daughter then comes back home,
>   The king's son comes away.
Slipping off her string of pearls,
>   The daughter goes to play.
Upon the road the jewels drop,
The king's son comes to pick them up,
Then hands her his own string of gems,
>   Forgetful in his turn.
The king's daughter then comes back home,
>   The king's son too returns.
The tired sun sinks to its rest
>   Beside the river bank;
Their studies over, both return
>   To their own native lands.

NIGHT

The king's daughter on a golden bed
    Dreams of a lovely face.
On a silver bed, the king's son dreams
    Of a smile of tender grace.
Around them joys and sorrows play,
To sudden fears the heart gives way—
The lips break in a sudden smile,
    Or sudden teardrops trace.
Whose smile is it the king's son sees,
    The king's daughter whose face?
The night is wild, the storm-clouds roar,
    The storm-winds toss and scream:
Pillowed upon dishevelled beds,
    They pass the night in dream.

Fragments

KNOWING LITTLE AND KNOWING MUCH

A thirsty ass went to a big lake's brink.
'This water's black!' he said, and wouldn't drink.
'Every ass sees I'm black,' the water cried.
'Only the wise man knows I'm really white.'

TRY FOR YOURSELF

'This honeycomb's so tiny,' said the wasp.
What makes the bee think it has cause to boast?'
'It's your turn now,' the bee replied. 'Do come:
Just try to make a smaller honeycomb.'

LITTLE HEARTS AND
GREAT HEARTS

A tiny flower, of no worth at all,
Was growing from a cranny in the wall.
'Measly beggar!' cried every plant that grew.
But the rising sun called, 'Brother, how are you?'

AUDACITY

'How bold am I!' the rocket says. 'I race
To the stars, and fling my ashes in their face.'
'It doesn't stick to them,' the poet calls.
'It simply drops behind you as you fall.'

THE TEST OF EXPERIENCE

The thunderbolt says, 'When I call from far,
The people think it is the clouds that roar.
When I flash, "Lightning!" they cry down under.
But when I strike, they know I am the thunder.

ON JUDGING OTHERS

The nose complains, 'The ear can't smell a thing:
It's good for nothing but to wear a ring.'
While the ear says, 'The nose can't hear a voice;
But when it sleeps, just listen to its noise!'

CAUSE FOR SUSPICION

Hear the fake diamond say, 'How big am I!'
That's why we think you might be just a lie.

WE ARE WHAT WE ARE

Turn and twist as you will, with all your might:
Your left hand's always to your left, your right hand to your right.

Bhajahari

I had an uncle working in Hong Kong.
He brought for us a Chinese thrush that whistled a fine song,
    Sitting in its cage under a cover—
    A present for my mother.
Bhajahari would comb Nichinpur Wood
To bring it bags of grasshoppers for food,
And every cage-bird on the street would stir
Their feathers as he passed, to hear their whirr.
Some birds he fed on bugs, some rice, some swill;
Sprayed them with turmeric-water when they were ill.
'Watch me,' he'd say, 'I fill the bugs with fright:
The dragonflies can't sleep a wink all night,
And at my sound, the beetles and the crickets
Hide in the leaves when I stomp through the thickets.'

One spring he came to Mother for to say,
'Tomorrow is my daughter's wedding day.'
    How funny seemed his words!
    That Bhaja of the birds
Should have a daughter, or that she should wed
With a red silken veil over her head!
'Will it be very grand?' I asked. He cried,
'Of course! Among my friends I have my pride.

Painting by Rabindranath, Rabindra Bhavan, Visva-Bharati.

Some sit on perches, some in cages barred—
I'll send them each an invitation card.
They'll feast on chick-peas, millet-flour with curds,
Juicy fat grasshoppers—why, all the birds
    Such an uproar will make,
      The neighbours all the night will lie awake.
I'll feed the mynahs chillies till they bawl:
The cockatoo will boom its loudest call,
The pigeons pout their throats out as they coo,
The crabby starlings add a squawk or two.
The parakeets and koels will be there,
Their screeches shutting out the marriage prayer.
    When the groom's father hears
The parrots scream, he'll turn and stop his ears!'

The Builder

I'm not so small as I might look:
    I'm thirty summers old.
I'm not your Shirish,[†] Mother dear—
    Noto is what I'm called.

On Tamiz Mian's bullock cart
    Each day to town I ride.
From then until the shadows gather,
I lay one brick upon another
    And build a wall, exactly as I like.

You think I'm only at my play,
Making houses out of clay—
    It's just not so, they're really proper homes.
And don't think either that they're small:
They rise to be three storeys tall,
    With columns and with domes.

But if you think of asking me
Why I should stop at only three,
    I really can't reply:
Why not sixty, seventy floors,

THE BUILDER

Brick on brick, until it rose
    Right up into the sky?

Higher and higher, yet more far
Until the rafters touch the stars
    And you can't see the top?
I puzzle over this myself:
    Why need I ever stop?

I clamber up onto the roof
    Along the scaffold-frame:
I really think it's better fun
    Than any sort of game.
The roofbeaters[†] sing at their work,
    While on the street down there
The cars rush by, the pedlar-man
Clangs upon his pots and pans,
    The fruitseller goes crying out his ware.

At half-past four, you hear a shout:
Boys come rushing, school is out—
    They raise the dust as down the road they run.
The light begins to fail at last,
The crows go flapping to their nest
    At the setting of the sun.

So when the day is at an end,
Down from the scaffold I descend,
    Back to my village come:

You see that post left of the pond?
    That's where I have my home.

But if you think of asking me
Why a straw hut my home should be
    When I build mansions high—
Why should my house not rise as tall,
Or be the biggest one of all?
    I really can't reply.

Madho

The landlord's goldsmith Jagannath was practised in his art.
To teach his son his wonted trade he wished with all his heart.
He'd call the boy to sit by him and help him with his tools,
Or sometimes make toy ornaments to put on children's dolls.
But if the lad should fumble as he stoked the furnace fire
Or poured the gold, he'd slap him hard, or pull him by the hair.
And so, when Madho had the chance, he'd simply run away
Where people couldn't find him if they searched for him all day.
Beyond the borders of the town, an ancient pond there stood,
Where Madho called the naughty boys of all the neighbourhood.
They'd tie their swings to branches tall, and romp and play and run,
And as for orchards full of fruit—they knew of every one.
They'd fashion sticks from shishu† sprigs, to make them fishing rods,
Or mount a pony that they'd caught, and dash off at a trot.
He had a dog called Batu, that by its master raced,
And if it saw a lizard or a squirrel, would give chase.
Mynahs he'd tame with dough-balls; at every kind of work
He'd toil all day, but only his father's orders shirked.

His father's master Kishenlal had Dulal for his son,
Whose rowdy ways struck terror in the hearts of everyone.
Swollen with pride because he had a rich man for his father,
He'd tyrannize the folks around with every kind of bother.

As Batu once went trotting to the river for a bathe,
He passed across the football field where haughty Dulal played.
Dulal came rushing with his whip, and made as if to flog.
'I'll knock you down,' said Madho, 'if once you touch my dog.'
But Dulal wouldn't heed him: he came on in a fit.
Madho snatched the whip he bore and broke it into bits.
Dulal was a coward: he'd throw his weight around,
But faced with Madho's challenge, he couldn't stand his ground.
Trembling with rage young Madho stood, and threw Dulal a dare:
'Do what you like,' he said to him, 'I simply couldn't care.'

Jagannath sent a band of men to go and catch the lad.
They brought him home, and trussed him up and tied him to his bed.
'You rascal,' said his father, 'that you should dare to beat
Your master's son, to whom you owe the very rice you eat!
To the market-place they'll take you in the evening, where Dulal
Will lay his whip across your back in the full sight of all.'
But when to carry out the threat the landlord's men came round,
They only saw the length of rope: Dulal could not be found.
'What's this?' they asked his mother. She said, 'With my own hands
I'd taken it upon myself to loosen Madho's bands.
He wanted to be free. "Why then," I said, "you'd better go:
It's better to be dead by far than be dishonoured so."'
Then, turning to her husband with a disdainful eye,
She cried, 'A thousand curses upon your slavery.'

Twenty years and more went by; to Bengal Madho came.
He found a girl of his own tribe, and settled down again.
The children too came one by one, his happy home to fill.
He had a job as foreman in a big jute-weaving mill.

But when the price of jute went down, the sahibs docked their wage:
Thousands of workers now struck work, and downed their
    tools in rage.
'Madho,' the sahib said to him, 'why should you come to grief?
Just stay out of this mischief, we'll see you find relief.'
'I'd rather die than be a traitor,' Madho answered back.
Policemen came; some went to jail, while others' skulls were cracked.
'Sahib,' said Madho, 'fare you well: I'll go back as I came.
My stomach never will submit to eat the rice of shame.'
They all set out towards the land that was his land no more:
His father dead, his mother dead, his ties snapped heretofore.
See them again upon the road, their hearts with hope made new.
Will the torn root find once again the soil from which it grew?

Two Bighas of Land

I'd lost my land to pay my debts: just two bighas† remained.
The landlord said, 'You know, Upen, I'm going to buy this land.'
'You're a great lord,' I said to him, 'with land on all sides lying;
But look at me, I'm only left with room enough to die in.'
'Look here, my man,' he answered me, 'you see my garden there:
It only wants two bighas more to be a perfect square.
You've got to give it.' So at last I tearfully besought,
With my hands pressed upon my heart, 'O save this poor man's plot!
My forefathers lived on this land! I count it more than gold,
A mother to me: and shall I, poor wretch, now have it sold?'
His eyes grew red; he held his peace a moment angrily,
Then told me with a cruel smile, 'Very well then, we'll see.'

In a few weeks I'd lost my home, was out upon the road:
He'd trapped me by a false decree, for debts I never owed.
It's they, alas, who've got the most who always grab for more:
The king of the land puts out his hand to rob the poor man's store.
I felt God would not have me among worldly troubles cast,
So gifted me the whole wide earth, for my two bighas lost.
From land to land, in sadhu's† robes I followed holy men:
How many pleasing spots I saw, how many pleasing scenes.
But land or sea, country or town, wherever I might roam,
There rose to mind the plot of land that once had been my home.

And having wandered far and wide, my heart began to yearn,
When fifteen years and more had passed, again there to return.

I bow before your lovely form, my mother, my Bengal!
The soft breeze by your Ganga's banks has comforted my soul.
You spreading plain, where the sky's brow bends down
    to kiss your feet,
Your tree-engirded villages, like little nests of peace,
Your mango groves beneath whose shade the cowherds
    come to play,
The silent love, as cool as night, within your dark deep lakes.
With hearts of nectar, village wives fetch water from the river—
My tears welled up to see it all, my soul longed to cry 'Mother'.
The second day, at last before my village home I stood:
There was the potter's shop, and there the festival-chariot's[†] route,
The rice-barn, market, temple-yard—all lay there as before.
I passed them by, and thirsting stood before my very door.

I gazed around on either side with aching heart, and saw
A mango tree that once I knew still standing by the wall.
I sat and wept beneath its shade; my aching heart was eased,
As one by one there rose to mind my childhood memories.
How in the month of summer storms, awake all night we lay,
Then ran to pick the windfall by the earliest light of day.
Or how on sweet, still afternoons, truant from school we ran:
Alas, I thought, I would not ever see those days again!
But suddenly the wind arose, the branches gave a clap,
And two ripe fruit fell from the tree and dropped beside my lap.
Here was a sign—the mother, then, has found her child, I said.
Devoutly I took up her gift and pressed it to my head.

But suddenly the gardener came, like messenger of death:
Top-knotted Oriya,† cursing me with all his power of breath.
'All that I've had,' I said to him, 'I've given silently,
And must you rave because you grudge two little fruit to me?'
He didn't know me: shouldered his stick, and marched me to his lord.
The master and his fawning crowd were fishing with line and rod.
He heard what passed, and shook with rage: 'I'll kill you straight,'
    he roared;
And what he said, his flatterers took up a hundredfold.
'Master,' I said, 'just two ripe fruit I beg for my relief.'
'He's dressed like a holy man,' he sneered, 'but he's a brazen thief.'
I laughed, and wept: was this the lot that fate for me decreed?
You, lord, are a moral man today, and I a thief indeed!

The Magic Stone[†]

❦

Sanatan,[†] by the river bank   at Vrindavan,[†] with mind intent
        Was saying his prayers.
When a brahman, poorly clothed,   fell at his two feet and adored
        Him, coming there.
'What's your name, sir?' Sanatan   raised his eyes and asked the man,
        'Where are you from?'
'What shall I say,' to him replied   the brahman; 'to obtain your sight
        Far have I roamed.
Jiban is your servant's name,   and in Mankar is my home,
        A village in Bardhaman.[†]
In all the world you'll never see   a wretched so beggared as I be,
        Such a poor luckless man.
Humbly I spend my days; I have   a little land, hardly enough
        To live upon.
Once I was a famous priest   at sacrifices, prayers and feasts,
        But that's all gone.
I tried to mend my destiny   by worshipping Shiva, that he
        A boon may grant.
Finally, in a dream at dawn   the god appeared, and said, "You'll gain
        That which you want.
Upon the Yamuna's bank you'll see   the sage Sanatan Goswami.
        Embrace his feet,

Call him 'Father'—he can teach   the very way for you to reach
         The wealth you seek."'
Sanatan was in quandary.   He thought, 'What might I have with me
         That's worth the giving?
Whatever wealth I had one day   I left behind and came away,
         I beg for a living.'
Then suddenly he gave a cry   at some returning memory:
         'Yes, truly told!
Walking beside the river-shore,   a stone I picked up long ago
         That turns all things to gold.
There in the sand I've buried it,   in case I find a person fit
         To give it to.
All your woes will disappear   upon its merest touch: good sir,
         Take it and go!'

To the river's edge the brahman ran,   with frantic hands dug in the sand
         The stone to hold:
No sooner was it lightly set   against two iron amulets,
         They turned to gold.
The brahman in amazement sank   down on the sandy river-bank,
         Submerged in thought.
Who knows what murmurs he could hear   the river pour into his ear,
         What strains it brought!
Beyond the river, in the west   the tired sun sank to its rest,
         Its beams blood-red.
The brahman sprang up from his seat,   and falling at the sadhu's feet,
         In tears he said:
'What is that treasure you possess   for which this stone beyond all price
         You can disown?
That wealth I humbly beg,' he cried;   and then, into the river's tide,
         He flung the stone.

The Fake Fortress[†]

'I won't let water pass my lips,' the Rana of Chittor vowed,
'So long as Bundi's fortress still stands above the ground.'
    'What vow is this you've made, O king!
    To stake your life on the one thing
No man can ever hope to do!' his courtiers all cried.
'I'll do it or I'll keep my vow,' the Rana still replied.

The fort of Bundi from Chittor is twenty-five miles' run.
The Haravanshis holding it are heroes every one.
    King Hamu is commander there:
    He doesn't know the taste of fear,
Of which the Rana is aware from only too much proof—
And Bundi's fort from Chittor is twenty-five miles off.

The Minister then made a plan: 'All night we'll work away
And, looking just like Bundi, make a little fort of clay.
    So then the Rana'll only need
    To raze it to the ground with speed—
Or else he'll have to end his life for just a hasty word!'
They set to work at his command and built the earthen fort.

Kumbha[†] was the Rana's man, a Haravanshi bold.
He came back now from hunting deer, and heard the story told.

'Who has done this?' he cried aloud.
'Will Haravanshi Rajputs proud
Be made to bow their heads in shame to see this sorry sport?
I, Kumbha, Haravanshi brave, will guard the dummy fort.'

The Rana now comes striding up to break the fort asunder.
'Keep out of here, your Majesty!' roars Kumbha like the thunder.
'I won't stand here and share the blame
To turn the battle to a game:
I'll fight to hold your phony fort, your wretched pile of clay.'
Kumbha roars to the Rana, 'Your Majesty, away!'

So holding up his hunting-bow and beaten to his knees,
Kumbha alone fights on to save the fort built to deceive.
The Rana's soldiers round him spread
And with their swords cut off his head—
Before the toy fort's lion-gate† it mingles with the mud.
The false fortress of Bundi is hallowed with his blood.

The Captive Hero[†]

Where the five rivers[†] flow,
The Sikhs awoke to the Guru's[†] word
   With hair knotted in vow—
   No qualms, no fear they knew.
A thousand voices break out, 'Hail, Guru!'
The newly-risen Sikhs, in that new dawn,
Gazed with steady eyes upon the rising sun.

'Hail the unbodied God!'[†] they cried together,
Dispelling every fear, breaking all fetters.
What joyful clamour rings from every sword
As 'Hail the unbodied God!' all Punjab roared.

   The hour is set
For a million hearts grown fearless, owing no man debt,
Flinging aside all care, beneath their feet
Trampling like vanquished slaves both life and death:
On the five rivers' ten banks, a great hour is set.

   In Delhi's castle-keep
The Emperor's son[†] is nightly shaken from his sleep.

Whose voices are those, cleaving through the night?
Whose flaming torches fill the sky with light?

> On the five rivers' shores
O what a tide of blood from pious bodies flows!
> From a million breasts
Flocks of souls take wing, like birds seeking their nests.
> With their life's blood, heroes
Anoint their mother's[†] brow, on the five rivers' shores.

> Mughal and Sikh are locked
In death's embrace, clutching each other by the throat:
A serpent struggling with a wounded hawk!
'Hail to the Guru!' deep Sikh voices cry,
> And thirsting for their blood,
'The faith! The faith!'[†] the enraged Mughals reply.

> In the Gurdaspur fort
Banda was taken prisoner by a Turkish force.
They chained him like a lion, brought him thence
> To the Delhi court:
Banda, taken prisoner in Gurdaspur fort.

See the Mughal army, in a cloud of dust
Marching along, severed Sikh heads on spearheads thrust:
And seven hundred Sikhs behind them, stumbling along,
Clanking the chains that bind them: how the people throng
The streets, and every window is wide open flung!
Heedless of death, 'Hail to the Guru!' cry the Sikhs.
Mughal and Sikh have stirred the dust of Delhi's streets.

Now a new strife
Breaks out among the Sikhs—who'll be the first
    To offer up his life?
Each morning they are brought forth, row on row:
A hundred brave hearts utter, 'Hail, Guru!'
    And then lay down
A hundred heads to the executioner's blow.

In seven days, seven hundred lives: when all was done,
The judge put into Banda's clasp Banda's own son.
'Kill him with your own hands,' he said—the little one,
Arms bound, flung on his father's lap: Banda must slay
    His very own son.

    He spoke no word,
But slowly drew the little boy close to his heart,
Laid his right hand upon his head for a brief thought,
And placed a single kiss on his red turban-cloth.
Then, bringing out his knife, he said
'Hail to the Guru!' in the boy's ear. 'My son,
    You mustn't be afraid.'

A flame of courage leaps in the young one's eyes:
His reedy voice 'Hail to the Guru!' cries—
The courtroom trembles: and then, undismayed,
'Father, I'm not afraid.'
    He looked him in the face;
And Banda, holding him in left embrace,
Plunges the knife with right hand: the boy calls
'Hail to the Guru!' one last time, and falls.

The court was hushed: the grim
Torturer tore Banda limb from limb
With red-hot tongs: without a groan he dies.
The hall was hushed: the courtiers closed their eyes.

The Representative[†]

One morning, as Shivaji sat   on the ramparts of Satara[†] fort,
        He looked across, and viewed
His holy Guru, Ramdas, go   begging for alms from door to door
        As though he starved for food.
'What do I see!' Shivaji thought,   'My Guru Ji, who lacks for nought,
        Holding a begging-bowl!
The man who has won everything,   holds under foot the very king,
        Can't satisfy his soul!

'A thirsty man might as well think   that he can have enough to drink
        By filling a leaking jug.
I must discover, as I live,   how much of alms I need to give
        That I might fill his bag.'
He asked that pen and ink be brought,   made up a letter—who knows what?
        Gave Balaji[†] the screed,
And said to him, 'As Guru Ji   beside the fortress door goes by,
        Let him have this to read.'

The Guru passes down the road: among the horses, chariots, crowds,
        He wanders, singing forth:
'Every human has a home—   me alone have you left to roam,
        O Shiva,[†] lord of earth.
Annapurna, giver of food,   has taken charge of all her brood—
        The whole world is content.

Me alone, O beggar-lord,   from the Mother's breast have you torn forth,
    To make me your servant.'

At midday, when his song was ended,   he bathed himself, and then descended
    To the fortress gate.
Balaji his obeisance made,   standing beside the path, and laid
    The letter at his feet.
The curious Guru stretched his hand   to take the letter up, and scanned
    The tidings that were there:
Humbly Shivaji did him greet,   and laid down at his lotus-feet
    His kingdom in entire.

Ramdas went when morrow broke   to see the king, and to him spoke.
    He said, 'Tell me, my son,
If all your land to me you give,   what means will you have left to live?
    What good can you perform?'
'I'll gladly tender all my days   in your service and your praise,'
    The king cried without qualms.
'Take then this bag,' the Guru said,   'and lay it on your shoulder straight:
    Let us go seeking alms.'

Shivaji with his Guru goes   making their way from door to door,
    Clutching his begging-bowl.
Terrified children turn in fear   and rush to call their mothers there,
    Astonished to their soul.
The lord of wealth beyond all count,   why should he now turn mendicant?
    Can a stone on water float?
They tremble as they give their mite,   abashed to see the very sight:
    The king must have his sport!

THE REPRESENTATIVE

The sun's on high: they strike the hour   at the fortress gate, and folk retire
        To seek their noontide rest.
The Guru breaks into a song,   to his one-string lute singing along,
        With joyful tears opprest:
'O God on high, I do not know   what you may seek from us below:
        There's nothing you need crave,
And yet, lord of the three realms,   you roam our hearts seeking for alms,
        Asking for all we have!'

At last they came at eventide   to the town's edge, by the riverside,
        And after they had bathed,
They cooked their rice† and sat to eat: the Guru took a part of it,
        His follower what was left.
The erstwhile king now smiled. Said he,   'You've brought me from proud royalty
        Down to a beggar's state.
I still remain your servant true: tell me what more you'd have me do,
        What suffer for your sake.'

The Guru answered, 'Hear me now.   You have just made an awesome vow:
        Your task must match the same.
Take in hand, as you had before,   this kingdom I give you once more,
        And rule it in my name.
This role to you destiny gives,   of beggar's representative—
        A destitute, unworldly king.
The royal task you undertake   know to be work done for my sake:
        Kingdomless in your kingdom reign.

'My saffron robes I give to you,   my son; and let my blessings too
        With them upon you pass.
Let the ascetic's garment be   the royal flag† that you shall fly,'
        Said the holy Ramdas.

With thoughtful brow and lowered head   the royal disciple silent sat
             Upon the river bank:
The cowherd stopped his flute, the kine   came back home; the setting sun
             Beyond the far shore sank.

To an evening raga,† all intent,   Ramdas tuned his instrument
             And sang again forthwith:
'Who are you, that amid this earth   has seated me in royal garb,
             Behind which you stay hid?
Your shoes, sign of your majesty,   I bear,† O king, even as I lie
             In the shelter of your feet.
Evening falls, the day is past.   To your own kingdom come at last:
             How much more must I wait?'

The Beggar's Bounty†

❦

When famine stalked Shravasti† town,
Filling the air with tears and groans,
The Buddha to his disciples came   and spoke in turn to each by name:
'Who will take on the load
To give the hungry food?'

The rich merchant Ratnakar Seth
Heard the plea, and hung his head.
'My lord,' he cried, joining his hands,   'to feed the vast and hungry bands
Of this great town of ours,
Is not within my powers.'

Next the warrior Jaysen spake:
'Your task I happily would take
Upon my head, and make it good   were it the shedding of my blood
Or my heart's flesh to carve:
In my own home, we starve.'

Dharmapal, next to relate,
Cried, 'Alas my hapless fate!
The spectre of the drought has killed   the golden harvest of my field—
I am nothing today.
My taxes I scarce can pay.'

Each at the others' faces stares:
Not one to make an answer dares.
Out of that silent meeting-place, only the Buddha's pitying gaze,
Like the evening star, looked down
Upon the suffering town.

Slowly at last then, blushing red,
With anguished tears and lowered head,
Anathapindada's[†] daughter rose. She touched the Buddha's feet, and spoke
In humble tones yet free
To all the company:

'I, Supriya, lowliest mendicant,
Take upon me your commandment.
All those who cry and lack for food, they are the children of my brood:
I take upon my head
The task to keep them fed.'

Amazement broke out in the ranks:
'Begging daughter of a begging monk,
Tell us what foolish pride of pelf has made you take upon yourself
A task so vast and grave.
What riches do you have?'

She answered, bowing low to all:
'Nothing except my begging-bowl.
Resourceless woman that I am, that very fact will make me claim
Largesse from all of you,
The master's will to do.

'I can command at every door
　　The treasure of my endless store.
You can perpetuate, if you wish,　the bounty of my begging-dish:
　　The world shall live through your alms,
　　And the famine's pang find calm.'

My Childhood

All the pieces in this section have been translated by Suvro Chatterjee.

My Childhood

I was born in the Calcutta of yesteryear. In those days horse-drawn carriages still rattled through the streets, leaving a trail of dust, the coachmen lashing the skinny horses with hempen whips. There were no trams, no buses, no motor cars. People weren't always in such a breathless hurry then; the days passed at a leisurely pace. The babus left for their offices after a long smoke on their hookahs, chewing on a wad of paan,[†] some in palanquins and some in shared hansom cabs. Rich men had their own carriages painted with the family insignia, draped with leather half-curtains; the coachman sat on the coach-box with a turban perched on his head; two pairs of footmen rode at the back with yak-tail fans tucked in their belts, startling pedestrians with their sudden cries. Women were shy of riding in carriages; when they went out it was always in the stuffy darkness of closed palanquins. They never used umbrellas in rain or shine. A woman who wore a chemise or shoes was mocked as a memsahib,[†] implying that she was a shameless creature. If a woman accidentally met a man other than a close relation, she would bite her tongue in embarrassment, turn aside and draw down the end of her sari beyond her nose. Their palanquins had closed doors, just like their rooms. When women of rich families went out, the palanquins were draped in thick curtains over and above the roof and sides, making them look like moving tombs. A darwan[†] walked alongside, brass-bound cudgel in hand. It was the darwan's duty to guard the front gate of the house, stroking his beard; to take money to the bank and womenfolk to their relatives' houses; and on festival days, to escort the master's wife for a holy dip in the river Ganga, palanquin and all. When pedlars came to the door with their boxes full of wares, they knew that Shiunandan, the darwan, would take his cut. Then there were the cabmen: if any of them thought that the darwan was asking for too much cut-money, he would make a great row at the gate. Our sergeant-at-gate, Shobharam, was a wrestler; every now and then he used to flex his arms and swing heavy clubs around his head, or prepare a bowl of siddhi,[†] or chomp raw radish, leaves and all, with great relish while we yelled 'Radha-Krishna!' into his ear. The more he protested and threw up his arms, the more lustily we shouted. He had hit upon this wile to hear the names of the gods he worshipped.

There were neither gas lamps then nor electric lights; when the first paraffin lamps arrived later on, we were amazed at their brightness. A servant came in the evenings to light our castor-oil lamps. In our study, there would be a double-wicked lamp.

By the flickering light of that lamp, our tutor[†] taught us from Pyari Sarkar's *First Book of Reading*. I would first start yawning, then begin to nod, and rub my eyes to keep awake. He never tired of telling me what a gem of a boy his other pupil Satin was, how keen he was on studies, how he rubbed snuff into his eyes if he ever felt sleepy. And I?—the less said the better. Not even the fear of ending up as the only ignorant boy of the group could keep me awake. When at last I was allowed to go, at nine o'clock, I could hardly keep my eyes open. The narrow corridor which led to the inner quarters was lined with slatted windows; a sooty lantern hung from the roof. As I went down that dark corridor I always imagined that something was following me, and the thought made me shiver. Ghosts and demons were plentiful in story and gossip in those days, as also in the crannies of people's minds. Often a maidservant would stumble and fall on hearing the nasal twang of a shankhchunni's[†] voice. That female ghost was a most ill-tempered thing, and she was

Rabindranath, his elder brother Somendranath and his nephew Satyaprasad with Shrikantha Sinha: photograph c. 1873–4.

a glutton for fish. There was a large leafy nut tree at the western corner of the house. Many people claimed to have seen a shape standing with one foot on the third-storey roof and another on a branch of that tree; there were also many people ready to believe it. When a friend of my elder brother's laughed at the story, the servants muttered darkly that he was a most irreligious man, and all his learning would prove of no use when the evil spirit broke his neck. The air was so thick with dreadful superstitions that one's flesh crept if one stretched one's legs under the table.

We didn't have mains water either. In the months of Magh and Phalgun,[†] the water-carrier would sling a bamboo pole over his shoulder, hang pitchers from it, and fetch enough drinking water from the Ganga to last us the whole year through. All that water was stored in huge pitchers, row on row, in a dark room on the ground floor. Everybody knew that the creatures who lurked in those dark, damp cells had huge gaping mouths, eyes on their chests, and ears the size of winnowing-fans; their feet pointed backwards. My heart pounded whenever I walked past those eerie shadows towards our back garden, and I would hurry as fast as I could.

At high tide the Ganga water used to come rushing through brick-lined channels by the roadside. Since my grandfather's time, some of that water had been allotted to our pond. When the sluice gate was drawn, the water fell foaming into the pond in a cascade, while the fishes tried to show their skill in swimming against the current. I would stand watching, entranced, clutching the rail of the southern balcony. At last one day the pond was filled up with cartloads of rubble. The disappearance of the pond marked the end of that mirroring of a country scene set round with green shadows. The nut tree is still there, but no one has talked about the brahman's ghost[†] for a long time.

There is more light everywhere these days, inside and out.

(*Childhood*, chapter 1)

The palanquin dated back to my grandmother's days. It was very capacious, in the old nawabi style. Each pole was long enough for eight bearers to hold. Those bearers used to wear gold bracelets, heavy earrings and bright red sleeveless jackets; but with the passage of old wealth, they have vanished like the brightness of clouds after sunset. The sides of the palanquin were painted with coloured designs; some of them had faded and stained with age, and the coir stuffing had spilt out of the torn seats. It was like a piece of rejected furniture thrown out of an office-room into the corridor outside. I was only seven or eight then. I had no responsibilities, and that old palanquin too had been retired from service, so I felt a natural kinship with it. It was like a quiet island in the middle of the sea. On holidays, I felt like Robinson Crusoe, hiding behind its closed doors from the prying eyes all round me.

Our house was full of people in those days, from close relatives to strangers. You couldn't keep tally of them. Every wing rang with the bustle of maids and servants.

Pyari the maid would be returning from the market, crossing the front courtyard with her huge basket of vegetables balanced on her hip. At the same time Dukhan the water-carrier would be fetching water from the river, the vessels slung from his shoulder-yoke. The weaver-woman would be visiting the ladies' quarters with a batch of saris in the latest fashion, and Dinu the bespoke goldsmith, who worked the bellows noisily in his little shop down the lane, would come to collect his dues from Kailas Mukherjee, who sat in the cash-room with a quill pen stuck behind his ear. The cotton-ginner twanged his bow in the courtyard, beating and fluffing a mass of cottonwool out of old quilts. Mukundalal the darwan practised wrestling-grips with our one-eyed strongman, rolling about on the ground, slapping his legs, doing push-ups by the score. A clutch of beggars sat at the gate, waiting for the customary alms.

The morning wore on, the sun grew hot, they rang the hours at the gate, but time inside my palanquin did not keep pace with the hours. In there, noontime was like in olden times, when the sentry at the palace gate struck a gong to dismiss the court for the day, and the king went to bathe in sandalwood-scented water. The people set to watch over me would fall asleep on holiday afternoons; I was left to my own devices. Within my mind, my idle palanquin started moving once more; the ghostly bearers were paid out of my imagination. The road, too, was built out of my fancy; it wound through strange and far-off lands, whose names I had found in books. Sometimes the palanquin entered a dense forest. Tigers' eyes gleamed in the bushes, making my flesh creep. Bishwanath the shikari† would be with me; he had only to fire his gun once—bang!—and all would be quiet. Then the palanquin would turn into a peacock-boat and strike out into the open sea, with no land in sight. The oars splashed in rhythm, the ocean heaved and swelled. 'Have a care, have a care!' the oarsmen roared, 'a storm's coming up.' At the helm was Abdul the boatman, with a pointed beard but a shaven head and moustache. I knew him well: he brought hilsa fish and tortoise eggs from the Padma† for my elder brother.

He told me a story once. One day towards the end of Chaitra,† he had gone fishing in his dinghy when a nor'wester arose. It was a terrific storm, and his boat was about to sink. Abdul took the towing-rope between his teeth and dived into the water, swam to a sandbank and dragged the dinghy to safety. The story ended too soon for my liking. The boat didn't sink, and he was saved too easily—what sort of story was that? I kept on pestering him: 'Go on, what happened then?'

So he carried on: 'Then there was a great to-do. I came upon a wolf—it had whiskers this long! During the storm it had climbed the pakur tree near the market jetty on the other bank. A great gust of wind toppled the tree into the Padma, and the wolf was washed along in the flood. Gasping and thrashing about, it somehow managed to crawl ashore on the same sandbank with me. The moment I saw it I made a noose with my rope. The brute rolled its eyes and barred my way. It had grown hungry after its swim: it put out its red tongue and began to slaver. Ah well, it might have met many types of men before, but it didn't know Abdul! "Come here, boy!" I called out. It rose on its hind legs, and at once I threw the noose over its head and pulled. The more it struggled, the tighter the halter became, until it began to choke.'

I grew very anxious at this. 'Did he die, Abdul?'

'He wouldn't dare die on me!' said Abdul. 'The tide was roaring up the river, and I had to go all the way back to Bahadurgunj. So I harnessed the big brute to the dinghy and made him tow it for forty miles at least. Every time it grunted and groaned, I jabbed it in the belly with my oar: the journey of ten or fifteen hours was done in just an hour and a half!—Don't ask me any more questions, son; you won't get a reply.'

'All right, so much for the wolf, but what about the crocodile?'

'I had seen its snout sticking out of the water now and then,' said Abdul. 'It would bask in the sun on the sloping river-bank, with a kind of leer on its face. I would have taught it a lesson if I had a gun, but my licence had expired. I had some fun all the same. One day Kanchi the gypsy woman was trimming a sliver of bamboo on the bank, her baby goat tethered beside her. The crocodile came quietly out of the water, took the goat by the leg and started dragging it into the river. The gypsy woman leaped upon the giant lizard's back and began to hack at its neck with her chopper. The monster let go of the goat and dived for its life.'

'And then—?' I asked breathlessly.

'The rest of the story's underwater too,' said Abdul. 'It'll take time to dive down and bring it up. I'll send a spy to find out and let you know when we next meet.'

But Abdul didn't come back again. Perhaps he's gone himself to find out.

Such were my journeys in the palanquin. Outside it, I sometimes played teacher; the railings were my pupils. They were always silent, though a few were naughty boys with no mind for lessons. I kept warning them they'd have to earn their living as coolies[†] when they grew up. They'd been beaten so often there were scars all over their bodies, yet they never stopped playing pranks, for else my game would have come to an end. I had another favourite game that involved my wooden lion. Having heard about animal sacrifices at puja[†] time, I had decided that sacrificing my lion would be a great feat, so I chopped away at it with a stick. I even made up a chant to go with the ceremony—you can't have a puja without a mantra:[†]

Uncle Lion cutoom
Andibose's butoom
Ulukoot dhulukoot pit-a-pat
Walnut pollnut rat-a-tat
Thud - bang - crack!

Most of these words were borrowed stuff, only 'walnut' was my own—I loved to eat walnuts. The 'rat-a-tat' told you that my sacrificial chopper was made of wood, and the 'crack' betrayed the fact that it wasn't at all strong.

(*Childhood*, chapter 2)

From a little before our time, well-to-do families were fond of putting on plays. Troupes would be made up of boys with reedy voices. Mejo Kaka† was the leader of one such group. He was as skilful at writing plays as at training young boys to act. Besides these home-grown productions among the rich, there was the commercial jatra† as well. In many neighbourhoods, jatra companies mushroomed under one renowned manager or another. Not all of them were well-educated or high-born. They had risen by their own merit. There were such musical jatras† in our house occasionally, but I was too young then to be allowed to watch. I could only watch the preparations for the show. The troupe would take over the verandah, which filled with clouds of tobacco-smoke. The boys were long-haired, with shadows under their eyes; though they were young, they looked hardboiled, and their lips were blackened with paan. There were coloured tin trunks full of costumes. The gate being open, hordes of curious people would pour into the courtyard; their clamour poured out of the house down our lane and onto Chitpur Road. Come nine o'clock and the servant Shyam would swoop down on me like a hawk upon a pigeon, grip me by the elbow with a horny hand, and say, 'Off to bed! Your mother's calling you.' I found it most demeaning to be dragged away in this fashion with everyone looking on, but I would concede defeat and slink off to bed. The din continued outside, the chandeliers burnt brightly; but my bedroom was very quiet, with only a faint light from a little brass lamp on a stand. I fell asleep listening to the applause every time a dance movement came to an end.

It's grown-up nature to constantly tell you not to do this or that. But just once, for whatever reason, my guardians relented and allowed us children to watch the show. It was the story of Nala and Damayanti.[†] We slept till eleven, until the play began—we had been repeatedly promised that we would be woken up in time. I didn't really trust grown-ups in these matters: after all, they were big and we were small. I dragged myself to bed that evening, partly because Mother herself had promised to wake me, and partly because I found it difficult to stay awake after nine. Anyhow, when the time came I was woken up and brought outside. My eyes were dazzled by the rows of coloured chandeliers, upstairs and downstairs. The courtyard, covered with white cloth, seemed huge. The men of the house sat on one side with the specially invited guests; the rest of the space was filled with people from anywhere and everywhere. Those celebrities, with gold chains dangling down to their chests, seemed to have come to the Western-style theatre; but at the jatra gathering on this side, everybody, high and low, sat together. Most of them were the sort of people that gentlefolk call riff-raff. Likewise those who had written the play had learnt to write with reed pens and never had use for English copybooks. The tunes, the dances, the stories that went into the making of these musical plays had been born among the fields and markets and river ghats[†] of village Bengal: no pandit[†] had polished their language.

When we sat down beside our elder brothers, they gave us some money tied up in handkerchiefs. It was customary to throw this money to the actors when you wanted to applaud them. It meant a little extra money for them, and honour for the householder.

The night might end, but it seemed the play never would. I didn't know when I fell fast asleep, who carried me away or where. That was just as well, for I would have felt very ashamed about it. How insulting it would be, to a person who had sat with grown-ups and tossed baksheesh[†] to the actors! When I awoke I found myself in my mother's bed. It was quite late: the sun was blazing. Never since that day have I risen after the sun was up.

These days, amusements flow through the city like a great river. There are no dry spots along its course. There are cinema shows everywhere at all hours, and anyone can walk in for a small price. In those days, watching the jatra was like digging for water in the sand every few miles along a dry river bed. The water lasts only a few hours; travellers pass by, cup their hands and drink their fill.

The old days were like a prince who made gifts of his wealth at festivals when it took his fancy. The present times are like a merchant's son who has laid out a dazzling pile of wares where two highroads cross. Customers come to him both from the main road and from the byways.

(*Childhood*, chapter 5)

Brajeshwar[†] was the head servant of our house, and Shyam was his second-in-command. Shyam came from Jessore.[†] He was a perfect rustic, and he spoke a language very different from Calcutta-style Bengali. He was dark, with big eyes, long well-greased hair, and a robust body. He was a gentle and simple soul, and he loved us boys. He would tell us hair-raising tales of bandits. In those days stories about bandits were as rife as the fear of ghosts. There are robberies aplenty even now; people are often killed and wounded, and the police don't always catch the real culprits either—but these are merely items of news, they don't give you the fun and thrill of a good story. The old-world banditry had crystallized into stories, told and retold for a long time. In our childhood there were still some people around who had been bandits in their youth. They were expert lathials—people who fought with lathis or long bamboo sticks—and their disciples followed them wherever they went. People saluted at the mere mention of their names. Banditry in those days was seldom a matter of mindless violence and slaughter. It called for large-heartedness as well as courage. Meanwhile, even people of respectable families had begun to practise self-defence with lathis. Even notorious bandits hailed the best of them as ustads, masters of the art, and avoided the places known to be under their protection. There were even some zamindars[†] who took up brigandage as a trade. I once heard a story about how one such robber-baron had stationed his gang at the mouth of a river. On a moonless night, at the feast of the goddess Kali,[†] his men brought him the freshly cut-off head of a man to offer to the goddess. He beat his forehead and cried out, 'It's my son-in-law!'

And then there were stories about Raghu Dakat[†] and Bishu Dakat. They were not vulgar rogues but honourable men; they would announce their raids in advance. When their war-cries were heard from afar, everybody's blood ran cold. Women were sacred in their eyes; they never touched them. There was a girl once who fooled the bandits by dressing up as the goddess Kali, blade in hand, and actually got offering-money out of them.

Some men once gave a display of bandits' skills in our house. They were big strong men, very dark and long-haired. They would sling a cloth around a threshing-stone, grip it between their teeth, and toss the heavy implements over their backs; or make a man hang on to their long hair and swing him round and round. They vaulted up to the first floor on a long bamboo pole, and slipped like a bird through another man's hands. They also showed us how they could rob a house twenty or even forty miles away, come back home the same night and go to bed like an innocent fellow. They used stilts—two immensely long sticks, with small footrests halfway along their length. When they stood on these footrests and gripped the tops of the sticks, each step they took was as long as ten ordinary ones, and they could outrun a horse. Though we had no intention of turning robbers, I once tried to train the boys at Shantiniketan to walk on stilts. But in my childhood, there were many evenings when I hugged myself to muster more courage, thinking of this bandit-show and relating it to Shyam's stories.

It was on a Sunday. The previous night, we had heard stories about Raghu Dakat, while the crickets sang among the bushes in the south garden. Our hearts had pounded as we sat among the flickering shadows cast by the faint lamplight. Next day I took advantage of the holiday to climb aboard my broken palanquin. It started moving (though of course it didn't really move) towards a nameless destination, sending a taste of fright through my heart, caught in that net of stories. In the pulse-beat of the still dark interior, I could hear the bearers panting and chanting away as they jogged along—Hai-hooi, hai-hooi—and I began to shudder. The fields stretched away as far as eye could see, the air shimmered in the heat, the black lake gleamed in the distance and the sand glittered. A pakur tree beside the water bent its branches towards the broken landing-place.

The terrors of the tales lurked among the dense cane bushes and the trees that dotted the unknown plain. The more I went on, the more my heart went pit-a-pat. I would see a lathi or two sticking out of the bushes. Now it was time for the bearers to stop for a minute and shift their load from one shoulder to the other. They would drink water and wrap wet towels round their heads. And then?—*'Re re re re re re!'* the bandits would fall upon us with loud yells.

(*Childhood*, chapter 6)

In our childhood there were virtually no provisions for luxury. On the whole, life was led much more simply than it is now. The modern age would cut off all relations with those times if it saw how little it took gentlefolk to keep up appearances in those days. It was the practice of the times; on top of it, our household was particularly free of the bother of paying too much attention to the children. The fact is, adults amuse themselves by pampering children; for children, it's simply a nuisance.

We were ruled by servants. In order to lighten their work, they forbade us nearly every kind of movement and activity. However stifling that may have been, neglect was itself an enormous freedom:

it left our minds free. Our souls escaped the grip of constant feeding and dressing and decking-up.

There was nothing even remotely elegant about our meals. Our clothes[†] were so meagre that it would be mortifying even to talk about them to the young folk of today. I never wore socks on any occasion before I was ten; in winter, one plain garment over another was considered enough. Nor did we ever see this as a misfortune. We only felt sad that our family tailor Niamat saw no need to put pockets in our clothes: there has never been a boy in even the poorest household without some movable and immovable possessions to stuff into his pockets. By God's grace, there is little difference in children's wealth between the rich and the poor. We had a pair of slippers each, but not where our feet would be. With every step we took, we kicked them ahead of us: the slippers moved so much more than the feet that the purpose behind the invention of footwear was frustrated all the way.[†]

Everything about our elders was remote from us—their movements, their clothes, their talk, their pleasures. We caught occasional hints of these things, but they were far beyond our reach. Nowadays youngsters treat their elders lightly: nothing holds them back, and they are given everything even before they ask. We never got anything so easily. Many paltry things were hard to get; we comforted ourselves with the thought that they would be ours once we grew up, and vouchsafed them to that remote future. Hence whatever small things were given to us, we enjoyed to the utmost: from the rind to the core, nothing went untasted. In well-to-do families these days, children so readily get all kinds of things that they take half a bite and throw away the rest. Most things in their world go to waste.

We spent our days in the servants' rooms on the first floor, in the south-east corner of the outer quarters.

One of the servants was named Shyam, a dark and well-built lad with long hair. He came from Khulna District. He would make me sit in a particular spot inside the room, draw a circle around me with a piece of chalk, and warn me with raised finger about the grave danger of stepping outside the circle. He never explained whether the danger was creatural or godly, but he frightened me all right. I had read in the *Ramayana* about the disaster that befell Sita[†] when she stepped out of her magic circle, so I could not laugh away Shyam's chalk circle either.

Just below the window there was a pond with paved steps leading down to it. Near the wall to the east of it stood a giant Chinese banyan tree; to the south was a line of coconut palms. Imprisoned within the chalk circle, I would part the window slats and look at the scene like a picture book nearly all day. Right from the morning, I would see the neighbours come one by one to bathe in the pond. I knew when each would come, and also everyone's bathing habits. One would stop his ears with his fingers, take several quick dips and leave; another would not immerse himself at all, but spread out his towel, fill it with water and pour it over his head again and again; one would sweep the water with his hands to remove any floating dirt, then suddenly dive in; while one plunged in without warning from the top step of the ghat, making a loud splash. Some muttered holy verses, all in one breath, as they entered the water. Some were in a tearing hurry to finish bathing and go back. Others were in no hurry at all—they bathed in a leisurely way, dried themselves, changed, shook out the ends of their dhotis two or three times, picked a few flowers from the garden and then set off home at a relaxed pace, spreading the contentment of their freshly-bathed bodies in the air. So the day wore on till one o'clock in the afternoon. The ghat became desolate and silent. Only the ducks and geese went on diving for water-snails and busily preening the feathers on their backs.

The great banyan tree would possess my mind once everybody had left the pond. It had a dark tangle of aerial roots around the main trunk. There was an enchantment in that shadowy corner of the world. There alone, nature seemed to have forgotten her usual laws: an impossible Age of Dreams seemed to reign there in broad daylight even in the present age, somehow dodging God's eye. Today I can no longer tell you clearly what sort of beings I saw there in my mind's eye, or what they did. It was of this tree that I would write one day:

> Standing there with matted locks through night and day,
> Ancient banyan, do you remember that little boy?

Where is that banyan today? Even that pond, the mirror in which the goddess of the tree viewed herself, no longer exists; many of the people who bathed in the pond have followed the path of the tree's vanished shadow. And that little boy has himself grown up, put down all kinds of hanging roots around him, and sits amid that vast maze counting the hours of joy and sorrow, sunlight and shadow.

We were forbidden to go outdoors; even inside the house we couldn't move freely everywhere. So we peeped out at the great world of nature from crannies and corners. There was something called 'the outside': a substance stretching endlessly beyond my reach, yet its sights and sounds and smells crept in from everywhere through chinks in the doors and windows. It would touch me for an instant, trying by sign-language to play with me through the bars of my prison. It was free while I was captive—there was no way we could meet, so the tie of love between us was profound. The chalk circle has disappeared today, but the barrier remains. What was then far-off remains far-off, what was outside is still so. I recall the poem I wrote when I grew up:

> The cage-bird had a golden cage,
> The forest bird lived free.
> They met one day—who can foretell
> The plans of destiny?
> The forest bird said, 'Cage-bird,
> To the forest let's away.'
> The captive bird said, 'Forest bird,
> In the cage we'll quietly stay.'
> The forest bird said, 'No,
> 'I shall never dwell in chains.'
> 'Alas!' sighed the captive bird,
> 'How can I freely range?'

The parapet around the roof above our inner quarters rose above my head. Once I had grown up a little and the servants' rule had relaxed somewhat, when a new bride had entered the household and was indulging me as her leisure-time companion, I sometimes went up there at midday. Everybody had finished lunch; there was a break in the routine of household chores. The women's quarters were sunk in rest; the saris, wet after the midday bath, had been hung out to dry; a flock of crows were crowding round the left-over rice thrown in one corner of the courtyard. In that lonely moment of leisure, the forest bird touched beaks with the caged bird through the openings in the

'Under that banyan tree...': Illustration for Jiban-Smriti *by Gaganendranath Tagore.*

parapet. I stood gazing outwards. There was the line of coconut palms at the end of the inner garden; glimpsed through them, a pond in the neighbouring quarter known as 'Singhis' Garden', and beside the pond the cowshed belonging to our dairy-woman Tara; and still farther away, jostling the treetops, ranged roofs of all shapes and sizes, high and low, gleaming in the midday sun till they faded into the pale blue of the eastern horizon. Here and there on those distant roofs a few stair-top rooms reared their heads, as though raising their immobile forefingers to tell me, with winks and signs, the secrets within them. Like a beggar outside a palace gate, dreaming of priceless jewels beyond all possibility locked up in the treasury within, I imagined those faraway houses as being packed with endless games and untold freedom. The sky blazed overhead, the kite's shrill scream came to my ears from its farthest end. In the lane running along Singhis' Garden, past the silent houses asleep by day, a pedlar went crying 'Bangles, toys, who wants my toys?'—and my mind filled with a great wistfulness.

My father often went travelling; he was rarely at home. His room on the second floor remained shut. I would part the door slats, reach inside and draw back the bolt. Inside, there was a sofa at the southern end. I would spend the whole afternoon sitting quietly on that sofa. To begin with, the room was kept shut for months on end, and was out of bounds; so it had a strong smell of mystery. Moreover, the sun beating down on the empty roof heightened the dreamy state of my mind. There was another attraction too. Mains water had just been introduced in Calcutta. It was a great novelty, still plentiful everywhere in the city, north as well as south; it was supplied unstintingly even to the Bengali quarter.† In that Golden Age of water mains, the water reached up even to my father's room on the second floor. I would turn on the shower and bathe to my heart's content—not for comfort, only to indulge my fancy. The joy of freedom blended with the fear of restraint—between the two, the Company's water rained on my heart like arrows of delight.

However little direct contact I might have had with the outdoors, I enjoyed its charms—the more, perhaps, for that very reason. Too many materials make the mind lazy; it comes to rely wholly on outward things, forgetting that a feast of delight is more an inward than an outward matter. That is the first lesson of childhood. A child's possessions are few and small, but he needs no more to give him delight. The wretched child who is given too many toys finds his play quite spoilt.

There was a little garden in our inner compound: it could hardly be called a garden. Its chief items were a shaddock, a jujube, a hog-plum tree and a row of coconut palms. There was a round platform of brickwork in the middle, among whose crevices grass and various lichens had trespassed and put up their flags like defiant squatters. Only such flowering plants as could survive without care carried on with their humble duty as best they could, laying no blame on the gardener. There was a threshing shed in the north corner; the womenfolk sometimes went there on housework. This shed has covered its face and vanished silently long ago, admitting the defeat of the village way of life in Calcutta. I do not believe that Adam's garden of Eden could have been in better array than this garden of ours. The first man's paradise was uncluttered—it had not wrapped itself round with artifice. Ever since humankind ate the fruit of the tree of knowledge,[†] his need for decoration and ornament has grown constantly, and will keep on growing till we have fully digested that fruit. The garden inside our house was my Eden, and it was enough for me. I remember that early on autumn mornings, I ran out into that garden as soon as I was awake. The smell of dewy grass and leaves rushed to greet me, and the dawn with its soft fresh sunshine thrust its face through the fans of coconut-leaves swishing above the eastern wall.

There is a piece of land near the northern end of our house which we still call the barnyard. This shows there must once have been a barn there to store the year's supply of grain. In those days, town and village were rather alike, like brother and sister in their childhood; now that they're grown up, you can hardly see any resemblance.

On holidays I used to run off to this barnyard—not so much to play, more out of a fondness for the place itself, though I cannot exactly say why: perhaps because, as a lonely waste space in the very corner of my home, it had an air of mystery. We neither lived there nor put it to any use; it served no need. It was outside the house, a bare and useless piece of land where no one had bothered even to plant a few flowers; so a child could give free rein to his fancy in that empty space.

Any day when I could give my guardians the slip and run away to this place seemed like a holiday to me.

There was yet another fascinating place in our house, but to this day I have not been able to discover its whereabouts. A girl my own age, whom I used to play with, called it the king's palace.† Every now and then she told me, 'I went to the palace today!' but I never had the good luck to accompany her. It was a wonderful place: the games they played, and the playthings they played with, were equally wonderful. I had the feeling that it was very close by, either upstairs or downstairs, but somehow I never could go there. I often asked the girl, 'Is the palace outside our house?' She would reply, 'No, it's right here.' I sat puzzling over the problem: I had seen every room in the house, so where could that palace be? I never asked who the king was, and I have yet to discover where his kingdom lay. All I ever learnt was that the king's palace was right inside our own house.

When I look back at my childhood, what I remember most vividly is that the world and life itself seemed to be filled with mystery. The unthinkable lurked everywhere: one never knew when one might encounter it. This idea was constantly in my mind. Nature seemed to hold out her closed fist and say with a smile, 'Tell me what's inside!'—and nothing seemed impossible for sure.

I remember how I planted a custard-apple seed in a corner of the south verandah and watered it every day. The very possibility that a tree might grow from the seed stirred my awe and curiosity. Custard-apple seeds sprout still, but they do not make the same wonder germinate in my mind any more. The fault does not lie with the seeds but in my mind. We stole rocks from the hillock in Guna Dada's† garden to make an artificial mountain in a corner of our study, stuck little flowering plants on it, and fussed so much over them that they put up with it only because they were plants, and lost no time in dying off. I can't tell what wonder and delight this little hill afforded us. We believed it would be equally wonderful to our elders; but the day we put our belief to the test, our indoor hill vanished somewhere with all its trees. We were full of grief at being taught so brusquely that the corner of a schoolroom was not the proper place to set up a mountain. Our hearts were crushed under the weight of all those stones when we realized that our game diverged so widely from our elders' wishes.

I still remember what an intimate charm the world held for me in those early days. Earth, water, plants and sky—they all spoke to me, they never let me remain indifferent. It hurt me to think that I could only see the surface of the earth and never underneath, so I made one plan after another to take off the earth's brown wrapper. It occurred to me that if a large number of bamboo poles could be driven into the ground one after another, I just might be able to reach the earth's core. At the festival of Maghotsav,[†] rows of wooden pillars were planted round our courtyard to hang chandeliers from. They starting digging holes for them from the beginning of the month. The preparations for a festival are always an exciting event for children, but these excavations had a special attraction for me. Year after year I saw holes being dug in the ground, deeper and deeper until the whole man vanished inside, and still there was nothing like a passage through which a fairytale prince or minister's son could successfully journey into the underworld; yet every time I felt as though the lid of a treasure chest had been thrown open. If only they were to dig a little further, I would think—but they never did: there was a little tug at the curtain, but it was never drawn aside. I wondered why the elders, who could do whatever they pleased, chose to stop at such shallow depths—if children like us could have had their way, the earth's deepest secret would not have lain underground in neglect for so long. I would imagine likewise that all the secrets of the sky were hidden beyond the blue that one could see. When our tutor said, while teaching us the *Bodhoday*,[†] that the blue dome of the sky was not an obstacle at all, it seemed utterly unbelievable to me. He said, 'You can build staircase upon staircase and go on climbing for ever and ever—you won't hit your head against anything at all!' I felt he was being miserly in planning his staircase. So I went on yelling to myself, 'More stairs, more stairs!' When at last I understood that would do no good, I sat stunned, convinced that this was such an amazing secret that only teachers knew about it.

(*Memories of My Life*, 'At Home and Out of It')

I can clearly see how times have changed when I notice that these days neither human beings nor ghosts walk about on rooftops any more. I have already told you how the big brahman ghost had been driven away by too much study in the house. The ledge where he was said to rest his foot is now a battleground for crows squabbling over mango stones, while we humans live boxed up between the four walls below.

I remember the walled-in rooftop of the inner quarters of our house. Mother would sit there in the evenings on a reed mat, chatting with her women friends around her. They didn't need to discuss any authentic news: they only wanted to pass the time. In those days, there were no spiced-up materials at various prices to fill up the time. The day was not tight-packed, but more like a large-meshed net. In both men's and women's company, the chatting and joking was very light indeed. The most prominent among my mother's companions was Braja Acharya's sister, whom they called 'Acharjini'. She would supply the group with its daily ration of news. Often she would bring along all kinds of weird reports—things she heard and things she made up. This led to expensive rituals to please and calm the angry stars. I sometimes conveyed to the gathering bits of book-learning that I had freshly picked up. I informed them that the sun was ninety million miles from the earth; I recited verses from Valmiki's original *Ramayana*[†] out of my Sanskrit reader,[†] nasals and aspirates[†] and all. My mother couldn't tell how correct my pronunciation was, but my learning struck her with amazement across all those ninety million miles. Who could have thought such Sanskrit verses could be uttered by anyone except the sage Narada?†

The rooftop above the inner quarters was entirely women's territory. It had close links with the larder. It got a lot of sunshine, so it was the best place to pickle lemons in the sun. The women used to squat there with brass pans full of lentil paste; they made little blobs of the stuff and laid them out to dry at the same time as they dried their own hair in the sun. The maids brought the washing and hung it up; the washerman didn't have much to do. Slivers of green mango were sun-dried in the same way, mango juice set to jell in patterned moulds of black stone, and young jackfruit pickled in mustard oil. Catechu paste† scented with screw-pine flowers was prepared with great care. I have a special reason for remembering this well. When our schoolteacher told me he had heard much about the catechu paste they made in our house, I easily understood the hint. He wished to see what he had heard so much of. So to keep up the family honour I had to—what shall I say?—it sounds better to say I commandeered some now and again than that I stole it. Even kings and emperors commandeer things when they feel a need, or even if they don't, while jailing or impaling those who merely steal.

It was the women's occupation to sit chatting on the rooftop in the mild winter sun, passing the time and shooing away the crows. I was my Boudi's† only young brother-in-law, protector of her drying mango jelly and her companion in all sorts of other tasks. I read aloud to her the story of King Pratapaditya,† and sometimes I cut supari† for her with a nut-chopper. I could cut them into very fine slices. Bouthakrun† wouldn't admit that I had any other virtues; she even found fault with my looks and made me angry with my Creator. But she could never praise me enough for my skill in cutting supari. Naturally this speeded up my work. Not having found anyone to encourage me since then, I've turned my talent for cutting supari so finely to fine-mincing other things.

There was a village flavour to all this women's work occupying the rooftop. It dated back to the days when there was a rice-thresher in the house, when coconuts were scraped to make sweets, when in the evenings the maids rolled cotton lamp-wicks on their thighs, and when the neighbours called you to eat eight kinds of fried lentils† eight days after a child was born. These days little boys don't hear fairy tales from the women any more, they have to read them on their own out of printed books. Pickles and chutneys have to be bought from the New Market in glass jars sealed with wax.

The chandimandap[†] added to the rural touch. Here the gurumashai[†] held his little school, where not only the children of our own house, but the neighbours' as well, first learnt to scrawl on palm leaves. I too must have formed my first letters here; but no telescope can bring that far-off boy back to my memory, any more than the farthest planet of the solar system.

The first books I remember reading were about myths: the dreadful goings-on at the school of the sages Shanda and Amarka, and how Vishnu's Nrisingha form—half-lion, half-man—tore out the guts of the demon-king Hiranyakashipu.[†] I think there was even an engraved picture of the latter scene. And I remember learning some of Chanakya's[†] verses.

In my life the open rooftop has always been holiday-land. From childhood to adult days, I have spent all kinds of times in all kinds of ways on rooftops. When my father was at home, his rooms were on the second floor. Peering from behind the stairtop room, I often watched him before the sun was up, sitting silently on the roof like a white stone statue, his joined hands on his lap. At times he would go away for long spells to the hills, and then going onto the roof held for me the delight of a voyage across the seven seas. I had always looked out at the passers-by through the railings of the verandah downstairs; but up on the rooftop, I could cross the boundaries imposed by people's houses. Once there, my mind could cross Calcutta with giant strides and head for the horizon, where the last blue trace of the sky faded away into the last green of the earth. I could see the high and low roofs of countless houses of all shapes and sizes, and the bushy tops of trees rising between them here and there. I often went up to the roof in the afternoons without telling anyone. The afternoon has always held a special charm for me. It was like night-time in the middle of the day, when the child-hermit could get away from the world. I would reach through the slats and unlatch the door. There was a sofa just inside the door, and I would settle down on it, intimately alone. Those who were supposed to keep guard on me were drowsing after a hearty lunch, stretched out on their reed mats.

The sun turned crimson by and by. The kites screamed overhead. The bangle-seller went calling down the lane. Those quiet afternoons are no more, nor do I hear the pedlars who belonged to that quiet hour.

Their cry would suddenly reach the room where the young wife lay sleeping with her hair spread across the pillow. The maid would call them in, and the old bangle-seller would press the girl's tender hand and ease in the glass bangles she chose. Today that young wife wouldn't be a wife at all—she'd be learning her lessons in middle school. And the bangle-seller might be trundling a rickshaw down the same streets.

The roof served for the hot desert that I read about in my books—a vast empty place, swept by dust carried along in the hot wind under a sky of a dull, pallid blue. But there was an oasis in the rooftop desert. Now the piped water doesn't carry upstairs, but in those days it even reached the second floor. I would creep into the forbidden bathroom like a child-Livingstone[†] of Bengal discovering a new land. I turned on the shower, and the water flowed all over my body. Then I dried myself on a bedsheet and sat around with nothing on.

Presently the holiday would draw to a close. The gong sounded at the gate: it was four o'clock. Though it was Sunday, the afternoon sky looked glum, as if the Monday that would eclipse it were already casting its shadow to swallow it in its gape. By now they would be searching downstairs for the boy who had given the slip to his jailers.

Now it was time for our afternoon snack: a very important time of day for Brajeshwar, since he was in charge of shopping for the meal. In those days the shopkeepers didn't make 30 or 40 per cent profit on bad ghee, whose foul smell and taste poison the snacks made with it. If we were given kachuri,[†] singara[†] or even alu dam,[†] we wasted no time in gobbling them up. But quite often, Brajeshwar would cock his crooked neck even more to one side and say, 'Look, babu, see what I've got for you today', and it would turn out to be peanuts in a paper bag. Not that we disliked them, but we judged such cheap fare at no more than its worth. Yet we never complained, not even when he brought sesame fritters in a palm-leaf packet.

The daylight would have begun to fade when I went up sadly to the rooftop one last time. Looking down, I could see that the ducks had left the pond. People had started gathering on the steps; the shadow of the giant banyan tree had fallen half across the pond, and the shouts of the footmen riding behind the coaches could be heard down the road.

(*Childhood*, chapter 8)

Sejo Dada made all kinds of arrangements for training me in various arts. None of them bore much fruit, owing to my own contrary nature. Ramprasad[†] must have had someone like me in mind when he sang 'My soul, you don't know how to till your land!' I never learnt to cultivate my powers.

Still, let me at least tell you what they tried to cultivate.

I had to get up while it was dark and prepare for wrestling. On winter mornings, I used to shiver. A well-known one-eyed wrestler of the town came to train us. There was a clear space to the north of the house which we called the barnyard. The name tells you that at one time the city had not quite stifled the village: there were some open spaces left still. In the early days of city life, that barnyard used to be stocked with the year's paddy crop; the tenant farmers also made over their shares. A shed alongside the wall here served as our wrestling-place. The mud floor had been dug up and a whole maund[†] of mustard oil poured over it to make the wrestling-floor. My wrestling lessons were little more than a game; I would get a good deal of mud over my person, then dress again and come back. My mother didn't approve of this wallowing in mud every morning—she was afraid it would make me dark. So she went to great trouble on holidays to repair the damage. Nowadays fashionable housewives buy skin lotions in little phials from Englishmen's shops; in those days they made up their own ointments from almond paste, cream, orange peel and all sorts of things—if I could remember them all and sell the stuff, under a catchy brand-name like 'Begum's[†] Delight', I daresay I could earn as much money as a sweet-seller. I was given a long massage on the verandah every Sunday morning, while I longed to run away and enjoy my holiday. A rumour spread among my schoolmates that in our family, newborn babies were dipped in wine: that was what made our skins glow like a sahib's.

By the time I returned from wrestling, a medical student would be waiting to teach us anatomy. An entire skeleton hung from the wall. It was kept in our bedroom at night; the bones rattled with every gust of wind. As we got used to handling the bones and learning their complicated names, our fears vanished.

The watchman at the gate would strike seven on his gong. My tutor Nilkamal was a stickler for punctuality; he never arrived a minute late. He looked wizened, but his health was as robust as his pupil's: he never complained of so much as a headache. I had to present myself before his table, book and slate in hand. He would start scribbling sums on the blackboard: arithmetic, algebra, geometry—all in Bengali. In literature, I passed in one leap from *Sita in Exile*† to *The Slaying of Meghnad*.† We learnt natural science as well. Sitanath Datta† came now and then; we picked up bits of science through little experiments. Heramba Tattvaratna† came for a while, and we got busy learning the *Mughdhabodh*† by heart without understanding a thing. As the morning wore on and the load of studies grew heavier, the mind slyly began shoving some of it aside. Much of what was learnt by rote slipped through the net and vanished, and Nilkamal-Master's† reports about his pupil became unworthy of report.

In another corner of the verandah sat the old tailor, thick glasses on his nose, bending over his needle, reading the namaz† at the proper times. I would look at him and think enviously, 'How happy Niamat must be!' When my mind was confused by sums, I would hold up my slate before my eyes and peer under it to see Chandrabhan sitting at the gate, combing his long beard with a wooden comb and training it in two bunches, one above each ear. The lithe young darwan sat beside him, bracelet on wrist, chopping tobacco. The horse had finished eating his day's ration of gram from a bucket nearby: the crows pecked at the spillover. Johnny the dog would suddenly remember his duty and chase them, barking furiously.

In the dust that the sweeper had piled up in a corner of the verandah, I had planted a custard-apple seed, and waited impatiently for it to sprout. The moment Nilkamal-Master left, I would run off to look at it and water it. But my hopes were dashed when the same broom which had swept the dust into the corner cleared it away again.

The sun would rise and the shadows shrink to only halfway across the courtyard. At nine o'clock Gobinda, short and dark and with a dirty yellow towel over his shoulder, would take me away for my bath. At nine-thirty the invariable daily feast of rice, dal and fish curry would be waiting for me. I had no taste left for it.

It struck ten. The green-mango seller's cry would be heard from the street, making me feel wistful. The pedlar of pots and pans passed by, the clank of his wares fading into the distance. On the open roof of the house beside the lane, the elder wife would dry her hair in the sun, while her two daughters played with cowries[†] for hours on end. They were in no hurry: girls didn't go to school in those days. I used to think it must be pure pleasure to be born as a girl. As for me, the old horse would drag me in the carriage to exile from ten o'clock till four. I returned home at four-thirty, by which time the gymnastics teacher had arrived. I had to swing my body up and around a wooden pole for an hour or so. No sooner had he left than the art tutor took over.

Gradually the rusty afternoon light would begin to fade. The city's blurred medley of sounds touched the body of the brick-and-wood monster with a dreamy music.

The oil lamp began to glow in the study. Aghor-Master[†] had arrived: the English lesson was about to begin. The black-bound Reader[†] on the table looked as though it was waiting to pounce on me. Its binding had come loose, some of the pages were torn, some marked over. Here and there I had practised writing my name, all in capital letters. I would doze off as I read, then jerk upright every now and then. I read only a little, and left out a lot more.

Only when I got into bed did I have a little idle time, all to myself. There I couldn't listen long enough to a never-ending fairy tale:

'The prince went riding across the vast empty plain'...

(*Childhood*, chapter 7)

After leaving the Normal School[†] we entered an Anglo-Indian school called the Bengal Academy. This added somewhat to our dignity: we felt we had grown up considerably, or at least ascended the first flight of steps to freedom. In fact, if we made progress of any sort at the Bengal Academy, it was solely in the direction of freedom. I could not follow the lessons, nor made any effort to do so—but nobody took heed. My schoolfellows were naughty but not contemptible: that was a great comfort to me. They would write 'ASS' in mirror-writing on their palms and pat you lovingly on the back while saying 'Hello!', so that you went around with the name of that socially despised animal stamped on your back. Or they might squelch a banana on your head and vanish, or suddenly take a swipe at you and turn away with an expression of great innocence, as though they were of saintly nature. Such little torments only hurt the body but never the feelings—they were a nuisance, but never an insult. I felt as if I had stepped out of oozy mud on to hard rock: you could cut your feet on it, but you would not get them soiled. A great advantage for a boy like me in such a school was that nobody harboured any impossible hope that we would improve ourselves through education. It was a small school making very little money; the Principal[†] loved us for one great virtue—we paid our fees regularly every month. That is why the Latin grammar never became too hard for us to bear, and our backs were spared the rod in spite of serious lapses in learning. Probably the Principal had warned the teachers not to be too strict with us: it was not out of loving-kindness on the latter's part.

Going to this school was hardly any trouble, but it was a school after all. Its rooms were pitiless, its walls like sentries—it didn't have the feel of a house, but was only a big box divided into pigeonholes. It had no decorations, no pictures, no colour: no one had made the slightest effort to win the hearts of young boys. The very idea that boys have likes and dislikes which are important to them, seemed to have been banished utterly from the school. My heart sank every time I stepped through the gate into the narrow courtyard. That is why my relationship with schools has always remained that of truancy.

There was one means of escape available to me. My elder brothers took lessons in Persian[†] from a man whom everybody called Munshi[†]— I forget what his real name was. He was an elderly man, all skin and bones. It seemed as though someone had wrapped his skeleton in black wax-cloth; there was no fat, no moisture inside. Perhaps he knew Persian well enough, and English reasonably well too, but that was not where he sought renown. He believed that he was an exceptionally talented musician as well as a superb wielder of the lathi or fighting-stick. He stood under the sun in our courtyard and brandished his lathi in all kinds of grotesque ways, with his own shadow as his opponent. Needless to say, the shadow could never win against him: when he beat it down with yells and stood smiling victoriously, it lay dim and mute at his feet. His tuneless droning songs sounded like ragas from a ghostly world, a hideous mix of raving and weeping. Our paid singer Bishnu sometimes said to him, 'Munshi Ji, you're robbing me of my bread!' He only smiled condescendingly, not bothering to reply.

You will understand from this that Munshi was not a difficult man to please. It needed only a little coaxing to make him write applications for leave to our School Principal. The Principal did not agonize over those letters either: he must have known perfectly well that whether we attended school or not, it would make no difference to our education.

Now I run a school of my own,† where the boys often commit many offences—because offending comes as naturally to boys as not forgiving them comes to their teachers. If someone grows too angry or alarmed at this, and impatiently wants to dole out fierce punishments for the good of the school, all the sins of my own youth line up before me, staring me in the face and grinning broadly.

I should write in some detail about another friend. What made him special was that he was fascinated by magic.† He had even published a small book on the art of magic and went around calling himself 'Professor' on the strength of it. Never before had I met a schoolboy who had published a book with his name on it. For this reason I began to regard him with great respect, at least as a conjuror, since I thought it impossible to lie in print. The printed word had always browbeaten us like a teacher: hence the awe. To write something of one's own in unfading ink—that really was something! It was under the full public gaze: it could not hide anything; it had to pass in rows of print before the world's eyes, with no chance of escape. Who could help respecting such unshakable self-confidence? I clearly remember that in the Brahmo Samaj† Press or some such place I once found some pieces of type that would spell my name: when, after being inked over and pressed down on a sheet of paper, they began to leave marks, it seemed a memorable event.

We took that author friend of ours to school every day in our carriage. Hence he began to visit our house all the time. He was keenly interested in acting too. With his help we built a makeshift stage in our wrestling-space by putting up some spliced bamboo poles, stretching sheets of paper over them and painting them with colourful drawings. I suppose it was because our elders forbade us that we could not act any play there.

But we did once manage to act a farce, even without a stage. You could call it a Comedy of Errors.† The author of this farce was my nephew Satyaprasad. Those who have only seen his calm, dignified presence today cannot imagine what an expert he was in childhood at working all kinds of disasters out of sheer mischief.

What I shall now narrate happened some time after the events described so far. I think I was then about twelve or thirteen. That friend of ours used to tell us such amazing things about the properties of matter that I would be left dumbfounded, and fretted for a chance to verify them for myself. But the substances he talked about were so hard to find that you had little hope of laying your hands on them unless you followed the track of Sindbad the Sailor. Once, no doubt out of carelessness, the Professor told me about some relatively easy way to work a miracle, and I determined to try it out. Who could have thought that if you smeared the gum of the manasasij tree on any seed twenty-one times and let it dry, the tree would sprout and bear fruit in just an hour's time? But one could hardly disbelieve a Professor who had published a book in print.

With the gardener's help, we collected a sufficient quantity of manasasij gum. Then one Sunday, we went up to our secret mystery-chamber on the rooftop to try out its effects on a mango stone.

I kept on rubbing the seed with gum and drying it in the sun with singleminded attention for a long time. I am sure no grown-up reader will ask me what the results were. But I had no inkling that Satya was busy raising a magic tree of his own, branches and all, in another corner of the second floor in that same hour. Its fruits were most curious too.

After the incident of the mango stone, the Professor began nervously avoiding my company, though I did not notice it for a long time. He did not sit beside me any more in the carriage, and gave me a wide berth everywhere.

One afternoon in our study, he suddenly said, 'Let's jump off this bench here: we'll compare our jumping techniques.' I thought that, since the Professor was learned in many mysteries of creation, he might know some secret about jumping too. Everybody leaped off the bench one by one; so did I. The Professor only said 'Hmm!' under his breath and shook his head solemnly. No plea could draw a more articulate comment from him.

Another day he said, 'Some boys belonging to such-and-such well-known family want to meet you. You must visit them.' Our guardians saw no reason to object, so we went.

The room filled with curious onlookers. Everyone expressed an eagerness to hear me sing. I obliged with one or two songs. I was very young then, so I didn't exactly sound like a roaring lion. Many people nodded and said, 'What a sweet voice!'

When we went in to dinner, everybody sat round to watch me eat. I had hardly met any strangers till then, so I was rather shy. Besides, being compelled to eat before the greedy gaze of our servant Ishwar at home, I had grown used to eating lightly. That day all the spectators were surprised to see how little I ate. If they had always observed every creature as closely as they did their young guest that evening, it would have led to notable advances in zoological studies in Bengal.

Not long afterwards, in the fifth act you might say, I received some curious letters from the magician which cleared up the mystery. The curtain fell after that.

Satya confessed that on the day I was trying to work magic with a mango stone, he had told the magician that my guardians sent me to school dressed like a boy for the sake of my education, but it was only a disguise. For the benefit of those interested in fanciful scientific discourse, I might mention that during the jumping test I had put my left foot forward as I leaped. I didn't realise at that time what a terribly wrong step that was.

(*Memories of My Life*, 'An End to Learning Bengali')

My father began travelling widely a few years before I was born. I hardly knew him in my childhood. He came home suddenly now and then, bringing with him servants from faraway places. I was always curious and eager to make friends with them. A young Punjabi servant called Lenu came with him once. The kind of reception that we gave him would have done Ranjit Singh[†] proud. He was from a strange land—moreover, from Punjab, which made him very special in our eyes. We held Punjabis in almost as much esteem as the mythical figures of Bhim and Arjun.[†] They were warriors: no doubt they had lost a few battles, but even for that we held their enemies to blame. Our hearts swelled with pride to have a person of such a race under our roof. In my sister-in-law's room there was a toy ship in a glass case: when you wound it up, the waves would rise and fall on a sea of coloured cloth, while the ship tossed on the waves to the music of an organ. I sometimes managed to borrow this marvellous object from Bouthakurani[†] after much pleading and whining, and amazed the Punjabi with it. Because I was caged within the house, everything foreign and faraway fascinated me. That's why I paid Lenu so much attention. For the same reason I felt excited when Gabriel, a Jewish vendor of perfumes, arrived at our gate in his gabardine sewn with little bells; and the giant kabuliwala,[†] in his loose grubby pyjamas and his bags and bundles, held a fearsome mystery for me.

Anyway, when father came home we youngsters only peeped and pried around his servants to satisfy our curiosity. We never managed to get as far as him.

The Russians were always the bugbear of the British government. I clearly remember that once in my childhood, the word went round

'My father sitting in front of the garden...':
Illustration for Jiban-Smriti *by Gaganendranath Tagore.*

that Russia was about to invade India. A well-meaning woman described to my mother the terrible dangers this implied, as elaborately as her imagination could fashion them. My father was in the hills at that time. No one could tell through which mountain pass the Russian hordes might pour in from Tibet, swift as a comet; hence my mother grew very worried. The rest of the family obviously did not share her concern, because she finally gave up hope of adult succour and turned to me, a slip of a boy. 'Write to your father about the Russians,' she told me. That is how I first wrote a letter to my father, telling him about my mother's anxiety. I knew nothing about the forms of letter-writing, so I in turn approached Mahananda Munshi[†] in the family office. The format that emerged was no doubt in perfect order, but the text smelt like the dry lotus-leaves of old papers, among which Saraswati the goddess of learning sat in our estate office. I received a reply to my letter by and by. My father wrote that we need not worry about him; he would chase the Russians away himself. I don't think even this tremendous reassurance really convinced my mother, but it certainly made me more bold about my father. I now began to visit Mahananda's office every day in order to write letters to him. Pestered in this way, Mahananda was obliged to draft them for a few days. But I had no money to pay for the stamps. I hoped that I would not have to worry after I had made the letter over to Mahananda: the letters would duly reach their destination. Needless to say, he was much older than me, and those letters never reached the Himalayan peaks.

(*Memories of My Life*, 'My Father')

Destruction

Destruction

❦

Let me give you some fresh news of the world, my dear.

There was this little cottage a few miles from Paris, and Pierre Chopin was its master. It was his life's passion to create new plants—matching strains, crossing pollen grains, fusing taste, colour and appearance. It was slow work: it took years to change the nature of a single flower or fruit. But his patience was matched only by his joy in his work. He seemed to work magic in that garden of his. Red turned to blue, and white to crimson; stones vanished from fruits, as did their rinds. Fruits that took six months to grow began to do so in two. He was a poor man, with no head for business: he would give away costly plants to anyone who uttered a word of praise. Anyone who wanted to cheat him had only to come and say: 'What lovely flowers you have on that tree there! People are coming from everywhere to see them—they're all amazed!'

He always forgot to ask them to pay.

There was another great love in his life, and that was his daughter Camille. She was the joy of his nights and days, and his fellow-worker as well. He had trained her to master the gardener's art. She could graft one plant on another no less skilfully than her father. She would not let him hire a gardener. With her own hands she dug the earth, sowed the seeds, weeded the beds, working quite as hard as her father. Besides all this she cooked for her father, did the sewing, answered his letters—in fact, looked after everything. Their little cottage under the chestnut tree was sweet with peace and hard work. The neighbours who came to tea in the garden would remark upon it. Father and daughter only smiled and said, 'Our home is beyond price. It isn't made with a king's treasure but with the love of two souls. You won't find another one like it anywhere.'

Jacques, the young man Camille was to marry, sometimes came to lend a hand with the work. He would whisper in her ear, 'When will it be?' But she kept putting it off, for she couldn't bear to marry and part from her father.

Then France went to war with Germany. The laws of the state were harsh and unbending. Even old Pierre was dragged off to the front. Camille hid her tears and told him, 'Don't worry, father, I'll look after our garden with my life.'

She had been trying to create a yellow variety of tuberose at the time. Her father had said it couldn't be done; she had insisted it could. She resolved to astonish him with it when he came back from the war, if she could make good her claim.

Meanwhile Jacques came home from the front on two days' leave to tell her that Pierre had been made a Commandant. He had been unable to come himself, so he had sent Jacques with the good news. Jacques arrived to find that a shell had landed in the flower-garden that very morning. The garden had been destroyed, along with the person who had guarded it with her life. That was the only mercy: Camille too was dead.

Everybody wondered at the advance of civilization. That shell had swept across the sky for all of twenty-five miles! Such was the progress of the times!

The might of civilization has been proved elsewhere too. The proof lies in the dust and nowhere else. It happened in China. That nation had to battle with two powerful civilized states.† There used to be a splendid palace in Beijing. It was full of enchanting works of art gathered over the ages. Such wonders had never been worked by human hand before, and never will be again. But China lost the war. It was bound to lose, for civilization is marvellously skilled in the arts of destruction. But alas for all that wonderful art, the loving labours of generations of master spirits! It disappeared who knows where, amidst the short-lived scratching and biting of civilization. I once went travelling to Beijing† and saw it with my own eyes. I can hardly bear to talk about it.

—Translated by Suvro Chatterjee

Explanations

OUR LITTLE RIVER

kash: a reed-like plant with white flowers.
mynah: a bird like a starling.

THE RUNAWAY CITY

Howrah Bridge: The most important bridge joining Calcutta with its twin city Howrah across the river Hooghly. The present bridge began to be built in 1937. When Rabindranath published this poem in 1931, there was only a pontoon bridge or 'bridge of boats'.
Harrison Road: a road in central Calcutta leading to the Howrah Bridge; now called Mahatma Gandhi Road.
Monument: the Ochterloney Monument, now called Shahid Minar (Martyrs' Column): a tall tower in the heart of Calcutta.
nagra: a kind of shoe with turned-up points, worn in northern India.

BHOTAN-MOHAN

banana-gourd: the thick skin or shell of a tight-layered bunch of banana flowers.

THE FLYING MACHINE

adjutant bird: a big ungainly stork that (like the common Indian or pariah kite) eats small animals and all kinds of rubbish.

THE TIGER

This poem shows how Rabindranath can bring serious social concerns even into a funny fantasy. Here he is mocking and attacking caste divisions. Putu belongs to a low caste: if the lordly tiger eats him, he will be defiled, so that other tigers will refuse to eat with him or marry his daughter.

Mahatma Gandhi (Mohandas Karamchand Gandhi, 1869–1948) was the most important leader and social reformer in the days of India's struggle for freedom. He carried out a crusade for the uplift of the lower castes; hence Putu calls himself a follower of Gandhi.

memsahib: a European woman.

THE PALM TREE

In the original, the tree is specifically the *tal gachh* or toddy palm.

THE HERO

red hibiscus: This flower is sacred to the goddess Kali, commonly worshipped by bandits with bloody sacrifices in olden times. See Rabindranath's own account in 'My Childhood' (p. 206).

THE WISE BROTHER

the washerman's baby donkey: Washermen used to (and sometimes still do) keep donkeys to carry their loads of washing.

Ganesh: the elephant-headed god of wealth and wisdom. People are often named after him.

BIG AND SMALL

Chariot Day: the Ratha Jatra, a festival when Lord Jagannath, with his brother Balaram and his sister Subhadra, are said to take a ceremonial ride in a chariot. The most important chariot festival is held at Puri in Orissa state, but fairs are held at many places in Bengal and elsewhere at the time.

Ashwin: the early autumn month when the Durga Puja, Bengal's most important festival, is held.

THE KING'S PALACE

The actual childhood experience behind this story is described by

EXPLANATIONS

Rabindranath in a section of *Memories of My Life*. (See p. 214.) It is also the subject of a poem in *Shishu*.

Nilkamal-Master: Nilkamal Ghoshal, Rabindranath's childhood tutor, who also features in the poet's accounts of his childhood.

MORE-THAN-TRUE

Ush-khush Mountains: Rabindranath moves between real and fantastic names at this point. The cities have real names, or something like them; but *ushkhush* is a Bengali word used of fidgety or restless people.

THE RAT'S FEAST

Kalikumar Tarkalankar: Kalikumar was the man's first name. *Tarkalankar* ('ornament to the art of logic') was a title or degree given him for his Sanskrit learning. The name sounds a little like *Kalo kumro tatka lanka*, 'Black pepper and fresh (i.e., hot) chilli'.

The Sacrifice of the Black Pumpkin: Vegetables, especially pumpkins, could be given to gods as offering or 'sacrifice'; but of course the boys are thinking of a more bloody kind of sacrifice.

sugar-balls...sweets: The Bengali refers to *kadma*, crunchy balls of sugar, and *khaichur*, sweetened popped rice rolled into balls.

WISHES COME TRUE

Krittibas's Ramayana: The *Ramayana* is one of the two great ancient Indian epics. Its most popular Bengali rendering is by Krittibas Ojha (born *c.* 1400).

jatra: the traditional popular theatre of Bengal.

paan: the betel leaf, garnished with spices and chewed by people in most parts of India.

THE WELCOME

zamindar: landlord. See Introduction, p. 9.

your daughter: a Bengali pun here. The Bengali word for 'girl' or 'daughter' is *meye*, which the zamindar confuses with 'MA'.

a marriage: another pun. *Biye* in Bengali means a marriage or wedding.

THE POET AND THE PAUPER

The names of the characters are significant. *Kunjabihari* means 'he who walks in the garden', while *Bashambad* means 'devoted, obsequious, flattering'.
dal: pulses, lentils.

THE ORDEALS OF FAME

Ganat parataram nahi: (Sanskrit) 'Nothing is greater than music.'
donation... throwing me out: a Bengali pun here. *Chanda*, a subscription, is linked by sound (though not origin) to *chand*, the moon. And to give someone an *ardhachandra* or 'half-moon' means to throw him out by the neck. Kangalicharan is saying something like 'I wanted the moon but you gave me only a half-moon.'
paan: betel leaf.
tanpura: a stringed instrument used as an accompaniment by Indian classical singers.
tabla set: the pair of small drums used to accompany Indian music.
khayal: one of the four major forms or modes of north Indian vocal music.
tappa: another of these major musical forms or modes.
Shori Miyan: the man who first developed and popularized the tappa. His real name was Ghulam Nabi (late 18th/early 19th century).

THE EXTENDED FAMILY

the Company: the East India Company, which administered British-held India till 1857. After that, India was ruled directly by the British crown, but the administration was still popularly referred to as 'the Company'.
bound up with others' support: a Bengali pun: *parer arthe*, which can mean 'to benefit others' or 'in the interest of others', but also 'at others' expense'.
two wives: Hindus were allowed more than one marriage at this time.
green coconut: which contains a sweet refreshing fluid or 'water'.
your nephew: In the Bengali, Paresh makes a reference to Sanskrit grammar at this point. This could not be rendered in English.

the fires of hell: The Bengali refers to 'Ravana's kitchen-fires'. Ravana, the demon-king of Lanka, was said to have so many people in his palace that its kitchen fires were always kept burning.
brother-in-law: Such joking torments were traditionally bestowed on brothers-in-law—though more usually by their sisters-in-law.

THE FREE LUNCH

Bhuto, Modho (a corruption of 'Madhu'), *Harey* (a corruption of 'Hari'): homely, rough-cut names, contrasting with the elaborate Sanskritic name 'Chandrakanta'.
right eye's been twitching: thought to be a lucky sign in men.
Company shares: shares of the old East India Company, considered a very secure investment.
amburi tobacco: a kind of superior scented tobacco.
tola: the weight of an old silver rupee. Only the most expensive kinds of tobacco were sold in such small quantities.
tobacco bowl: the part of the hookah that actually holds the tobacco.
Lord Shiva: in one of his characteristic veins, held to be addicted to drink, drugs and wayward behaviour.
Nandi and *Bhringi:* two of Shiva's followers.
green coconut: with its refreshing 'water'. See notes to 'The Extended Family'.
in the Company's domain: under British rule. See notes to 'The Extended Family'.
when the ocean was churned: In Hindu mythology, the gods and demons were said to have together churned the ocean, using Mount Mandar as the churning-rod, and drawn from it the goddess Lakshmi and many celestial creatures and substances. They then churned it again to draw a deadly poison, which Shiva drank up so that it could not destroy the universe.
Udo: a corruption of 'Uday'—could be friendly, but is obviously sarcastic here.
Uday...disappearing act: a Bengali pun. *Uday* literally means 'rising', as of the moon. *Chandra* means 'moon', and the Bengali word used here means 'to set'.
baksheesh: a tip.
Hamilton's: a famous jeweller and silversmith's shop in Calcutta.

THAT MAN

Mahabharata: one of the two great ancient Indian epics.
Tepantar: a vast field traditionally mentioned in Bengali fairy tales.
malai: a sweet made from cream.
Barabazar: a market area in central Calcutta.
in these parts: i.e., around Shantiniketan, with reddish soil.
jamewar: a kind of expensive shawl, embroidered all over, made in Kashmir.
Just think, Shrikanta etc.: From a traditional Bengali song called a *panchali* by the famous poet Dasharathi Ray. The song had been taught to Rabindranath in his childhood by Kishorinath Chattopadhyay (see note below).
Chitragupta: the secretary or assistant of Yama, the god of death. It was his task to record everyone's good and bad deeds, to judge them by after their death.
Hindustani ustad: a master-singer of North Indian classical music.
Mohan Bagan: a famous Calcutta football club.
Bhim Nag: a famous Calcutta sweet-maker.
Din-da: Dinendranath Tagore (1882–1935), Rabindranath's great-nephew: a notable musician, one of the chief musical members of the Tagore circle. *Da* is short for *Dada*. Dinendranath was Nandini's elder cousin.
rasgullas: a sweet consisting of balls of curd in sugar syrup.
Barabazar, Bowbazar, Nimtala: parts of Calcutta.
Kumbha Mela: a great religious fair held at Prayag (Allahabad) and Hardwar, and less famously at some other places of pilgrimage—not, of course, at *Kanchrapara*, whch is an industrial town near Calcutta.
Doctor Nilratan Sarkar: (1861–1943), one of the most famous physicians of the time.
jalebis: a kind of lacy fritter dipped in sugar syrup.
chamchams: a kind of sweet.
supari: betel-nut: the nut of a kind of palm, chopped up finely and used as an ingredient with betel leaf or paan.
ghee: a kind of thick butter.
dirty water from his hookah: a chamber of the hookah contains water.

EXPLANATIONS

sinful age: the Kali Yuga, the last and worst of the four yugas or ages into which human history was divided in Hindu myth and philosophy.

black face: The hanuman or langur (specifically mentioned in the Bengali) has a black face.

Rai Bahadur: a title given by the British government to Indians who were particularly loyal to them—even (as implied here) by giving them information about those fighting the British to win independence for India.

Smritiratna: a scholarly title: 'the jewel of the smritis' (certain religious texts). *Mashai (Mahashay)* is a term of courtesy or respect. Smritiratna Mashai is a traditional Sanskrit scholar or pandit, thus necessarily a traditional-minded brahman. This makes his fastidiousness about touch and diet quite appropriate, but his playing football or chatting with a doorman just as unlikely.

Ochterloney Monument: See notes to 'The Runaway City'.

Senate Hall: a famous building belonging to Calcutta University, now demolished. It was actually a long way off from the Monument.

The Statesman: an English newspaper published from Calcutta. Its office is close to the Monument, as is the Indian Museum.

Comment vous portez-vous, s'il vous plaît?: (French) 'Please, how are you?'

Sankhya philosophy: one of the six great schools of ancient Indian philosophy.

remedy: There were many traditional penances to remove pollution and loss of caste. Of course these would be found in the Sanskrit scriptures or Hindu almanacs, not in Webster's English Dictionary.

Bhatpara: a town near Calcutta, traditionally the home of many Sanskrit scholars. The pandits there would have been able to advise Smritiratna Mashai.

twig toothbrush: specifically of the neem tree: a traditional practice.

Ganesh: See note to 'The Wise Brother'. Ganesh is also held to have written the ancient epic *Mahabharata* to the poet Vyasa's dictation; so the Man is actually paying the writer a compliment by comparing him to Vyasa.

to Cardiff for a game of cards: The Bengali, necessarily, has a different pun: 'I went to Tasmania to play *tas*' (Bengali for 'cards').

Privy Council: the highest judicial authority of the British Empire, where lawsuits could be referred from India in the days of British rule.

bizarre story: The Bengali refers to *adbhuta rasa.* This is one of the nine *rasas* or poetic veins prescribed in ancient Sanskrit poetic theory. The *adbhuta rasa* is the poetic vein of the marvellous or wonderful. But *adbhut* in Bengali commonly means 'strange' or 'bizarre', and Rabindranath is jokingly using the word in this everyday sense.

Kishori Chatto: Kishorinath Chatto (i.e., Chattopadhyay or Chatterjee) was actually an employee of the Tagores in the poet's own childhood. He was the particular assistant and travelling companion of the poet's father Debendranath. Once a professional folk singer, he taught the young Rabindranath many songs. Rabindranath is fancifully transferring to Pupe his own childhood companion.

Ravana: The demon-king of Lanka in the *Ramayana*, who stole away Sita and was defeated by Rama. He was said to have ten heads. Presumably Pupe had heard the account of Ravana's death in the *Ramayana* the previous evening.

a rabbit fancier: The dark spots on the moon are sometimes thought to make up the shape of a rabbit.

Brahma's zoo: Brahma, the first of the three main aspects of the Hindu godhead, is the creator of all things. (Vishnu is the preserver, and Shiva the destroyer.)

Bangama bird: Bangama and his wife Bangami are a mythical bird-couple appearing in Bengali fairy-tales.

Seven Sages: the Indian name for the constellation of the Great Bear or Plough.

fields of sleep: The Bengali refers to Tepantar. (See above.)

Jatayu bird: a legendary bird, featuring in the *Ramayana.* A friend of Rama, he tried to prevent Ravana from carrying Sita away, but was killed by him. He did, however, convey the news to Rama before dying.

squirrel...Rama's bridge to Lanka: In the *Ramayana*, Rama builds a bridge across the sea in order to reach Lanka and destroy Ravana. (A line of rocks in the sea at this point is supposed to be the remains

EXPLANATIONS

of the bridge.) All the animals helped Rama to build the bridge: even the little squirrel brought small pebbles.

Diwali: the festival of lights.

Chhatrapati: a word meaning 'king' or 'ruler', specially applied to the Maratha ruler Shivaji. (See notes on 'The Representative' below.) But it literally means 'lord of the umbrella' (i.e., royal canopy), and thus suits Sukumar's make-believe horse.

Satya Yuga: Literally, 'age of truth': the first, ideal yuga or age of human existence according to Indian legend. (See note on 'Kali Yuga' above.)

MOVING PICTURES

Nawab: a Muslim ruler.

Pathan: a member of certain races of present-day northern Pakistan. They served traditionally as soldiers and guards.

shehnai: a wind-instrument, played especially at weddings.

chanda, hilsa, chital: types of fish.

Santhal: a tribe of the forest regions of east-central India.

AT SIXES AND SEVENS

quicklime: spread on paan or betel-leaves before adding spices.

chapatis: a kind of flat round bread, very common in India.

THE INVENTION OF SHOES

pandits: men of classical Sanskrit learning.

THE BUILDER

I'm not your Shirish: The little boy speaking in this poem is pretending he is a real builder as he makes his toy houses. But his account of the builder's work is very realistic, and of course the question he asks at the end even more so.

roofbeaters: A roof was traditionally made waterproof by covering it with a layer of special mortar, and having workmen (or often women) beat it with bats until it was hard-packed.

MADHO

shishu: a species of tree.

TWO BIGHAS OF LAND

bigha: a measure of land, a little less than half an acre.
sadhu: a holy man. However, the word can also mean an honest or upright man, and the zamindar puns sneeringly on the two meanings in his last speech in the poem.
festival-chariot: See note on 'Chariot Day' in 'Big and Small'.
Oriya: a man from the state of Orissa.

THE MAGIC STONE

This story is taken from the *Bhaktamal*, a Hindi work (later rendered in Bengali) on Vaishnav doctrines and the lives of Vaishnav saints and holy men. The Vaishnavs (literally 'followers of Vishnu') were the exponents of the Bhakti movement, a great spiritual movement of medieval India.
Sanatan Goswami: (*c.* 1488–1558) was a famous Vaishnav saint. Hailing from Bengal, he finally sought spiritual retreat at Vrindavan.
Vrindavan: a famous place of pilgrimage near Mathura in the present state of Uttar Pradesh, beside the river Yamuna. It is holy because of its associations with the god Krishna, and is specially revered by Vaishnavs.
Bardhaman: a district in western Bengal.

THE FAKE FORTRESS

Narrates an incident of late 14th-century Rajput history. Rabindranath took his material from *Annals and Antiquities of Rajasthan* (1829–32), a great collection put together by the British soldier and administrator, James Tod.

Lakha Rana, the Rana or king of Mewar, was the pre-eminent Rajput ruler of the day, with his capital at the great fort of Chittor. But he could not subdue the Hara or Haravanshi race under King Hamu, with his stronghold at Bundi. Shortly before the events described here, the Rana had besieged Bundi and been badly defeated by Hamu's far smaller army. (This is mentioned in the second stanza.) The Rana then resorted to this childish and ignoble trick to make good his vow of revenge. (Tod, however, only says he vowed not to eat.)

Kumbha: Kumbha Bairsi, one of a band of Haravanshis in the service of Chittor, but basically more loyal to the general honour of his race. What offends him about the Rana's trick is the implied insult to the actual fort of Bundi, the Haravanshi stronghold.

lion-gate: the main entrance to a fort or palace, often decorated with images of lions.

THE CAPTIVE HERO

Narrates an incident of early 18th-century Sikh history, in the reign of the Mughal Emperor Farrukhshiyar. The Sikhs were fighting to preserve their independence against the Mughals. After the death of their tenth and last leader, Guru Govind Singh, the command passed to the ascetic Banda. He built a strong fort at Gurdaspur, to which he was finally beaten back after a long struggle. This poem describes the events that followed.

Rabindranath took his material from J. D. Cunningham's *A History of the Sikhs* (1849). He follows Cunningham quite closely, except for leaving out an exchange between the captive Banda and a Muslim nobleman. Also, Cunningham says Banda was 'silent and unmoved' as he killed his son; Rabindranath shows him as displaying more paternal feeling.

five rivers: 'Punjab' literally means '(the land of) five rivers' flowing through it: the Jhelum, Chenab, Ravi, Beas and Satluj.

the Guru: Guru Govind Singh (died 1708). It was he who enjoined five vows on the Sikhs, one of them being to keep their hair unshorn (and hence 'knotted').

'Hail the unbodied God!': *Alakh niranjan*—a religious cry of the Sikhs, literally 'the invisible and uncoloured God'—i.e., a pure spirit without material form or attributes.

Emperor's son: So in the Bengali (*badshahzada*). Seems to be used loosely of the Emperor and his family.

their mother's: i.e., their motherland's.

The faith! The faith!: Arabic 'Din! Din!'—upholding, of course, the Muslim or Islamic faith.

THE REPRESENTATIVE

Describes an event in the career of Shivaji (c. 1627–80), the great Maratha ruler and warrior. Ramdas the famous poet-saint was his spiritual guide or guru.

Rabindranath took the story from the Introduction to Harry Arbuthnot Acworth's collection, *Ballads of the Marathas* (1894).

Satara: a place in the south of the present state of Maharashtra: one of Shivaji's chief strongholds and centres of administration.

Balaji: Balaji Abaji, Shivaji's chitnis or chief writer. According to Acworth, Shivaji dictated the letter; Rabindranath makes him write it himself.

Shiva: The god Shiva is presented as ascetic, wandering, even wayward, unconcerned with material goods and pleasures. He balances the image of his consort Parvati or Durga as Annapurna, 'giver of food' and mother to the world. These two deities present the two aspects of human life. Most people, says Ramdas, follow one, but he the other.

they cooked their rice: Acworth says 'Ramdas baked two cakes, one of which was eaten by him and one by Shivaji.'

royal flag: Saffron is the colour of spirituality and sacrifice. Shivaji made his guru's saffron banner his flag, 'as a sign that the kingdom belonged to an ascetic' (Acworth).

evening raga: The raga cited is purvi, actually sung just before evening.

Your shoes...I bear: a reference to the ancient epic, the *Ramayana*. Rama, rightful heir to the throne of Ayodhya, has to go into exile. His brother Bharata rules in his place but does not sit on the throne: instead, he places Rama's shoes there, to indicate his respect for the rightful ruler whose place he is taking.

THE BEGGAR'S BOUNTY

This event from the life of the Buddha (i.e., from the 6th or early 5th century BC) was taken from a collection called *Kalpadrumavadan*. Rabindranath found it in Rajendralal Mitra's collection, *The Sanskrit Buddhist Literature of Nepal* (1882). The poet has greatly simplified a long story, leaving out many supernatural details, to make a striking moral point.

Shravasti: an ancient city in the present-day state of Uttar Pradesh. The Buddha lived for long on the outskirts of the city, so that it became a great centre of Buddhist religion and culture.

Anathapindada: A merchant of Shravasti. His real name was Sudatta. He was called 'Anathapindada' or 'provider to the poor'. His unlimited gifts to the Buddha and his religion, and his generosity to the poor, finally left him poor himself. He also joined the Sangha or Buddhist order, so that Supriya could be described as the daughter of a *bhikshu* or 'begging monk'.

MY CHILDHOOD

Rabindranath was born on 7 May 1861 in the large family mansion belonging to a branch of the Thakur or Tagore family. It was located in Jorasanko, a quarter of north Calcutta bordering Chitpur Road, the oldest road in the city. The road has now been named Rabindra Sarani after the poet.

The Tagores were a wealthy and well-established clan with several branches. Their wealth came from land, and sometimes from business ventures of varying success. Rabindranath's grandfather Dwarkanath (1794–1846, called 'Prince' because of his wealth, luxury and refinement) was one of the first Indians to set up business enterprises along Western lines and with British collaboration; but he suffered a great crash. By contrast, the poet's father Debendranath (1817–1905) soon outgrew his self-indulgent youth to become a spiritually-minded person known as the 'Maharshi' or 'great sage'. Debendranath was one of the early founders of the Brahmo Samaj, a Hindu reform movement. Rabindranath's mother was named Sarada Debi. He was her fourteenth child and eighth son.

However old-fashioned and tradition-bound the poet's childhood home might seem to us, the Jorasanko Tagores became the most enlightened and progressive family among the Bengali aristocracy of the age. This showed in their commitment to education and new thought, including the education of women and their entry into wider society and occupations. These developments became prominent as the members of Rabindranath's generation began to grow up: the poet's account of his childhood suggests little or nothing of the process. But the account has a double fascination: as a vivid, intimate portrayal of upper-class Calcutta life in the 1860s, as well as a record of the early thought and experience of one of the world's great poets and thinkers.

paan: betel leaf.

memsahib: a European woman, supposed to be lacking in the traditional modesty of Indian women.

darwan: a doorkeeper, hence a guard.

siddhi: a kind of home-made intoxicating drink.

our tutor: This was Aghornath Chattopadhyay (Chatterjee), a medical student who taught Rabindranath English from 1869. 'Our' refers to Rabindranath, his elder brother Somendranath and his nephew Satyaprasad Gangopadhyay (Ganguly), son of the poet's sister Soudamini. Both these boys were two years older than Rabindranath. The three were brought up and schooled together.

shankhchunni: a kind of female ghost.

Magh and Phalgun: i.e., late winter and early spring.

brahman's ghost: a *brahmadaitya:* the ghost in the nut-tree referred to earlier.

shikari: hunter.

Padma: a river in eastern Bengal; the largest of the branches or distributaries making up the joint delta of the Ganga and Brahmaputra rivers.

the end of Chaitra: This time, and the ensuing summer, sees violent evening storms or nor'westers in Bengal.

coolies: labourers, load-bearers.

puja: worship. Sacrifices were specially common during the great festival of Durga in autumn and the Kali Puja that follows.

mantra: a holy chant or prayer.

Mejo Kaka: i.e., the second younger brother of one's father. This was Girindranath Tagore (1820–54—i.e., he died well before Rabindranath's birth).

jatra: See notes to 'Wishes Come True'.

Nala and Damayanti: an old legend. Nala, king of Nishadha, loved Damayanti, princess of Vidarbha. He sent his love-message through a swan he had spared from killing. Damayanti too loved Nala so much that she preferred to marry him rather than one of the several gods seeking her hand.

ghats: jetties or landing-places. Bengal, especially its eastern part, being riverine, boats were a major (sometimes only) means of transport. Hence the ghats were of great importance in the life of the land.

pandits: men of classical Sanskrit learning.

baksheesh: tip, gift of money.

Brajeshwar: Though Rabindranath refers to the man by this name, he actually seems to have been called Ishwar Das.

Jessore: a district in eastern Bengal, now in Bangladesh. (The Bengali text gives some examples of Shyam's dialect, which obviously cannot be rendered in English.)

zamindars: See Introduction, p. 9.

the goddess Kali: of grim and violent attributes, hence commonly worshipped by old-time bandits.

Dakat: 'dacoit' or bandit.

our clothes: Actually, the Tagore household accounts show that the young Tagores' clothes were not as few or austere as suggested here.

all the way: a Bengali pun on *pade pade*—literally, 'at every step'.

Sita: During their forest exile, Sita was once left alone by her husband Rama and his brother Lakshmana. Lakshmana drew a line round her for her safety and forbade her to cross it. But she stepped across it and was snatched away by Ravana.

even to the Bengali quarter: The northern part of Calcutta, where Bengalis and other Indians chiefly lived, had far worse services and amenities than the European quarter to the south; but there was enough water even to supply this 'Black Town'.

ate the fruit of the tree of knowledge: a reference to the fall of Adam and Eve as told in the Bible.

the king's palace: See notes to 'The King's Palace'.

Guna Dada: Gunendranath Tagore (1847–81), younger son of Rabindranath's uncle Girindranath (see above) and father of the artists Gaganendranath and Abanindranath (see Introduction, p. 10).

Maghotsav: a festival set up by the Brahmos (see note above), held in the month of Magh.

Bodhoday: a primer of knowledge for children written by the great scholar and reformer Ishwarchandra Vidyasagar.

Valmiki's original Ramayana: the Sanskrit *Ramayana*, attributed to the poet Valmiki.

Sanskrit reader: The Bengali text names *Rijupath*, a collection of simple Sanskrit pieces compiled by Ishwarchandra Vidyasagar.

nasals and aspirates: These sounds are very common in Sanskrit, so that people who do not know the language take them as the hallmark of good Sanskrit.

Narada: a very learned sage of legend, supremely skilled in music and poetry.

catechu paste: khayer, a paste smeared on the betel leaf or paan.

Boudi: elder brother's wife.

Pratapaditya (*c.* 1560–1610), a ruler of Bengal. He defied the power of the Mughals but was finally defeated by them. The Bengali text refers specifically to a book about him, *Bangadhip Parajay* (*The Defeat of the King of Bengal*) by Pratapchandra Ghosh (2 vols, 1869, 1884).

supari: See notes to 'That Man'.

Bouthakrun, Bouthakurani: elder brother's wife (like *Boudi* above).

eight kinds of... lentils: a popular observance called 'atkouri'.

chandimandap: originally a place for the worship of the goddess Chandi or Durga, but by extension a structure used as a meeting-place in a village or within an estate.

gurumashai: teacher, especially at the traditional primary school or *pathshala*.

Shanda and Amarka: Two brothers, teachers of Prahlad, the son of Hiranyakashipu, the ruler of the demons. In the war between the gods and demons, they first fought for the demons but later for the gods. Hiranyakashipu swore vengeance against Vishnu for having killed his brother. Finally Vishnu, in the shape of the Nrisingha or half-man half-lion, killed Hiranyakashipu by disembowelling him with his claws.

Chanakya or Kautilya (4th century BC): a great political thinker, adviser to the Emperor Chandragupta Maurya. Besides his political writings, he is said to have written some moral verses in simple Sanskrit, commonly taught to children.

child-Livingstone: i.e., a child explorer. David Livingstone was a famous explorer of Africa.

EXPLANATIONS 251

kachuri, singara: types of fried savoury food (the latter called *samosa* in Hindi).

alu dam: a savoury dish made from potatoes.

Ramprasad: Ramprasad Sen (*c.* 1720–81), a poet and singer. A devotee of the goddess Kali and famous for his songs in her praise. The quoted line opens a well-known song by him.

maund: a measure of weight, about 37 kilograms or 82 pounds.

Begum: an aristocratic Muslim lady.

Sita in Exile: Sitar Banabas, a simple retelling of part of the *Ramayana,* written for children by Ishwarchandra Vidyasagar.

The Slaying of Meghnad: Meghnadbadh Kabya, an epic poem by Michael Madhusudan Datta (Dutt) based on part of the *Ramayana.* (Meghnad was Ravana's son.) It was a long work in elaborate, rhetorical language, a contrast to *Sita in Exile.*

Sitanath Datta: Rabindranath's memory betrays him here. The teacher was actually called Sitanath Ghosh, a preacher of the Brahmo faith and an enthusiast in science and technology. He invented a weaving machine and experimented with novel ways of treating illness.

Heramba Tattvaratna: Nothing has been found out about this man. *Tattvaratna* ('Jewel of Philosophy') is a title or degree awarded for Sanskrit scholarship.

Mugdhabodh: a Sanskrit grammar attributed to the ancient scholar–sage Bopadeva.

Nilkamal-Master: See notes to 'The King's Palace' above.

namaz: the prayers offered by Muslims five times a day.

cowries: a kind of shell, once used as money but by that time only as a plaything.

Aghor-Master: See note on 'our tutor' above.

Reader: This may have been the *First* or *Second Book of Reading,* a celebrated textbook of the age, composed by Pyaricharan Sarkar. But in *Memories of My Life,* Rabindranath specifically cites, as being black-bound, a book from Macculloch's *Course of Reading.*

Normal School: established in early 1855 under the supervision of Ishwarchandra Vidyasagar (see above). This was the second school to which Rabindranath went, the first (which still exists) being the Oriental Seminary.

the Principal: In a piece in *Galpa-Salpa*, Rabindranath names the Principal of the Bengal Academy as a Mr De Cruz.

Persian: The language still had importance in India at that time as a relic of Mughal rule.

Munshi: the subject of a piece in *Galpa-Salpa*.

a school of my own: This was, of course, the school at Shantiniketan.

another friend...fascinated by magic: The subject of another piece in *Galpa-Salpa*, where the boy's initials are given as H.Ch.H. His name was Harishchandra Haldar.

Brahmo Samaj: the formal organization or 'church' of the Brahmo community (see above).

Comedy of Errors: The Bengali word here is *Bhrantibilas*, the title of a prose retelling of Shakespeare's play *The Comedy of Errors* by Ishwarchandra Vidyasagar. (The Bengali text has been slightly compressed at this point, to leave out a reference to earlier passages not included here.)

Ranjit Singh: (1780–1839), a great Sikh leader and ruler of Punjab.

Bhim, Arjun: two of the five Pandava brothers, heroes of the *Mahabharata*.

Bouthakurani: elder brother's wife (the full form of *Bouthakrun* above).

kabuliwala: an Afghan trader or pedlar. Rabindranath has a famous short story about a kabuliwala.

Mahananda Mushi: The Tagores' 'munshi' or clerk. His name was Mahananda Mukhopadhyay (Mukherjee). Prashantakumar Pal, Rabindranath's recent biographer, has found evidence that the mother's anxiety lay elsewhere. She had been alarmed by an unfounded report in the magazine *Somprakash* that her husband had given up his family and worldly concerns to lead a spiritual life in the Himalayas. Unable to express her fears openly, she had thought of this means to get news of her husband. It also appears that Rabindranath's immediately older brother, Somendranath, was involved in the letter-writing. (See Prashantakumar Pal, *Rabijibani* vol. 1, Bhurjapatra: Calcutta, 1389/1982, pp. 136–7.)

DESTRUCTION

As this piece was written on 6 March 1941, the setting could be either the First (1914–18) or Second (1939–45) World War. [Of course it must have been the latter, going on at the time, that moved Rabindranath to tell the story.]

two powerful civilized states: We cannot be quite certain which two states Rabindranath has in mind. One, no doubt, is Britain; the other might be the United States, Russia or even Japan.

I once went travelling to Beijing: in April–May 1924.

Notes on Texts, Dates, and Publication

❦

The Bengali text followed is that in the original Visva-Bharati edition of Rabindranath's Collected Works *(Rabindra-Rachanabali)*, Calcutta, Ashwin 1346– (September–October 1939–). Departures and changes have been noted below.

Dates beginning 12... or 13... follow the Bengali calendar; the international equivalents according to the Christian era are given alongside. The Bengali era is 593 years behind the Christian. In other words, to change to the international style, you must add 600 and then subtract 7. But because the Bengali year begins in mid-April, you have to subtract only 6 for the last three and a half Bengali months (mid-Poush onward).

The English titles given in this book are not always exact translations of the Bengali ones.

'Grandfather's Holiday' *(Thakurdadar Chhuti)*—first published in the Puja annual *Parbani*, ed. Nagendranath Gangopadhyay, 1 Ashwin 1325 (18 September 1918); collected in *Palataka* (October 1918).
'Flowers' (first line: *Kal chhilo dal khali)*—from *Sahaj Path* Part I (Vaishakh 1337, April–May 1930).
'Our Little River' (first line: *Amader chhoto nadi)*—from *Sahaj Path* Part I (Vaishakh 1337, April–May 1930).
'The Voyage' (first line: *Nadir ghater kachhe)*—from *Sahaj Path* Part I (Vaishakh 1337, April–May 1930).
'The Runaway City' (first line: *Ek din rate ami swapna dekhinu)*—from *Sahaj Path* Part II (Vaishakh 1337, April–May 1930). Another poem called *Chalanta Kalikata* ('Calcutta on the Move'), in a similar vein and even with some language in common, was published from a manuscript after Rabindranath's death in the *Visva-Bharati Patrika*,

Shravan–Ashwin 1351 (July–September 1944), and then in *Chitra-Bichitra* (1954).

'Bhotan-Mohan'—written on 5 September 1938 at Shantiniketan; first published in the Supplement to *Khapchhara (At Sixes and Sevens)* in the Visva-Bharati edition of Rabindranath's Works, vol. 21.

'The Flying Machine' *(Uro Jahaj)*—first published in the children's magazine *Sandesh,* Vaishakh 1338 (April–May 1931); collected after the poet's death in *Chitra-Bichitra* (1954).

'The Blaze' (first line: *Tolpariye uthlo para)*—first published in the Supplement to *Khapchhara (At Sixes and Sevens)* in the Visva-Bharati edition of Rabindranath's Works, vol. 21. Here, the servant's name is given as Tinkari, and the poem printed as a dialogue between master and servant. Reprinted in *Chitra-Bichitra,* where it is entitled *Agnikanda* ('The Blaze').

'The Tiger'—first printed in the children's magazine *Mukul,* Vaishakh 1341 (April–May 1934) under the title *Bagher Suchita* ('The Tiger's Purity'); later included in *Se (That Man),* section 6. A similar poem occurs in an essay for adults, *Sahityatattwa* ('The Philosophy of Literature', 1934). There is also a short version in *Pashchimjatrir Diary (The Diary of a Traveller to the West),* serially published between Agrahayan 1331 and Jyaistha 1332 (November–December 1924 and May–June 1925), Rabindranath's account of a journey to South America.

'The Palm Tree' *(Talgachh)*—from *Shishu Bholanath* (1329/1922).
'Sunday' *(Rabibar)*—from *Shishu Bholanath* (1329/1922).
'The Unresolved' *(Sangshayi)*—from *Shishu Bholanath* (1329/1922).
'The Stargazer' *(Jyotishi)*—from *Shishu Bholanath* (1329/1922).
'The Hero' *(Birpurush)*—from *Shishu* (2 Ashwin 1310, September 1903).
'The Wise Brother' *(Bigna)*—from *Shishu* (2 Ashwin 1310, September 1903).
'Big and Small' *(Chhotobaro)*—from *Shishu* (2 Ashwin 1310, September 1903).
'Astronomy' *(Jyotishshastra)*—from *Shishu* (2 Ashwin 1310, September 1903).
GALPA-SALPA (CHATS) was published in Vaishakh 1348 (April–

May 1941). Nearly all the pieces, including all those included here except 'The Rats' Feast' *(Indurer Bhoj)*, were written in 1941, the last year of Rabindranath's life. 'The Rats' Feast' had appeared in the magazine *Bangalakshmi* in Asharh 1346 (June–July 1939) under Nandini's name. Rabindranath would sometimes tell her the outline of a story and let her write it out in full for him to look over and put into final shape. The piece finally appeared in Rabindranath's name in a new edition of *Galpa-Salpa* published in Agrahayan 1372 (November–December 1965).

The Bengali titles of the other pieces are:
'The Scientist': *Bignani*
'The King's Palace': *Rajar Bari*
'The Big News': *Baro Khabar*
'The Fairy': *Pari*
'More-than-True': *Aro-Satya*

'Wishes Come True' *(Ichchhapuran)*—first published in the children's magazine *Sakha o Sathi*, Ashwin 1302 (September–October 1895); collected in *Galpaguchchha* (1934 edn., vol. 2).

PLAYS: See the Introduction (pp. 2–3) for the circumstances of first publication. Most of the plays included here were collected in *Hasyakoutuk* (1907), while 'A Free Lunch' was placed in *Byangakoutuk* (1907). They had appeared earlier as follows:

'The Welcome' *(Abhyarthana)*—*Bharati*, Shravan 1292 (July–August 1885).

'The Poet and the Pauper' *(Bhab o Abhab)*—*Balak*, Agrahayan 1292 (November–December 1885).

'The Ordeals of Fame' *(Khyatir Birambana)*—*Balak*, Magh 1292 (January–February 1886). Adapted under the title *Dukari Datta*, it was acted five times at the Emerald Theatre in Calcutta, the first performance being on 6 April 1895. It was produced by the famous actor-manager Ardhendushekhar Mustaphi, who might himself have acted as Dukari.

'The Extended Family' *(Ekannabarti)*—the combined magazines *Bharati* and *Balak*, Vaishakh 1294 (April–May 1887).

'The Free Lunch' *(Binipayshar Bhoj)*—*Sadhana*, Poush 1300 (December 1893–January 1894). This monologue-drama was popular on the stage. Rabindranath seems to have written it with the well-known actor Akshaykumar Majumdar in mind: the latter performed it several times at various gatherings.

SE (THAT MAN) appeared in Vaishakh 1344 (April–May 1937). Some parts had appeared earlier in the children's magazines *Sandesh* and *Rangmashal*, and short sections elsewhere.

'Moving Pictures'. *(Chalachchitra)*—composed around 27 March 1940; found in a manuscript in the poet's hand and first published in *Chitra-Bichitra* (Shravan 1361, July–August 1954). A rather similar poem, with many lines in common, was composed just over a month later during the poet's stay in Mangpu and first published in *Chhara* (Bhadra 1348, August–September 1941).

'The Invention of Shoes' *(Juta-Abishkar)*—written in 1304 (1897–8); published in *Bharati*, Jyaistha 1305 (May–June 1898) and then collected in *Kalpana*, 1307 (1900).

'The King's Son and the King's Daughter' *(Rajar Chhele o Rajar Meye)*—written in Chaitra 1298 (March–April 1891); published in *Sadhana*, Asharh 1299 (June–July 1892) and then collected in *Sonar Tari* (Poush 1300, 2 January 1894).

Kanika ('Fragments') was published on 4 Agrahayan 1306 (19 November 1899). The short poems were written over the preceding year or more. No details are available about specific dates of composition.

'The Builder' *(Rajmistri)*—first collected in *Shishu Bholanath* (1329/ 1922). A part of the poem was included in *Sahaj Path* Part II (1931).

'Bhajahari', written Jyaistha 1344 (May–June 1937) and 'Madho', written Shravan 1344 (July–August 1937) were published in *Chharar Chhabi* (Ashwin 1344, September–October 1937).

'Two Bighas of Land' *(Dui Bigha Jami)*—written on 31 Jyaistha 1302 (mid-June 1895). First published in *Sadhana*, Asharh 1302 (June–July 1895); collected in *Chitra* (29 Phalgun 1302, 11 March 1896), then in *Kahini* in the collected works *Kabyagrantha*, vol. 5 (1310/ 1903–4), and finally placed in *Katha o Kahini* (1908). We have followed a slightly abridged version of the poem given in the collection *Sankalita*.

'The Magic Stone' *(Parashpathar)*—written 29 Ashwin 1306 (mid-October 1899); 'The Fake Fortress' *(Nakal Gar)*—written 7 Kartik 1306 (23 October 1899); 'The Captive Hero' *(Bandi Bir)*—written 30 Kartik 1306 (15 November 1899); 'The Representative'

(Pratinidhi)—written 6 Kartik 1304 (mid-October 1897) while travelling by boat to Orissa. All four poems first published in *Katha* (1 Magh 1306, 14 January 1900); then in the somewhat different group entitled *Katha* in vol. 5 of the collected works *Kabyagrantha* (1310/1903-4), and finally included in the now standard collection *Katha o Kahini* (1908).

'The Beggar's Bounty' *(Nagarlakshmi)*, composed 27 Ashwin 1306 (13 October 1899), has a similar publishing history, except that it was not included in *Kabyagrantha*.

The autobiographical extracts are taken from *Jiban-Smriti (Memories of My Life,* Shravan 1319, 25 July 1912), and *Chhelebela (Childhood,* Bhadra 1347, August–September 1940). The specific chapters are cited at the end of each section.

'Destruction' *(Dhwangsa)*—composed 6 March 1941 and first published in *Galpa-Salpa* (Vaishakh 1348, April–May 1941).

List of Illustrations

Cover: Painting by Rabindranath. Rabindra Bhavan, Visva-Bharati.

Frontispiece: Painting by Rabindranath. Rabindra Bhavan.

Introduction:
Rabindranath and his eldest daughter Madhurilata. Pastel drawing, 1887.
Open-air class at Shantiniketan, taught by W. W. Pearson. Woodcut by Ramendranath Chakrabarti from *Shantiniketaner Brahmacharyashram*, Visva-Bharati (1395/1988).
Painting by Rabindranath. Rabindra Bhavan, Visva-Bharati.
Nandalal Bose hugged by a bear: Mural by Nandalal and pupils. Santoshalay, Visva-Bharati.

'Grandfather's Holiday': 'The old man was like a ripe mango...': Picture of Shrikantha Sinha. Illustration for *Jiban-Smriti* by Gaganendranath Tagore.
'Flowers': Woodcut by Nandalal Bose, *Sahaj Path*, Part 1 (1930).
'Our Little River': Sketch of the Ajay river by Nandalal Bose, *Chharar Chhabi* (1937).
'The Voyage': Illustration by Asit Kumar Haldar for the poem entitled 'The Merchant' in *The Crescent Moon* (1913).
'The Runaway City': Illustration for the poem by Nandalal Bose in *Chitra-Bichitra* (1361/1954 edn).
'The Tiger': Illustration for the poem by Nandalal Bose in *Sahaj Path*, Part 3 (1941).
'The Palm Tree': Illustration for the poem by Nandalal Bose in *Sahaj Path*, Part 3 (1941).
'The Stargazer': Woodcut by Nandalal Bose, *Sahaj Path*, Part 1 (1930).

'The Hero': Illustrations by Sukhen Gangopadhyay for a special edition of the poem (*Birpurush*), Visva-Bharati (1369/1962).
'The Wise Brother': Painting by Rabindranath. Rabindra Bhavan.
'Big and Small': Woodcut by Nandalal Bose for *Sahaj Path*, Part 1 (1930).
'The Big News': Illustration by Nandalal Bose for 'Jalajatra', *Chharar Chhabi* (1937).
'The Fairy': Painting by Rabindranath. Rabindra Bhavan, Visva-Bharati.
'The Rats' Feast': Sketch by Rabindranath for *Galpa-Salpa*.
'Wishes Come True': Illustration by Nandalal Bose for the poem 'Makal', *Chharar Chhabi* (1937).
'The Welcome', 'The Poet and the Pauper', 'The Ordeals of Fame', 'The Extended Family', 'The Free Lunch': Woodcut by Nandalal Bose, *Sahaj Path*, Part 1 (1930).
'That Man': All drawings for *Se* by Rabindranath.
'Moving Pictures': All illustrations by Nandalal Bose. Woodcut of fish from *Sahaj Path*, Part 2 (1930); all other woodcuts selected from *Sahaj Path*, Part 1 (1930), chiefly the series illustrating the Bengali alphabet.
'At Sixes and Sevens': All illustrations by Rabindranath for *Khapchhara*.
'The Invention of Shoes': Drawings by Rabindranath. Rabindra Bhavan, Visva-Bharati.
'Fragments': Paintings by Rabindranath. Rabindra Bhavan, Visva-Bharati.
'Bhajahari': Painting by Rabindranath. Rabindra Bhavan, Visva-Bharati; illustration by Nandalal Bose for 'Bhajahari', *Chharar Chhabi* (1937).
'The Builder': Illustration for the poem by Nandalal Bose in *Sahaj Path*, Part 2 (1930).
'Madho': Illustration for the poem by Nandalal Bose in *Chharar Chhabi* (1937).
'Two Bighas of Land': Illustration by Nandalal Bose for 'Talgachh', *Chharar Chhabi* (1937).
'The Fake Fortress': Illustration by Nandalal Bose in *Sahaj Path*, Part 2 (1930).

LIST OF ILLUSTRATIONS

'My Childhood':
Rabindranath, his elder brother Somendranath and his nephew Satyaprasad with Shrikantha Sinha: photograph *c.* 1873–4.

Painting by Rabindranath. Rabindra Bhavan; Visva-Bharati.

Illustration by Nandalal Bose for the poem *Kather Singi* (The Wooden Lion) in *Chharar Chhabi* (1937).

'Under the banyan tree...': Illustration for *Jiban-Smriti* by Gaganendranath Tagore.

Illustration by Nandalal Bose for the poem *Atar Bichi* (The Custard-Apple Seed) in *Chharar Chhabi* (1937).

Illustration by Nandalal Bose for *Akash* in *Chharar Chhabi* (1937).

'My father sitting in front of the garden...': Illustration for *Jiban-Smriti* by Gaganendranath Tagore.

Doodles from Rabindranath's manuscripts used as space-fillers.

Poetry

"The Gift" ["I want to give you something"...]
"The Home" [I paced alone on the road...]
"The Journey [The morning sea of silence broke
"The Judge" [Say of him what you please, but
186   I know my child's failings..]

196
The Source [The sleep that flits on baby's eye
203
Unending Love [I seem to have loved you
              in numberless forms...]
206
Unyielding   When I called you
               in my garden
210
When And Why [When I bring you coloured
              toys my child
211

When Day is done

Where the mind is without fear